Death Date
Heartless Fate

David Cunliffe

Grosvenor House
Publishing Limited

This book is published by
Grosvenor House Publishing Ltd
Link House
140 The Broadway, Tolworth, Surrey, KT6 7HT.
www.grosvenorhousepublishing.co.uk

This book is a work of fiction. Any resemblance to
people or events, past or present, is purely coincidental.

A CIP record for this book
is available from the British Library

ISBN 978-1-83975-963-5

A special thanks to Alan Norman the
company director of Mersey print,
for the help now and in the past

Death Date Heartless Fate

A travelling theatre production, the stars of the show, Dylan and Erica embrace. Erica a slim blonde in her early twenties, her beauty was truly intoxicating. Dylan, her partner in and out of theatre, smiled – he was tall, dark and handsome, complete with dark piercing eyes.

They began to kiss each other in a small dressing room. Erica gazed into Dylan's eyes and then began to laugh. Dylan shrugged his shoulders and became annoyed, but held her hand and spoke, "Why are you laughing?"

"Oh, I fear I displease you, oh Master."

Dylan began to laugh. They were then interrupted by a loud bang on the door. The door opened and a face appeared. It was Nicholas, the Production Manager. His face was extremely haggard, with bushy eyebrows and a soft black moustache. His face was bright red with anger.

Erica turned to Dylan and spoke, "Why, if it isn't our boss, Saint Nicholas. Does this mean the curtain is coming down?"

Nicholas shook his head. Erica was conscious of his annoyance as he began to speak, "Okay, you both know the score. One by one everyone's left, including the audience. The play isn't bringing in any revenue anymore. The people ain't interested in Count Dracula anymore. In fact, I am losing money on this production, that's why I am calling time on it."

Dylan reflected a shade of terror and said, "You what?"

"I am but the master of the theatre, if you know what I mean."

Nicholas shook his head and then spoke in a heightened voice, "Sorry, Count Dracula and his Bride is over. Look, if it makes you feel any better, I'll let you keep your costumes. The rest of the cast have been informed and everyone has been paid up. Look, let's depart and say our goodbyes – who knows, maybe one day Count Dracula might come back into fashion again."

Dylan shook his head in disgust and then put on a brave face, "Oh well who cares, me and Erica have each other. Let us leave now and fly off to better pastures - what do you say my fair lady?"

"Shut up Dylan. I am not going to work in no field. Just take me to the bar, I need a drink."

Nicholas began to laugh and then turned around and left the room.

A draught of fresh cold air suddenly ran down Dylan's spine. He then began to talk fluently in a heightened voice, "Come on Erica, we don't need this, Hollywood is calling out our names. It's time to hit the road."

Erica smiled as Dylan picked up his costume. She then spoke softly, "Babe, let's give Hollywood a miss for now and just go to the bar."

"Okay Erica, your wish is my command."

Dylan took Erica's hand and escorted her to his awaiting car. It was an old car, full of wear and tear. Erica called it the rust bucket for obvious reasons.

As they made their way out of the theatre, the light faded rapidly. Suddenly Erica stopped in her tracks as she gazed upon the rust bucket parked up in the car park. She turned to Dylan, "My God, I am so embarrassed. Is it your turn to drive or mine?"

Dylan tried hard to control his anger, "Why, I believe it's my turn to drive our vintage automobile."

Erica became angry and began to speak in a heightened voice, "My, are you for real? it's just a rust bucket and a total embarrassment."

There was a moody and dogged silence as they walked closer toward the car. Dylan laughed and then spoke, "You just described my car in considerable detail did you not? You, my dear have enlightened me, which I believe is a good thing."

Erica smiled, "Does this mean we are headed for the scrapyard?"

"Look, Erica, first we need a drink, I reckon my vintage automobile will get us that far."

Erica laughed, "I wouldn't bet on it."

Dylan smiled as he reached inside his pocket for his car keys. He opened the door which was a struggle as it was full of rust. He gritted his teeth and put on his usual false smile.

Erica had the same problem. She got into the car and turned to Dylan, "Okay, what day is it?"

Dylan looked into her eyes in confusion.

"Okay Dylan, it's Groundhog Day."

With a sudden feeling of repulsion, he glanced at Erica and spoke, "Look, it's not Groundhog Day, it's nightfall and if you don't give it a rest I will put on my costume and bite you."

Erica smiled, "No, save the play for later."

Dylan laughed and put the key into the ignition. After three attempts his automobile started up. Dylan tapped his steering wheel and then laughed, "This car always starts the third time."

Erica yawned, "Yeah, the third time lucky automobile."

A sudden crunch of the gear stick and they were on their way. Erica closed her eyes in anxious silence and then, Erica's worst nightmare – Dylan turned on the dreaded radio.

With a sudden feeling of repulsion, Dylan looked to Erica. His mind began to fill with excitement "Listen babe, you love this song – Don McLean's American Pie." Dylan, without warning, broke out into song – *"Good old boy drinking whisky and rye, singing this will be the day I will die."*

Erica nudged Dylan and spoke, "Look, if you love me, please don't sing and keep your eyes on the road."

Dylan smiled, "Look, you sit quietly and listen; I've improved."

Erica quickly placed her hands over her ears as Dylan began to sing again – *"The day the music died. So, bye, bye Miss American Pie."* Dylan just could not resist the temptation – he sang his heart out even though he couldn't sing. The man said the music would not play.

Erica finally lost her patience - his singing voice had that effect on her, "Look Dylan, shut up or it will be you that will be DEAD on a permanent basis." She then lost her cool and reached over, turning the radio off.

Dylan had a look of disbelief on his face, "What the hell are you doing turning off my radio?"

"Look, Dylan, it was sheer misery. I've got to think about my poor ears, after all you said you like my ears."

Dylan regained his composure and began to see her point of view, "Oh sorry, is my singing really that bad?"

Erica shook her head, "How many times have I told you, your singing is worse than bad."

"Oh, it's my memory. I keep telling myself my singing voice has improved, but I guess it never will."

Dylan weaved his way in and out of the traffic.

Erica calmed down and regained her composure. She closed her eyes once more. The echo and sounds of the streets rang out in her ears, lights gleamed all around and then there was a disagreeable damp smell. Erica suddenly opened her eyes and began to sneeze. Dylan laughed and spoke in a calm voice, "Why bless you dear. Look we are here." They had reached their destination, Big Dave's Bar and Grill.

Dylan parked up his automobile. They both struggled to open the car doors at the same time – the usual struggle. Erica slammed the door behind her. Dylan shook his head in disbelief, "Look, Erica, my vintage automobile has feelings. Was there any need to slam the door like that?"

Erica was not in the mood for confrontation and just answered, "Yes" and then made her way to the bar.

Dylan locked the door and then began to play catch up. "Wait for me babe, I was just saying…"

Erica stopped in her tracks, "Hurry up Dylan, you're paying."

Erica felt a cool breeze on the back of her neck. She took hold of Dylan's hand as he escorted her into the bar and grill. They gazed around at the bright neon signs and the pictures of Hollywood heroes. This was their favourite hangout.

Dylan and Erica made their way toward the bar. Erica looked at the barman in disbelief, "Look Dylan, it's a new man. Oh my, those shoulders, what muscles."

Dylan became annoyed, "Keep your eyes off him. Remember what you told me. You prefer brains to brawn."

Erica laughed out-loud, "Why the hell am I with you then? You don't have either."

Suddenly his anger rose like an erupting volcano, "Goddam shut up. Go sit over there – you're embarrassing me."

Erica smiled, "does this mean I displease you? Maybe I ought to go and sit down over there." Erica winked at the barman and then turned around before she was exposed to Dylan's wrath. She moved to the far corner of the room.

The Bar and Grill was pretty much empty, the way they liked it. The barman looked into Dylan's eyes, conscious of his annoyance. Dylan tried hard to regain his composure. He looked back into the barman's eyes. His inner mind kept repeating itself – Goddam caveman, goddam caveman.

And then it spoke, "What would you like to drink, sir?"

"Oh" Dylan shook his head, "I was miles away there."

"Yes sir, I believe you were."

The barman scanned his memory – he had seen this customer somewhere before. He remembered the poster. This is the guy in the poster, none other than Count Dracula. He then spoke as he smiled, "Is that two chilled red wines, sir?"

"No, one ice cold beer and one red wine."

"Okay, coming straight up."

The barman served Dylan with the drinks. Dylan handed the barman the money. The barman could not resist himself and held the money in his hand and said, "Oh, I love to count" ha, ha, ha.

Dylan picked up the drinks and then gazed into the barman's eyes, "No need to count, dumbo, it's the right money, and another thing, keep your eyes off my babe."

The barman laughed and turned away.

As he walked over to Erica, he mumbled to himself, "They ain't real muscles, it's steroids, an artificial man with no brain."

Dylan sat next to Erica, handing her a glass of red wine. He then looked into Erica's eyes. She was conscious of his annoyance. She remained totally calm.

Dylan chewed his bottom lip and then, with an edge of coldness, he spoke, "Don't you ever say I haven't got no brain. I am an actor, of course I have a brain. I remember all my lines, don't I?"

Erica interrupted, speaking in a low voice, "I'm sorry - you have got brains. Sometimes I forget about your sensitive nature. I was just jesting. Will you forgive your fair maiden? What is more, you are the greatest actor of all time. I bow down to your genius and intellect."

The smile returned to Dylan's face. He relaxed in his seat and began to sip his ice-cold beer. She sensed Dylan was now at ease, "Does this mean you forgive me? After all, you, Dylan are my destiny. I will always love you."

Chapter 1

Dylan gazed all around. He noticed a newspaper of sorts on the table next to theirs. Dylan stood up and reached over and picked up the newspaper. On the front cover was a picture of an old man.

Dylan sat back down and gazed at the picture. He began to read the story below the picture. Suddenly his eyes peered with curiosity. He began to think and then, in a low voice, he spoke, "An old man died of a heart attack and left all his money to his new Mexican bride as he had no other kin."

Erica shook her head, "So, that sort of thing happens all the time."

Dylan closed his eyes and drifted into a trance-like state.

Once again, Erica's eyes peered with curiosity. She thought to herself, Dylan has a plan.

A few minutes later Dylan regained his usual composure. He then became excited, "You know what, Erica? I have the perfect plan to make us rich. I want you to sit quietly and listen to my plan."

Erica's eyes lit up; her mind began to fill up with excitement.

"Right, Erica, this is my plan. Imagine if we did the same. We find out the names and addresses of all the rich, lonely old men with no kin and most of all, they've got to have heart conditions. You, my darling, date them. No man on earth could resist your charms. You then marry them. As soon as you are married, I appear in my vampire costume, or even better, imagine if you pretended to be dead, fake blood on your neck! The fright will induce a heart attack and then the money is all ours. What do you reckon?"

Erica gazed at his magnificence, "Alright, this does sound like one of your better plans. What's the first move then, Dylan?"

"Oh, I need to go to the bar and get us another drink."

"Oh, that sounds like another good plan."

Dylan stood up and walked over to the bar. On this visit nothing could upset him. He smiled at the barman and said, "Same again."

"Same" the barman laughed. He nodded in confirmation and then spoke in a loud confident voice, "You can count on me, Drack."

Dylan just laughed it off. The barman was moving, lightning fast and soon placed the drinks on the bar.

Dylan handed the barman the money. He then spoke, "Keep the change, Fred."

The barman looked at Dylan in confusion. Dylan winked at the barman and said, "You work it out for yourself, caveman."

As Dylan walked away with the drink, the barman let out a cry, "Yabba dabba do, where's Thelma?"

Dylan began to laugh as he made his way back to Erica.

Erica sat reading the paper. As Dylan sat down and placed the drinks on the table, Erica gazed into his eyes, "My God, that Mexican bride is now one rich lady. Okay, Dylan I require enlightenment. How on earth are we going to find these rich old guys?"

"Well, my dear, I have also thought of that. Remember William the Geek?"

"Oh yes, I remember William the Geek."

"I call him the information man and he does owe me a favour. We will visit him. He has lots of those fancy computers. He could use them to find out the locations of all the rich old bachelors with heart conditions. That guy can hack into anything."

Erica smiled to herself in contentment, "Once again I must apologise. You leave me mesmerised by your higher degree of intelligence, but can we trust William the Geek?"

Dylan grinned, "Yes, that guy owes me his life. I still remember the day when William was being bullied. The poor guy was always being bullied. One day some guys went too far and pushed him into a river. What made things worse was the poor guy could not swim. I dived in and saved his life. Later, he paid me protection money. I gave each one of those bullies a good beating. William swore then that if ever I needed a favour, he would repay me. He also said he would also be my loyal servant."

Erica's eyes were attractive, big and blue. A tear came in her right eye.

"Oh my Dylan, that was such a sad story."

Dylan shook his head in disbelief, "What are you doing? I've told you this story before."

"Oh, sorry Dylan I cannot remember." Erica took hold of Dylan's hand and smiled. "We are, my lover, on the same wavelength. My memory just ain't what it used to be."

Dylan smiled, "Oh don't worry, I believe it's just a blonde thing."

Erica twisted Dylan's hand as they both began to laugh out loud. Erica moved closer to Dylan. She then kissed him passionately on the lips.

Dylan finished off his drink. He gazed into Erica's eyes, "I know what's next. You're hungry are you not? I guess you require one of Big Dave's special burgers."

Erica licked her lips, her eyes and taste buds were filled with passion, "Oh and I'm sick of wine, get me a nice cold beer in the way of a change."

"Oh yes, now you're talking Erica, let's celebrate my perfect plan. I reckon after just three victims I will be able to hang up my Count costume forever."

Dylan stood up as Erica winked at him. The bar was now busier. Without warning, the music was raised. Dylan joined a queue for food.

Erica sat listening to the music, her eyelids began to flicker spasmodically. She then closed her eyes for a few minutes and then a familiar voice rang out.

"What are you doing? Are you asleep? I've got your food."

Erica slowly opened her eyes on Dylan, "I was just thinking of what to do with all the *money, money, money*".

Dylan placed a tray on the table "Oh I remember that, wasn't that an Abba song?"

Erica knew what was coming next, "Oh no, please the last thing we need is rain." It was too late - Dylan burst out into song *"Money, money, money, it's so funny, in a rich man's world. Imagine all the things I could do, if I had a little money..."*

Erica sat with her head bowed down. Dylan sat with true concern in his voice and spoke, "Are you okay? Does my singing have such a negative effect on you?"

Erica looked up and slowly began to clap, "Thank God for that. You don't know the lyrics, do you?"

Dylan shook his head, "You're right, I must confess I don't."

Erica shook her head, "I'm just glad we don't go to any karaoke bars, or I would be in trouble with the bar. I reckon your singing voice would clear it."

Dylan shook his head, "Okay, eat up and shut up."

Erica took hold of her burger and then took a big bite out of it. She smiled with content, "This burger sure tastes good."

Dylan began to eat his and nodded in agreement. After a couple of minutes both burgers were gone. Erica sipped her ice-cold beer and gazed out of a window.

"Look outside Dylan, it's a full moon. Do you reckon we ought to get ourselves some blood?"

Dylan shook his head in disbelief, "My, I reckon this vampire thing is going to haunt us for the rest of our lives."

Erica laughed, "Oh Dylan, I ain't serious – just having a laugh. I know I can always count on you to laugh along."

Dylan took a drink of his beer, "Look you can count on me. Hey, let's get the hell out of here. Our car awaits."

Erica finished off her drink and stood up. She laughed, "Dylan, you mean our royal rust bucket awaits."

Dylan laughed, "One day it will be replaced by a brand-new sports car."

Erica moved closer to Dylan, kissing him on the cheek. She whispered in his ear, "The sooner the better."

Dylan laughed and took hold of Erica's hand as they left the bar. Outside they could hear a wailing, choking scream which echoed all around. A fight had broken out. A mysterious stranger with death cold eyes pulled out a semi-automatic pistol and opened fire on two men. A bullet penetrated one man's temple, the other had two bullets pumped into his chest. The sound of the gun fire echoed around the night air. Dylan began sweating furiously.

Erica reflected a shade of terror as she moved closer to the car.

Dylan turned to Erica, "My God, let's get out of here quick."

Erica was gripped by a hot flush panic as Dylan wrestled with the car door. Erica turned for a brief second. There lay two dead men. The killer looked towards Erica and then started to proceed towards her. She pulled open the car door and jumped in. She turned to Dylan, "My God, the killer is coming towards us."

Dylan began to panic. The car started up, the second time. Dylan then pulled away at great speed. Behind them they could hear police sirens. Dylan took a deep breath, "My God, that was a close call."

Erica's bottom lip trembled. She began to speak, her words full of panic and fear, "My God, that was a fully-fledged killer, and he was coming for us next."

Dylan shook his head and continued to drive. Erica sat motionless, frozen with true fear. Her mind was paralysed by the hideous sight. Suddenly her anger rose. God damn the killer, he spoilt the perfect night out.

Dylan put on a brave face, "All I can say is thank God the rust bucket started."

Erica laughed and then put on a brave face, "You're so right, Dylan, we were very lucky to get away from that situation alive; Divine Destiny, our guardian angels played their part."

"You reckon, Erica, we were saved by guardian angels?"

Erica regained her composure and answered in a calm voice, "Why yes, our angels are looking over us."

Dylan looked up into the night sky, "Look, Erica, at the stars, are they looking out for us?"

"Why yes, remember I have a degree of psychic potential."

"My God, Erica, if that's the case why didn't you see that one coming?"

"You know why, I have told you once before, having the power is one thing, controlling it is a different ball game."

"Yeah, I see what you mean. Remember that time you dreamt of a birth and my Aunty Sally died. Also, that time you won the bingo twice, and all the competitions you have entered and won. Was that not a sign of your psychic potential?"

Erica shook her head, "No, all of that was just luck."

Dylan looked confused, "What, are you saying - the death of my Aunty Sally was just luck?"

"Heavens not, my darling Dylan, that was just a vision or a dream."

"Oh, that's okay then."

The noise of the traffic echoed in Dylan's ears as they reached their destination. Dylan parked his automobile near their apartment.

Erica turned to Dylan, "My darling, I have just had a thought. Should you have been drinking and driving?"

Dylan laughed out loud, "Look love, I won't tell anyone if you don't."

They then both got out of the car. Dylan struggled as usual. He got out and stopped abruptly and then he lost his cool. With wild strength he slammed the door behind him. Erica laughed, "Oh Dylan, why that's no way to treat your vintage car."

Dylan shook his head. He turned to Erica and spoke in a funny voice, "Come here and say that."

Erica started to run towards the apartment, Dylan locked the car door and was soon in hot pursuit. He soon caught up with her, wrapping his arms around her waist. Erica laughed out loud. The neighbourhood suddenly came to life. Dogs started to bark in the distance. Erica struggled to get away and then turned to face Dylan. He pulled her closer, recalling the words he had used lots of times whilst playing the part of Count Dracula.

"Look into my eyes. Escape is out of the question."

Erica laughed, "Go on, bite me if you must, Count Dylan."

Dylan began to laugh, "How about a kiss instead."

The pale moon shone down and radiated an atmosphere of love. Dylan was quite taken aback by her beauty, the emaciation of her features, such an engaging smile. Dylan kissed Erica on the lips. Moisture shone all over her face.

Erica pulled away, "Come on Romeo, don't you know the streets ain't safe after dark?".

As soon as she finished her sentence, distance screams echoed in the night air.

Dylan looked at Erica, 'You're right, we are surrounded by mutants. The dark seems to bring out an abundance of creatures."

Erica agreed as they moved swiftly to the safety of their apartment. Erica stepped over a small chain link fence as Dylan moved forward with the door key. He opened it with great speed and very soon they were both inside. Dylan moved gingerly towards his medicine in the shape of a litre bottle of Jack Daniels. The apartment room was small and cosy. It served their needs for now.

Erica watched as Dylan poured himself a drink. She then spoke in a quiet voice, "Haven't we got a busy day ahead of us tomorrow? Let's get some shut eye. If we get up early, we could put the plan in motion."

"Okay Erica, I am only having one drink. We have had one crazy night. That guy was one crazy killer."

Erica agreed, "I turned around and I reckon he was heading straight for us."

"Yeah, but our car saved us, what a vintage car."

Erica smiled, "Yeah, if you say so."

Erica turned around entering the bathroom. She then brushed her pearly white teeth and undressed. Her body was perfection. She gazed into the mirror and smiled. She returned to the bedroom to find Dylan stark naked, ready for some action, standing next to the bed, his clothes hanging of the back of a chair.

Erica began to laugh, "Why on earth are you standing there in your birthday suit?"

Dylan smiled, "Well babe, funny you should say that – it's my birthday and I am waiting for my treat."

Erica shook her head, "But I planned on going straight to sleep."

Dylan smiled, "Once we have made love you can go straight to sleep."

Erica knew Dylan would not take no for an answer. She gently removed her bra and panties.

Dylan became aroused and moved closer and closer to Erica. He kissed her sweetly. She captivated his eyes. Dylan continued to kiss her tenderly and then drew a deep breath. Very soon they lay on the bed and began to make love.

Afterwards Erica fell into a deep sleep whilst Dylan got out of bed and finished off his glass of Jack Daniels. He did not sleep much – such an active mind, always seeking answers. He had dozens of books about the supernatural, Nostradamus and, of course, vampires. He considered himself a true thinker. It was knowledge and wisdom he sought.

Dylan picked up a book and began to read it. His mind ordered him back into bed. Dylan placed the book back down and then slowly got into his bed. After several minutes he joined Erica in the Land of Nod.

Several hours later Erica dreamt of the task at hand. Her dream soon became a nightmare. She met up with a macabre, mysterious stranger, complete with death cold blood-filled eyes and pale skin, the creature of the night. It called out her name, "Erica, Erica." When she did not answer the creature became red with rage. Erica dreamt she had to escape. She began to run from the beast but lost her footing and toppled over head-first. She slowly lifted herself up off the cold stone ground. She caught sight of her reflection in an old dirty mirror. She gazed all around. She was standing in the corridor of an ancient castle surrounded by cobwebs and a disagreeable damp smell. She was shaken and dazed, anxiety twisted her face as she heard again the dark sinister voice.

"Erica, blood – I want your blood. You shall be my bride."

Erica turned around and out of the shadows appeared a walking corpse. She gazed into its blood-filled eyes. The creature then revealed its razor-sharp fangs. Erica faced her worst fear. She should not be beaten and spoke out in her nightmare, "No, vampires don't exist. You are but an hallucination."

The vampire spoke back to her in the dream, "I wish that were so. I am cursed to walk in the shadows of the night seeking blood. Now my dear, I want you to concentrate. Look into my eyes."

Erica knew what was coming next and began to scream at the top of her voice, "No, never; no never."

She then felt herself being vigorously shaken. She opened her eyes to a familiar voice, "Erica wake up, wake up."

Chapter 2

It was now morning, the glorious sun started to peep through the curtains. Erica sat up and shook her head in disbelief. Dylan put his arm around her, "Are you okay? Sounds like you were having a bad nightmare."

"Yes, it was a horrible nightmare about being chased by a mysterious stranger. He got closer and closer."

Dylan laughed, "Don't tell me it was the mail-man."

Erica's eyes began to glisten with a tear or two, "Dylan, I wish sometimes you would take me seriously."

"My. Erica, I am sorry. You are still shaking. What did you see?"

Erica closed her eyes and answered slowly, "I saw an old vampire. He was after my blood. His razor-sharp fangs and blood red eyes – it felt so real."

"Look, calm down Erica, it was just a nightmare. We all have them."

"Yeah, but sometimes mine come true. Remember that time I dreamt of that woman stepping out in front of a bus. One week later it happened. Some of my dreams seem to predict the future."

"No, Erica, I disagree. What about last night, you didn't see that one coming – two guys shot dead in front of us."

Erica wiped her eyes. Dylan offered to make the coffee as Erica sat in bed motionless, her mind whispered vampire. She shook her head and rubbed her eyes. A draught of cold air suddenly ran down her spine.

Dylan appeared minutes later with the coffee. Dylan smiled and gave Erica a cup of coffee. She took a sip and then placed the cup onto her bedside table. She then turned to Dylan and spoke in a low voice, "Why is it you always make the coffee too strong and sweet?"

Dylan laughed and then replied, "Because that's what we are together, strong and sweet."

Erica smiled, "How romantic, lovely words from the heart."

Dylan laughed.

Erica finished her coffee, then announced she was going to have a shower.

Dylan showed his approval and with a cheeky smile he said, "Is there room in the shower for one more?"

Erica shook her head, "Why ask, you know the answer before you ask."

"Oh, that's a definite refusal then?"

"Yes, it's the same as ever, No."

Dylan sat down with his coffee and picked up a book whilst Erica made her way to the bathroom. She stood in front of the mirror, gazing at her face. She felt her life flashing before her. She had been with Dylan for eight years. Nothing had ever changed, same old rusted automobile and rented apartment. They were now both unemployed. What would happen if his plan failed?

She felt so confused and then a thought entered her mind – maybe the dream was a message of doom. Should I leave him before it is too late? But she had nowhere to go. She was an only child, her parents died when she was young. Tragedy was all she had known until Dylan, her knight in shining armour, appeared. She knew she was stuck. Money was the key out of this poor existence. Erica turned on the shower. She waited until it was the right temperature and then entered it.

Meanwhile, Dylan sat reading a book on vampires.

Erica was soon out of the shower. She dried herself and then turned on her hairdryer as Dylan continued to read. After she had dried her hair, she re-joined Dylan. She smiled and then spoke in a low voice, "What are you reading?"

Dylan felt a bit sensitive, "Er, I'm reading a book on…"

Erica shook her head, "Let me guess, it's about vampires, isn't it? Okay, smart ass, enlighten me – what have you learnt?"

"Well, did you know Bram Stoker's Dracula, Vlad the Impaler, was a fifteenth century warrior and did you know that today there are an estimated ten thousand real vampires in the United States, but they ain't real, they are just cult members, and that Goths see themselves as a sub-species, alienated from the mainstream of humanity."

Erica shook her head, "Such a lot of information in a short period of time."

"Babe, I am a fast reader."

"So, you're an intelligent man, what is your conclusion on all of this vampire business?"

"Well honey, I reckon it is all there just to spread the contagion of fear."

"What is your favourite vampire movie?"

Erica answered straight away, "Well it's got to be Interview with the Vampire. My favourite actor was in it, Tom Cruise. Oh, and I like all the old Hammer movies starring Christopher Lee and Peter Cushing. I also like Buffy the Vampire Slayer."

"Okay, let's change the subject now".

"Oh, Erica, did I tell you your beauty is so divine?"

"Yeah, I reckon I have heard that one before. Where would I be without you?"

Dylan laughed out loud, "I don't know, maybe rich, happy and famous."

Erica, without warning, walked over to Dylan and affectionately embraced him and kissed him on the cheek, "Okay Dylan, get in that shower whilst I fix us a quick snack; we are wasting valuable time."

Dylan agreed and made his way to the shower. He suddenly stopped in his tracks, "My, what have I forgotten to do?"

Erica looked at Dylan, "Have you called William the Geek?"

"No, I figured he would still be in bed."

"Well lover boy, time is ticking. I reckon he might be up now."

"Yeah, I was thinking the same."

Dylan picked up a pad and then located William's number. After a moment Dylan dialled the number. William did not drink much or smoke, all he had was his computers. He was a true geek.

After a few minutes William answered, "Hi, who is this please?"

"It's me, Dylan."

"Oh, hi Dylan, long time no see."

"No, William, I am on the telephone, you can't see."

"Oh, you know where I'm coming from."

"Yeah, I know".

"How are things anyway – still got your computers?"

"Yes, you know me, I'm William the Geek. Why?"

"You sure are, in fact that is why I'm calling. I need some information. You are the greatest hacker of all time."

William laughed, "Flattery will get you everywhere, Dylan, my friend."

'Oh good, you speak my kind of language and that, my friend, is cash."

"Okay, Dylan, what do you require? I owe you a favour as I recall."

"Say, so you do as I recall. The information I require is a small list of old guys that are all alone, have no kin, are rich and above all, they must all have heart conditions."

"My, Dylan, this is going to take a while".

"Can it be done, William?"

"Yes, you know me, I'm a wizard. Anything is possible."

"I'll come around in three hours or more, is that okay?"

"I don't see why not."

"I will get you the data and seal it in a brown envelope, is that okay?"

"Yes."

"May the Force be with you, William the Geek."

"Cheers, Dylan, you're a dipstick."

Before Dylan could answer, William had hung up.

Erica looked over at Dylan, "Well Dylan, can he, do it?"

Dylan shook his head in disbelief, "Yes, he can do it. Do you know what William called me before he hung up?"

"No. But I bet he was speaking the truth."

"Well not really, the Geek called me Dylan the Dipstick."

Erica laughed out loud, "So I was right. Maybe I have psychic ability after all."

Dylan laughed as he headed for the shower. Erica headed for the kitchen. She opened the fridge door, reaching inside for the pure orange juice. She poured the juice into a glass and then began to drink it.

Dylan was in and out of the shower like a flash.

Erica made some pancakes as Dylan rushed, drying himself at great speed. He got dressed quickly and entered the kitchen, "Well, Erica, something smells nice. Is that pancakes I can smell?"

"Sure, is Dylan, help yourself".

Dylan picked up a plate full of fresh pancakes. He sat down on a small kitchen table and began to eat them. Erica joined him with a warm smile, "So Dylan, William can do it?"

"Yeah Erica, he is going to put the information in a sealed envelope. How about that for service?"

"So far so good," Erica smiled, "We need to pull this off. I am sick of our lifestyle. We need more money – the more the merrier."

Dylan nodded his head and then spoke, "You know you can count on me – oh that reminds me, I left the costume in the car."

Erica laughed and then spoke, "Reckon it still fits?"

Dylan smiled, "Has it been that long? It only seems like yesterday."

Erica finished off at the table, "Right, lover boy, I need to return to the bathroom and fix my hair and makeup."

Whilst Erica was in the bathroom, Dylan turned on their small 28-inch television. He switched channels until he arrived at the local news. After a few minutes the story was read out – *Two men, shot dead. Police believe the guy was a hitman and was not related. Police are appealing for witnesses.*

Dylan switched off the television quickly. He was a lot of things, but he was no rat. His brothers Ralph and Eddie were both criminals. He was taught by his brothers the code of the street – 'Don't mess with the mob.' His brother Ralph did a bit of driving for the mob. His friend Franco tried to double-cross them. He ended up in a concrete overcoat. Dylan had not heard from his brothers for a while. Erica had a notion they were a bad influence on him. Crime was their way of life and if you hung around with them you would get sucked into that kind of lifestyle.

Erica returned from the bathroom, "Okay, Dylan, what's with the face?"

"Oh, I have just been watching the news, it seems it was a mob hit. I reckon those two guys had it coming to them."

"No, that's your brothers talking. You're not like them, you're a good man."

Dylan shook his head, "We are planning to knock off some old guys – does that make you and me good?"

Erica sat down in deep thought, "Well maybe, but these old guys are all living on borrowed time. All we will be doing is giving them a few months of happiness and then putting them out of their misery."

"My, Erica, you got it all worked out – so professional and you're right, we are going to be doing them a service. Okay, Erica, I just need to brush my teeth and then we hit the road."

Dylan entered the bathroom, he picked up his toothbrush, added a bit of paste and then gazed at himself in the mirror. He then took a deep breath and opened his mouth. He imagined he was back in the theatre. He then began to talk to himself in the mirror "I am Count Dracula."

Erica sneaked up behind him. She saw him gazing at himself in the mirror. Erica suddenly shouted out in a loud voice "What are you doing you freak, you ain't Count Dracula, get a grip of yourself."

Dylan laughed out loud "Erica, do not insult my intelligence. Of course, I am the Count. I love to count one, two, three, four. I love to count ha, ha, ha."

"Dylan you're a dipstick. Let's get serious, the Geek awaits."

Dylan finished off brushing his teeth and then turned to Erica, "Okay, you want to get serious, my name is Dylan, not Dipstick and the Geek as you call him is William. How would you like it if I made up a name for you?"

Erica laughed, "Go ahead think of one, bet you can't."

Dylan stood motionless thinking for a few minutes. He then gave up, "Sorry I can't think of any, you're perfect."

Erica smiled, "I thought as much, perfection can't be ridiculed."

"Okay, Erica, you won, now let's go and visit William the Geek."

Erica started to laugh, "You just called your friend William a geek."

"Oh sorry, it's just a bad habit." Dylan picked up the car keys.

"Okay Dylan, this is it, destiny awaits us millionaires in the making."

"My, Erica, you say such pretty words."

"Yes, I have my moral responsibilities to talk like an intelligent lady."

"That you are, Erica, and what's more, you are a rare catch, intelligence and beauty."

Erica shook her head, "A rare catch, I ain't no fish."

"Yeah, that's it, I've thought of a nickname for you."

"What, Dylan the Dipstick?"

"Oh, how about Erica Fish-face?"

Erica put on a serious face and pretended to be a gangster, "Look, Dipstick, you carry on talking like that and you will be swimming with the fishes."

Dylan laughed, "Come on Marlon Brando, let's go."

Erica took hold of Dylan's hand then embarrassed, they then kissed as they left the apartment.

Dylan wore a navy-blue cotton short sleeved shirt. Erica was wearing a pale blue dress which complimented her blonde hair and blue eyes and as usual she had an amazing gleaming smile.

Chapter 3

Dylan locked the door, and they then left the apartment hand in hand. They made their way toward the car. The sky was now cloudy and overcast with the sun trying its best to make a guest appearance. A short stroll and they were next to the car. Dylan reached for his key and took a deep breath before wrestling with the driver side car door. He opened it after a struggle.

Erica looked to Dylan, "My God, why on earth don't you buy some oil and administer it? Believe me, the sheer effort and cursing would surely come to a halt."

Dylan agreed, "You're right, my destiny is calling. It's a new car, that's what I need, along with a big property and lots of money."

Erica attempted to open her door. It was a miracle it opened without a struggle.

"Maybe we don't need a new car after all."

Dylan laughed and then climbed into the driver's seat.

Erica sat back and relaxed. Oh, how she craved silence. She closed her eyes as Dylan started up first time.

"First time. My, I reckon this car is trying to tell us something."

Erica laughed keeping her eyes closed, "Yeah, please don't scrap me."

Dylan gently pulled off and then, to Erica's annoyance, Dylan turned on the radio. Erica listened to Dylan as he said, "My, this is one of my favourite songs, Bob Marley" and without warning Dylan broke out into song, *"No woman, no cry. No woman, no cry."*

Erica leaned over and turned the radio down. She craved peace and tranquillity. Suddenly her anger rose, "Look, Dipstick, carry on singing and you won't have a woman. I've told you on several occasions that you're singing it totally out of tune.'

There was a calm silence for a second and then Dylan shrugged his shoulders, "Yeah, you tell me all the time."

"Well, Knucklehead, why don't you take any notice? Do you want me to have nightmares about your singing?"

"Heck no, Erica. From now on you won't hear a peep out of me."

"Good, it's about time you listened to reason."

Dylan went all quiet and then rain started to patter against the windows. There was a moody and dogged silence. Erica looked to Dylan, "Look what your singing has gone and done, it's raining."

Dylan ignored Erica's remarks and concentrated on his driving, taking a left turn and then a right. Dylan was a slow-moving driver due to his automobile.

Suddenly, the silence was broken, "My God, this car ... can't you move any faster?"

Erica began to speak words of wisdom, "Look, don't you dare lose it. Stay calm, take a chill pill."

"Oh okay," Dylan reached inside his pocket and then popped something into his mouth, "Oh by the way, Erica, I took your advice and took a chill pill."

Erica shook her head, "What on earth is a chill pill?"

"Oh, I just took a mint, it originated from the UK. I believe it's called a Polo Mint."

Dylan stuck out his tongue. On the end of it sat a Polo Mint.

"Dylan, it's got a hole in it."

"I know, Polo Mints have a hole in the middle of them."

"Oh, how strange."

"Do you want to try one? Just reach inside my pocket and help yourself."

Erica reached inside Dylan's pocket. Dylan began to wriggle in his seat, 'No that's not the packet of mints."

"Are you sure? It's small and minty."

Dylan shook his head in disbelief, "Look stop messing about. How can I concentrate on my driving?"

The rain stopped as soon as it started. Erica could hear the noise of the traffic as she closed her eyes once more. The last thing she needed was a mint. Memories came flooding back to her. She opened her eyes, "Hey Dylan, remember that time we went on vacation to Marina Sand Hotel?"

Dylan shook his head, "Yes, I remember. It was our first and our last. We saved our money and got ripped off."

"Remember mealtimes? My God, what a nightmare, people pushing into our queue. Remember those Mexicans trying to push in? You just wouldn't budge. In the end they gave up. You gave the Manager a good talking to, did you not? It said entertainment, three bars and a whole list of extras. Four star it said. In fact, it was hardly two stars."

Dylan shook his head, "And the worst part about it was the long walk to the beach. Anyway, Erica how are you feeling now?"

"Well, okay I suppose. You stopped singing and the rain has stopped."

"Do you still think vibrations influence our lives? Either the dark shadow side negative experiences or the light positive experiences?"

"Dylan remember that book I read".

"Which one, dear?"

"You know, Five Fives: Beyond Imagination."

"Was that a British Author?"

"Yes, David Cunliffe. His author's note was so enlightening as was his book."

"Yes, the book was full of hidden meanings."

Erica took over the radio station until she came across one of her favourite songs, the one she loved to sing when she was younger – *Da Doo Ron, Ron* by the Crystals. Suddenly it was her turn. She burst into song, *"I met him on a Sunday and my heart stood still da doo Ron, Ron, Ron da doo Ron, Ron. Somebody told me that his name was Bill, da doo Ron, Ron, Ron, da doo Ron, Ron"*.

Dylan reached over and turned the radio down, "Sorry, I just turned down the radio so I could speak. You're singing isn't that good either. I prefer Bob to Bill."

"You mean Bob Dylan?"

"No, Bob Marley, *No Woman No Cry.*"

"Well, Dylan, for your information your singing is enough to make any woman cry. Look out of your window, the rain has stopped, there ain't a cloud in the sky and the sun has got his hat on."

Dylan shook his head, "Well hip, hip hooray some sunshine."

Erica pinched Dylan's leg and they both began to laugh out loud.

"My God, Dylan, where on earth did I dig you up from?"

Dylan shook his head "You didn't, I found you."

"Well, that sounds about right. You must have seen the light."

"Oh, what a hypnotising display of words, a great description of when you first laid eyes on me."

"Sure, was, babe, sure was."

Dylan continued to drive as the sun shone in all of its glory. Dylan began to sweat furiously. He opened his car window as he did, Erica became annoyed.

"Dylan are you sure we are going the right way? I don't remember it being this far."

"Oh, don't worry, we ain't lost, it's but a couple of more miles."

Erica scratched her head in confusion. A thought entered her head, "Hey, Dylan what is the surname of the Geek?"

"Oh, it's Shatner."

"What, you're having a laugh ain't you? So, it is all so clear, the Captain of the Star Trek Enterprise. Beam me up, Dylan."

Dylan shook his head, "No, you've got it all wrong."

"Why ever so, my dear?"

"The ship's engineer wasn't called Dylan; his name was Scotty on account of him being from Scotland."

"Oh, my Dylan, we are a wealth of information, but I jest as I already knew."

Dylan smiled, "Oh I see, you, as ever, were only joking."

"I'm right about one thing, William is a big Star Trek fan, isn't he?"

"Well yes, he is, but that don't make him strange, does it?"

"No, you're right, I once had a friend who was a bit of a Klingon."

Dylan laughed out loud, "My Erica, you do have a wicked sense of humour."

"I know, I've been with you for eight years – it's either laugh or cry."

Dylan pulled over to the side of the road and put his handbrake on. He turned to Erica with a serious look on his face, "What's that supposed to mean?"

"Oh, just means I am having a laugh. Remember you said I had a wicked sense of humour."

Dylan took off the handbrake and carried on with the journey. He turned to Erica, "I'm glad to hear it straight from the horse's mouth."

Erica pinched Dylan's leg.

"Ouch, what was that for?"

"I ain't no horse, maybe more of a pony."

"Well, Erica, the Pony Express has just arrived at our destination."

Dylan pulled into William's driveway. He parked up and then turned to Erica.

Chapter 4

"Right, we are finally here. Try not to mess about. Remember best behaviour."

Erica laughed out loud. Dylan got out of the car after a brief struggle with the door. Erica laughed as her door opened fine. She turned to Dylan, "I think I am falling in love with this car."

Dylan shook his head and then banged shut his car door. He locked the car door. Erica pulled a funny face. Dylan shook his head, "Erica this ain't no theatre, show a little respect."

Dylan and Erica walked to William's front door – five knocks – no reply. Erica began to giggle, "Where art thou, William?"

Dylan knocked again. There was a brief delay and then the sound of several locks opening. Dylan and Erica looked at each other in confusion. The door opened slowly and then a strange voice echoed all around, "Who is it? Who is it?"

Dylan smiled at Erica and then replied, "It is Dylan. It is Dylan. Is it safe to let us in?"

William opened the door slowly and then revealed himself. Erica and Dylan could not believe their eyes. They looked at William and then gazed at each other in total disbelief. William was wearing a Captain Kirk shirt. Erica totally lost control and burst out laughing. Dylan bit his bottom lip and turned to Erica, "So what's so funny?" Suddenly, he totally lost it, roaring with laughter.

William stood at the door with his hands on his hips, totally confused, "What's so funny? Is it something I said? No, it can't be, I haven't said much, have I?"

Dylan smiled, "I'm sorry William, you haven't changed a bit."

William became all paranoid, "So how do you mean? Am I a funny guy to look at?"

William was very small, skinny with a pale complexion. The reason for this was he never ventured outside of his strange world.

Dylan held out his hand. William moved closer and shook it.

"How are you doing my old friend?"

"Not bad, no use in complaining, no-one ever listens. No-one cares, but I guess it's today's society."

Erica smiled, "Is it okay if I introduce myself? I'm sure we have met once before."

William was not used to female company and was quite shy, "Oh what can I say? You're such a pretty lady. Do come in and you Dylan, I've prepared your envelope."

Dylan and Erica entered William's domain, closing the door behind them. Inside the room was a typical shrine to the Geek Movement, posters of various conspirators, UFOs and lots of Star Wars toys. William had lots of computers and gadgets on display.

"Okay you two, welcome to my humble abode. Do you two fancy a couple of ice-cold beers?"

Dylan smiled, "Yes, William, the heat has left us dry."

"Okay, two bottles of Bud coming up."

William left the room and then ventured into his kitchen. He opened the fridge and got out three bottles of Budweiser. He knew they were coming and was ready to provide. William reached inside a cupboard and produced three glasses. He then opened each bottle and poured the beer into the glasses.

Erica whispered into Dylan's ear, "My God, this must be a sad and lonely experience."

William appeared with the drinks. He looked into Erica's eyes and spoke, "No whispering. It's okay to communicate with me."

Erica smiled, "Oh William, I was just saying to Dylan what an amazing variety of computers you have."

"Yes, you're right, I am a computer geek, it's in my blood. My father was a geek. I belong to a long line of geeks."

Erica smiled, "There is nothing wrong with geeks. Where would we be without geeks? I'll tell you where, back in the Dark Ages. Most ladies would prefer a geek to a caveman."

Finally, William for once started to feel good about himself. With a gleaming smile he returned the compliment, "My God, Dylan is so lucky to have such a beautiful, wise woman as you."

Erica laughed and spoke, "Why thank you William for your kind words."

William put the drinks onto a small table. Dylan picked up his drink and spoke, "Okay, let me propose a toast to William."

Erica and William raised their glasses.

"Okay, ready, here's to William, a God amongst the geeks."

They all laughed and raised their glasses.

"Cheers, my friend Dylan. Oh, I forgot are you still acting? Made it to Hollywood yet?"

"You can count on it my friend. One day I will be amongst the Hollywood greats."

"Oh, it's great to be visited. I got out the barbeque just in case you pair fancied a burger."

"Why, you're so sweet William." Erica felt good, "beer and a burger what more could a girl ask for William."

"You know that's the first time I have ever been called sweet."

Erica replied, "Oh there is always a first time for everything, sugar."

William, after some hesitation, replied, "I sometimes wish I could meet someone as beautiful as you."

Erica gazed into William's eyes – they looked so miserable in their perplexity, "Look, William, look to the light. Escape this domain of darkness. Think positive and you will meet the woman of your dreams."

William's eyes peered with curiosity, "You reckon I could find myself someone as beautiful as you?"

"Yes, the lady of your dreams awaits."

Dylan joined in the conversation with his own brand of sense of humour, "Look, William, are you trying to hit on my girlfriend?"

"Why no, Erica is just giving me some advice."

Erica shook her head as Dylan explained he was only joking.

"Alright, William, look around, you have all of these computers. There must be hundreds of websites you can go on to meet a beautiful lady."

"I guess you're right. I just need to be more positive. To be honest with you I have tried dating sites. I met a lady called Delilah. She kept cheating on me and I left her. I guess I just couldn't take it anymore."

Erica produced her usual cheeky smile and said, "Who was the guy - it wasn't Tom Jones was it?"

William looked confused, "No, the guy's name was Richie Jones, he was a local bar singer."

Dylan began to laugh out loud. This was not what he expected. "Did you actually see him perform with Delilah?"

"Why yes, he kept coming over to our table. He sang in her ear several times. Looking back now, I should have complained about his behaviour."

Suddenly a memory came flashing back to William, "Oh, I remember the guy. He was a Tom Jones tribute act and he ended up taking my Delilah to his green, green grass of home."

Erica looked to Dylan, "Is William having us on or what?"

"No Erica, don't be ridiculous, the guy is a prize geek."

William agreed, "You're right, God loves a trier, so I went on to another site. I met Esmeralda in a burger bar. The pictures of her were not up to date. She was French. She was a complete yak."

Erica looked confused, "What on earth is a yak?"

"Oh, it's an unattractive fat female and to make matters worse, she turned up with her father and they both expected to get fed, with me paying the bill. Her father looked a bit like Quasimodo. Does that name ring any bells?"

Dylan looked to Erica then burst out laughing, "My God, your stories sure are funny."

"Oh, I have gone on a bit, let's go into the garden. Oh, and help yourselves, the beers in the fridge."

Dylan finished off his beer and then helped himself to another.

William opened several locks to gain access to his garden. He finally opened the door and stepped out into the light. The sun dazzled his eyes. He reached inside his pocket and produced a pair of shades, "Sure gone nice now hasn't it, Erica?"

"Yes" Erica scanned all around to the right there was a selection of weeds and on the left concrete. Sitting on the concrete was a barbeque and attached to the barbeque a gas bottle. There was also a plastic white table and four chairs.

Dylan then appeared with some beers. He placed the bottles on top of the table and then sat down.

"Okay, I will get the food. Could you start up the barbeque, Erica?"

"Oh yes, it would be my pleasure."

Erica opened up the gas bottle as Dylan shouted, "Boom."

Erica shook her head, "Dylan, stop being a dipstick." She then ignited the barbeque.

William reappeared with the burgers. He handed them to Erica and spoke, "Do you fancy playing chef, as I always burn them?"

"Oh okay, nothing worse than burnt burgers."

William returned to the kitchen and came back with a tray of batches and various sauces.

Erica turned the burgers over, making sure she did not burn them.

William stood next to Erica admiring her beauty, "My, them burgers smell nice."

"Yeah, I reckon they're cooked now."

Erica slowly picked up the burgers placing them carefully onto the batches. A minute later her task was completed. She turned off the barbeque and the gas and then took a seat at the table. She picked up a glass of beer and quenched her thirst. Dylan added sauce and began to eat a burger.

William shook his head, "I'm missing something. I know, atmosphere! I'll be back in a minute"' He went back into the house and then returned with a small battery-operated stereo. He placed it on the table and then pressed play.

Erica and Dylan had no idea what sort of music William was into.

"Oh, it's the greatest hit of the Beach Boys, one of my favourites."

Dylan jumped out of his seat and pretended he was on a surfboard, "Come on join me. Look at those waves."

William stood up as did Erica. All three of them pretended they were on surfboards. Dylan shouted, "Let's go surfing USA."

A couple of minutes later they sat back down drinking beer and finishing off their burgers. William turned to Dylan, "Okay, tell everything about yourself. What have you been up to? Anything supernatural? Do you know, I love that show? Sam and Dean are such cool dudes."

"Well, William, Erica has psychic potential. She dreams of celebrities she watched or listened to as a child. Lots of times she has told me of her dreams, and I have turned on the television to find the person she had dreamed about had passed away."

"My, that is supernatural. I bet she does a lot of things supernatural."

Erica turned to William, "I could write a book on the strange things that have happened to me. Remember that time when we were on vacation playing cards?"

Dylan scanned his memory, "Yes, I remember. One night we were sat together bored due to the lack of entertainment in our hotel. We played cards. I placed the deck on the table and said to Erica "pick me out the ten of hearts." She picked it out. I shuffled the pack. She picked out four tens. I then shuffled the pack and asked her to pick out all the kings. She did it. People looked on in disbelief. One came over, he said he was a magician. The guy wanted to prove a point. He shuffled the deck, placed the cards on the table and then said, "Pick out the queen of spades." All eyes were on Erica. She picked out the Queen of Spades. The guy turned to Erica and said, "Oh my God, how on earth did you do that?""

"She did it. I just wish I had filmed it."

"My God, fancy a game of cards, I could fetch a pack?"

Erica shook her head, "No point, I have this gift, but I have no control over it."

"Oh, my dear, that's such a shame."

"I have also written lots of poems, some of which have predicted future events."

"What about 9/11, no-one saw that one coming."

"Look, don't tell anyone, but I joined a secret society, it's called the Order of Geekhood. We all chat about conspiracy. We reckon it was our own people that carried out the 9/11 attack."

"You reckon, William?"

"Yes"

"But why?"

"Oh, can't say, it's a secret."

"Okay, what about UFO's, unidentified flying objects, I reckon they are real?"

"I met a geek on the internet who was once abducted by aliens, he claimed he was force-fed cold baked beans for a week. He claims the aliens returned him back to earth because he was full of gas and wind. I guess they didn't take too kindly to the smell."

Dylan shook his head, "I hate cold beans, that must have been an ordeal. What do you think about all of these vampire cults?"

"Oh, funny you should say that; I met a really upset guy on the internet. His mum had simply disappeared without trace. The strange thing about all of this was the guy's mother was a reporter investigating a group of vampires."

Dylan shook his head, "My God, she must have found out something."

"I know, it's quite shocking. Should have sent Sam and Dean to sort them out."

Dylan looked to William and said, "What about Big Foot?"

William turned to Dylan and said, "My feet ain't that big."

Dylan laughed, "You got to be having me on."

"Well maybe I am. It is not often I hear laughter. A geek's life is one of loneliness and solitude."

Erica put on a sympathetic look, "I guess you don't get out much then?"

"No, I am lost between these four walls. Do you know, if it hadn't been for Dylan, I reckon I wouldn't be here today? Dylan saved my life and to this day I haven't forgotten."

With an expression of sadness William stood up and hugged Dylan, "Thank you for saving my geek life."

William then hugged Erica and then spoke, "I want to also thank you for your words of wisdom. From now on I will stay positive and look to the light. I shall endeavour to escape this pit of darkness."

Erica embraced William and kissed him on the cheek.

Dylan finished off his drink, "Okay, we must be on our way."

William smiled, "Okay, it's brown envelope time."

William returned to the house and then turned around, "Okay, this way."

Erica and Dylan followed William to the house. William opened a drawer and then produced a brown envelope. He then turned around and handed it to Dylan.

William laughed and then spoke in a low voice, "Whatever you are up to my friend, I hope it all works out for you. The information you required is in the envelope and remember, I never supplied you with this information."

Dylan smiled, "Look, William, as far as I am concerned, I never visited this humble abode."

"Oh okay, I guess this is it. We will never meet again."

"William, maybe we will in the not-too-distant future." Dylan shook his hand as he handed over the envelope.

Erica once more embraced William, "Remember, William, stay loose and look to the light."

William opened the front door, and they said their final goodbyes. The door closed. As they walked away, they could hear all the locks closing. Erica looked to Dylan, "My God, he is security conscious, isn't he?"

"Yeah, I reckon he thinks the Government is out to get him because of all those fancy computers."

"No, I reckon it's all those conspiracy theories."

"Don't you believe in them?"

Erica shook her head and said, "Well sugar, you would have to give me an example."

"Okay, what about JFK?"

"Yeah, I reckon he was assassinated by our government."

"See there you go, another conspiracy theory put to bed."

Dylan looked to his car, "I've got another conspiracy theory for you."

"Yeah, what?"

"Why on earth is it me that always ends up driving? You have insurance and a driving licence too."

"You're ever so right, honey. Next time we go out, I'll drive."

"Good, it's been that long, are you sure you know how to?"

Erica laughed as Dylan opened his car door with gritted teeth. He pulled it open, and Erica got in the car. Her door seemed okay. She sat down as Dylan handed her the envelope. Erica put on her usual cheeky smile and said, "Okay fella, let's hit the road."

Chapter 5

Dylan started up the car. It started up first time and they slowly drove off. Erica turned to Dylan and said, "Your mate William – his shirt, now that was funny."

"No, it wasn't funny, the word you are looking for is sad. All over America there are thousands of William's, geeks looking for answers."

The sky was overcast and cloudy, but the traffic was flowing. Dylan suddenly stopped at a set of traffic lights.

Erica noticed a sign in the back window of the car they were behind. She read it out loud, "We are all being watched."

Erica shook her head, "How sad there are no aliens and no monsters, just us humans. We are the biggest monsters of all."

Dylan shook his head, "My God, you ain't developing a conscience before our first crime, are you?"

"Why no, we need the money."

Erica began to play with the radio, flicking through the station until she found the song of her choice, "I'm in a good mood, fancy a sing song?"

"Why yes my dear, a song by the Animals, *we got to get out of this place.*"

They both began to sing, "*We got to get out of this place, if it's the last thing we ever do.*"

Dylan turned to Erica and sang, "*Girl there's a better place for me and you. In the dirty old part of the city, where the sun refuses to shine…*"

Suddenly it started to rain. Dylan stopped singing and began to laugh, "My, Erica, why is it whenever I sing it starts raining?"

"Oh, that's easy, your voice opens up the heavens, thus whenever you sing it rains."

"Erica, I just want to say thank you for honouring me with a duet."

Erica shook her head, "Don't worry, it ain't going to be habit forming."

Erica flicked through the channels as they cruised along until she found one of her all-time favourite songs. Erica started moving her arms and feet to the beat and she broke out in song to Tina Turner, "*Rolling on the river.*" She, pretended she had a mic in her hand as she sang, "*Rollin, rolling, Rollin on the river.*"

Dylan looked in the rear mirror, behind him was a patrol car. Dylan began to panic and quickly turned off the radio.

Erica became annoyed and then expressed her anger, "Why on earth have you turned the radio off?"

"Look behind us."

Erica looked behind and laughed, "So what, it's a patrol car."

"Yeah, but it's on our trail."

Panic and fear began to fluster his mind. He turned his attention to the envelope, "What happens if they pull us over? Erica quick, place the brown envelope in the glove compartment."

As Erica did as she was told, the patrol car began to flash at them to pull over.

Dylan's heart was now pounding. He pulled over to the side. Erica shook her head in disbelief, "My God, get a grip of yourself. Remember you're an actor."

Dylan was gripped by a hot flush panic attack. He began to frown in confusion.

Erica shook her head, "Snap out of it and stay cool. Wind your window down."

Dylan shook his head and then regained his usual composure. He began winding down the car window.

Two large police officers appeared before Dylan. One of them was tall, middle aged and well groomed. He was the one who was doing all the talking.

"Hi sir, my name is Officer Anderson and this big young guy next to me is Patrolman Jones. I have picked you out at random as I need to show this raw recruit the ropes."

Dylan smiled and said, "Thank you officers, only too happy to help."

"Okay, Patrolman Jones, what is it you require?"

"I require this guy's driving licence. Sir, can I please see your driver's licence and keep your hands where I can see them."

Dylan took a deep breath and then reached inside the glove compartment and produced his driving licence. Officer Jones dropped his hand within easy reach of his revolver.

"Okay Sir, can you step out of your vehicle, nice and easy, cool and calm."

Dylan shook his head in disbelief.

Officer Anderson laughed, moving his hand slowly towards his revolver. The rookie patrolman was in his early twenties, fresh faced and wide-eyed.

Dylan opened the car door, it creaked due to the rust.

Officer Anderson smiled, "My, your car is in need of some lubrication, especially that door."

Dylan put on a false smile and got out of the car. He handed the driving licence to the patrolman who looked at the licence. Officer Anderson noticed hesitation from Patrolman Jones, "Okay, is everything in order Patrolman?"

"Well, sir, I just caught a whiff of Bud on this man's breath. I reckon he's been drinking."

Dylan again shook his head in disbelief. The words 'Why me?' kept repeating again and again in his head.

Officer Anderson turned to the patrolman and spoke in a deep calm voice,

"Look, patrolman, check out his car for evidence whilst I pop the question to him."

Officer Anderson stood next to Dylan and said, "Right sir, my colleague has reason to believe you have been drinking. If that is the case, how much? Let me see you walk in a straight line."

Erica had seen enough. Suddenly, she got out of the car ready to save the day. "Good day to you, officer."

Officer Anderson looked at Erica with her tender looks and gleaming teeth. She put on a big smile and then spoke, "Why officer, me and my driver but shared one bottle of Bud."

Dylan looked to the officer, "Yeah, just the one bottle."

Officer Anderson looked to Dylan, "Look here you driver, you speak when you are spoken to. Me and the pretty lady are having a conversation. Please remain silent."

The patrolman turned to Officer Anderson, "Sir, nothing to report, no evidence of any criminal activities."

"Okay, patrolman, why don't we go find us some real criminals and leave this nice lady and her driver to continue to their destination."

"Yes sir, right away."

Officer Anderson and Patrolman Jones got into their patrol car and were soon on their way. Dylan breathed a sigh of relief. He then turned to Erica, "Beauty never lies, who the hell is he trying to kid?"

Erica laughed out loud. "I believe he was just kidding himself. My, Dylan, is that the first time you have been pulled over?"

"Would you believe me if I said yes?"

"Why Dylan, I would believe anything."

They both climbed into the old car. Erica began to laugh out loud, "Officer Anderson spoke the words."

Dylan's eyes opened wide with curiosity, "What words?"

"Lubrication."

Dylan shook his head, "One day, doll, I am going to get us a new car."

He then turned on the radio, moving the volume to high. *A Bat out of Hell* was playing, "Oh, one of my favourites, Malt loaf, Bat out of Hell."

Erica shook her head in disbelief, "The group was called Meatloaf – not Malt loaf."

"Oh babe, well pointed out." Dylan pulled off slowly. Just as he was about to burst out into song, Erica leaned over and turned the radio off. Dylan shook his head and then turned to Erica, "What the hell. Why have you turned the radio off?"

"Darling, that's simple. I do not require a headache. Am I right in thinking you were about to burst out into song?"

"Yeah, you must have read my mind."

"No not really, you're just very predictable."

"Okay, smart ass Erica, what am I going to do next?"

"That's easy, you're going to sulk and then attempt to turn the radio back on."

"Yeah, you're right and why shouldn't I? It's my car."

"Yes dear, but these pretty things are my ears. Do you really want to burst them?"

Dylan shook his head, "Why no, I guess you're going to need them to pull this thing off."

"What was that, Dylan?"

"I said, you're going to need them to pull this thing off."

"I can't hear you."

Dylan laughed and said, "Erica, you're just messing around."

"Oh of course I am, dear, it's what I do best."

Dylan turned and smiled at Erica, "Babe, you are the best."

"Yeah, Dylan, don't I know it."

Dylan breathed a sigh of relief, "Here we are, babe, home sweet home."

Dylan parked up and they both got out of the car. Dylan slammed the car door and then gazed up into the dark sky. He began thinking to himself 'if only I was rich, a new car, a large property and no money worries.'

Erica turned to Dylan and shouted, "Stop daydreaming and get a move on."

Dylan began to run towards the apartment. He overtook Erica and then stood by the door. There was a brief delay and then he opened the door. Dylan then remembered the envelope. He slowly turned to Erica and handed her the keys to the car.

"Oh, what are these for, daydreamer?"

"Oh, would you believe me if I said the envelope was still in the car?"

"Okay, I'll get it whilst you make us a coffee."

Dylan nodded in agreement.

Erica stepped into the darkness. She made her way to the car. She opened the car door and then the glove compartment door. She reached inside and picked up the envelope. She shut the car door and was then startled by a sinister looking black cat. Erica felt a bit shaken and then her anger erupted like a volcano, "You damn stupid cat." She picked up a stone and then threw it in the direction of the cat. It was a hit. The cat cried out in pain and ran in the opposite direction.

Chapter 6

The light began to fade rapidly as Erica returned to the room. She began to hear screams in the distance. A couple of seconds later she was back in the safety of the apartment. She entered the room and looked to Dylan. "Okay, where is the coffee you promised?"

"Oh, I figured you might want a cold drink."

Erica shook her head, "Oh, sometimes I just wish you would listen to what I am saying."

"Okay, I'm sorry, but can we please open the Goddamn brown envelope? The suspense is killing me?"

"Okay Dylan, let us both sit down and open it together."

They both sat down next to each other. Erica opened the brown envelope slowly then proceeded to pull out a piece of paper. Dylan looked at the piece of paper and then spoke with a shade of impatience in his voice," How many old guys are on the list?"

"Oh, I count six."

Dylan smiled, "That's not a problem as long as they are all rich. I must admit I don't plan on hanging around here. Where would you like to retire, babe?"

"Oh, some beautiful island in the Caribbean."

"Yeah babe, I could just picture you topless on the beach and then strolling out of the sea, the sun beating down on your bare breasts.".

Erica shook her head, "Shut up you pervert. No wait, you're right, we are both on a nudist beach."

"Yeah babe, now you're talking."

"We make mad passionate love amidst the golden sand as the sun beats down on our naked bodies."

"Erica, my love, shall we retire to the bedroom?"

Erica shook her head, "No, don't be stupid. Let's make a plan instead."

"Okay Erica, back to business."

"Yeah, business before pleasure."

"What's the name of the first guy on the list?"

"Oh, it's Henry Jones, that surname again."

"Yeah, you're right it is a common surname. What age is he, Erica?"

"Oh, he's sixty-seven."

"Where does he live?"

"Oh, it's about thirty miles away from here, his address is Number 5, Glen rose Mansion. I once had an aunt that lived up that way, up there in the hills. It's really rich up there. Oh look, how sweet, William left extra information. Henry was once a top mechanic and restorer of old vintage cars. That's how he made all of his money."

Dylan's eyes perked up with curiosity. After a brief delay Dylan announced triumphantly, "I've got a great plan. Imagine you're driving along, and you just happen to breakdown outside that old fella's mansion. The old maiden in distress routine – it never fails. The old knight in shining armour appears and helps you start the car and then, bingo, you've got him hooked. What do you think of the plan so far, Erica?"

"Yes, it's good. You possess such an extraordinary gift for planning."

Dylan smiled. With an air of superiority, he began to speak, "Erica you are right. You are witnessing a high degree of intelligence in operation."

Erica shook her head in disbelief, "No, no, let's not get carried away. After all it's me that is the brains of this outfit. Right, Dylan, it's my turn. I am a lonely orphan just split up with violent boyfriend, no money and nowhere to stay. All I've got is my kind nature and my beautiful looks."

"Outstanding, Erica. When we get through all of this you will be my bride."

"No, you must be joking. You are The Count, remember. I believe you would suck me dry."

Dylan laughed and then finished off his Budweiser. He then put on his favourite CD, *American Heartbeat.*

Erica drank her cool beer. Dylan smiled as he looked to Erica, "Babe, fancy another beer?"

"Oh, I'm not sure. Oh, go on then. Why don't we talk about the old days, Dylan?"

"Okay Erica, here's your beer." Dylan produced a bottle of Budweiser. He removed the lid and placed the bottle next to Erica.

The next song on the CD was an all-time favourite by Survivor, *The Eye of the Tiger.* Dylan began to dance, spinning around and moving backward and forward. Erica laughed and then spoke, "My what a mover, what a groover. I like your dancing. Just don't start singing Rocky or it will rain." Erica shook her head, "Okay that's enough, just sit down, and we will do some talking."

Dylan stopped dancing and then turned the volume down. He then sat down and turned his full attention to Erica.

"Right, lover-boy, do you want to start?"

Dylan smiled, "Okay, well let me think. Yes, remember that guy you used to date before you met me, wasn't his name Henry?"

"No stupid, his name was Harry."

"Oh, I knew it began with an H."

"Yeah. My, he was a big guy, six foot five."

"Wasn't he a basket-case?"

"No Dylan, I believe he was a basket-ball player. Didn't you and he come to blows?"

"Yeah, I took him out with a baseball bat. Erica, I confess to doing wrong, but that guy had it coming. When he heard I was dating you he threatened to break every bone in my body."

"I guess you're right, Dylan, Harry was a complete hothead. I witnessed him beat up lots of guys that made a pass at me. I should have left him earlier, but I was lonely. He was the jealous type. You're right, he had it coming. What goes around comes around. Anyway, Dylan what about that girl you dated before you met me, Hot Legs Lulu?"

"Yeah, Erica I must admit she was a mistake. Her father pulled a gun on me, he said if I were to date her again, he would shoot me. The rest is history."

"Yeah, and what a colourful history. Dylan, I must admit you took the safe option. You dumped her and started dating me."

Dylan gazed into Erica's eyes. His mind whispered, 'My God she possesses such appealing beauty'. "I reckon I made the right choice, a bullet or a broken bone."

Erica smiled and spoke, "Dylan it was your baseball bat that saved the day."

"Yeah Erica, it was a smashing investment. I've just remembered, Erica, didn't you once work with old people in a Care Home?"

"Yeah Dylan. My God, what a horrible job that was."

"Yeah, but that work experience will come in handy, all you need to do is pretend to be kind and considerate."

"What are you trying to say, Dylan, I can't act?"

"No Erica you're a great actress, that's why I know we will pull this thing off."

Erica smiled and then spoke in a soft voice, "All I need to do is pretend those old guys just require friendship, someone to talk to."

"That is right Erica, you get them to marry you and on your wedding night I will appear and give them a fright. I am a natural born vampire, ready to unleash the fangs. In my costume I would give any old guy the fright of his life."

"Okay Dylan, enough said, it's time for bed."

The next song came on REO Speed wagon, *keep on loving you*. Without warning Dylan broke out into song, *"I do not want to sleep, I just want to keep on loving you."*

Erica shook her head, "Yeah alright, goodnight." Erica ignored Dylan and made her way towards the bed. Dylan appeared completely naked wearing only a smile, "Erica are you in the mood for mad passionate love?

Erica looked at Dylan's naked body, "Well I am not sure. It's getting really late."

Dylan started playing with his manhood, "It's never too late. Come on Erica, come out to play."

Erica laughed and then pulled off the covers, revealing her naked body – a body no man could resist. "Okay Dylan, kiss me all over you sex machine."

Dylan climbed onto the bed and began kissing her tenderly. Soon after they were making love. Afterwards Erica fell into a deep sleep. She dreamt of living on a Caribbean Island. She sat in a large mansion and had people waiting on her day and night. Such a happy dream. Erica awoke to the sound of a spoon turning in a coffee cup.

"Wakey, wakey Princess, your coffee awaits."

Erica opened her eyes; the coffee was a welcomed sight. Erica sat up as Dylan handed her the coffee. Dylan smiled, "I have cooked you a breakfast."

Erica sat amongst the satin sheets whilst Dylan returned with the breakfast. Dylan handed Erica a large wooden tray. Upon the tray sat two plates, one with eggs, bacon and sausage – the other plate had three muffins on it.

Erica took hold of the tray and then spoke, trying her best not to laugh, "Okay Dylan this looks lovely, all cooked to perfection."

Dylan began to laugh, "Perfection deserves perfection."

"Look, I'm not going to argue with you Dylan, after all you're always right, but have you forgotten something? I'm not going to eat this food with my fingers."

Dylan scanned the tray – no knife and no fork. Dylan laughed out loud, "How stupid am I?"

"Dylan, you said it, come on hurry up and bring me the sauce."

Dylan turned and raced into the kitchen. Within minutes Dylan had returned with the items she required. Dylan then disappeared back into the kitchen to finish off his muffins.

Dylan made some more coffee and then joined Erica in the bedroom. He placed a cup of coffee on the tray as Erica finished off her breakfast.

"Oh, Dylan, it's like that dream I had last night."

Dylan shook his head, "No, babe, that was all real."

Erica laughed out loud whilst shaking her head, "No that was alright, but I dreamt I was in the Caribbean sitting in a large mansion being waited on night and day."

Dylan produced a wide grin, "See babe, what happens when you make love to me."

Erica shrugged her shoulders in confusion, "No, what?"

"Why, sweet dreams of course."

Erica looked to Dylan feeling enlightened, "Yeah, wise words Dylan. I reckon you're right."

Dylan became excited, "That means same again tonight?"

Erica shook her head, "No, it doesn't, sorry. We have got to get back to the plan. Concentrate Dylan, we have a lifetime of making love together. Once we have pulled this off, I reckon making love will be the order of the day."

Dylan burst out into laughter, "Now you are talking."

"Yeah, babe, action speaks louder than words."

"Okay Erica, I have an idea; why not drive up to the mansion? I will disconnect one of the batteries leads so the car won't start. I will leave you and get a taxi back to town."

"Dylan my darling, one small detail – what happens if I can't get in contact with you?"

Dylan put his arm around Erica, "Don't worry, I've got this old mobile phone, it's fully charged, and it's got credit."

Erica began to have doubts about the plan, "Okay Dylan, let's go through the plan one more time. I win the old guy over; tell him I am homeless and unemployed and appeal to his kind nature – that is if he's got one. And what happens if he doesn't want to get married? Plus, what is the time limit on all of this?"

Dylan shook his head, "I know what you really mean. You're going to miss me as I am going to miss you. The time limit is one month, and you get the hell out of there. Just think of all that lovely money. I reckon more than half a million for one month's work. What do you reckon, Erica?"

"Yeah, when you put it like that, I wouldn't earn that kind of money in a lifetime. I am going to earn me some big money - by the end of the year we could be millionaires."

"Erica, that's what I want to hear, positive words. All we need now is action."

"Okay Dylan I need a shower whilst you wash up."

Dylan laughed, "Okay boss, I'll wash up."

"Good, I need to look good for Henry."

Dylan picked up the tray with the cup and plates on it and then proceeded towards the kitchen. Erica wasted no time and was soon in the shower, in and out was the order of the day.

Chapter 7

Dylan had done the washing up and was now sitting down watching television. He flicked through the channels until he got to the news. He watched it for a few minutes and then turned it off – the same old news, job losses and murders.

Dylan could hear the noise of the hairdryer in operation. He picked up one of his horror books and began to read about werewolves. He read about different encounters. One story Dylan found interesting was about a werewolf that was attacking people during full moons. Two tramps were slaughtered by the beast. One guy was found with his head ripped off and another guy had his face and ears missing. Cattle and horses were found eaten. A witness saw the creature and described it as a weird looking animal that reared up on its hind legs like a human being, its tongue lolling out of its huge mouth, its jaws dripping with blood. Its eyes were emerald green and seemed to reflect an intelligence that was almost human.

Erica suddenly appeared. She turned to Dylan, "Werewolves ain't real. Why on earth do you like reading about man-made monsters?"

Dylan closed the book. He then announced triumphantly that he was to one day become an author – the new Stephen King, a master of the horror books.

A draught of cold air suddenly ran down Erica's spine. She could not believe what she was hearing. Dylan wasn't the most intelligent guy, he struggled with basic grammar. Erica said nothing; for once she was speechless. Dylan smiled anyway, "How did you know I was reading about werewolves?"

Erica answered in a low voice, "Oh that's easy. I'm psychic, remember."

Dylan shook his head. "Whatever, don't insult my intelligence."

Erica felt a red mist descending but kept her composure. She looked into Dylan's eyes and said, "Don't be stupid Dylan, there is nothing to insult."

Dylan laughed, "Oh that's alright then. You're not insulting me."

Erica laughed out loud, "Dylan you're a star, the man of the moment."

A thought flashed through Dylan's brain. He remembered the past predictions Erica had made and they had all come true. Dylan began to talk fluently with a heightened voice, "I'm sorry Erica, communication between minds. You have demonstrated your powers in the past. Remember the solar eclipse you predicted, or the deaths of all of them celebrities. You dreamt about them and the following day they were dead. And the times you have mentioned a song you haven't heard for a long time. I have turned on the radio and the song was being played. My favourite was when you picked out all the cards from the deck. There were plenty of witnesses – a million to one, magic."

Erica smiled and replied in a low voice, "Okay, from now on I want you to think before you speak."

Dylan looked to Erica with a fixed expression, "Look, right, sometimes I don't think, and I say such stupid things. Question is, do you forgive me? Shall we get back to the plan?"

Erica closed her eyes for a brief second and then said, "Yes."

Dylan looked to Erica, "My, that pink top looks lovely – pretty in pink."

"Yeah, Dylan are you going to have a shower?"

"No, I had a wash when you were asleep."

"Okay Dylan does that mean we are all ready?"

"Yeah, and you're driving."

Erica nodded in confirmation. Dylan was not expecting that. After some hesitation Dylan spoke his mind, "I wasn't expecting that, you haven't driven for a while, ever since that near miss. Remember that gutter punk pulling out his revolver?"

Erica shook her head, "Oh such blasphemous language. It was so small I could hardly see it."

"Oh, I must admit, I turned away, just not my scene."

"Mine neither Dylan, mine neither."

"Okay, less of the chit chat, we need to hit the road, Jack."

"Yes, we sure do, Jill."

They both stood up and then collected the items they needed for this operation to be a success. They left the apartment and made their way to the car. Erica put the key into the door of the car and opened it with ease. Dylan could not believe his eyes.

"How on earth did you do that?"

"Oh, it's a woman's touch."

Dylan got in the passenger side and watched Erica close the door and start the car up for the first time.

Dylan laughed as his eyelids flickered spasmodically. The sun had appeared in all its glory. Dylan reached for his sunglasses and placed them over his eyes with great haste.

Erica shielded her eyes expressing annoyance and spoke, "Pass my sunglasses. I'm driving remember."

Dylan reached inside the glove compartment and produced Erica's shades. He quickly handed them to her. Erica placed them over her eyes. The sun shone bright, livid with wrath. Erica closed her eyes and then spoke, "My, what's with this weather. It must be all that global warming business."

Dylan rolled his sleeves up as Erica pulled off. Dylan then spoke with a look of bewilderment on his face, "My God, this car must love you."

"Yeah, cars love the ladies as they look after them."

Dylan nodded in agreement. With a feeling of enlightenment he spoke, "Erica, you say the most intelligent things, no wonder my car likes you."

Erica was administering total concentration. She adjusted her speed and began to smile. Erica stopped at a set of traffic lights. Dylan scanned all around – he disliked the noise of the traffic. Suddenly a thought flashed through his brain – the radio – why not turn on some music. After all it was his car.

After some hesitation Dylan turned to Erica, "My darling Erica, may I turn on the radio?"

Erica pulled off from the traffic lights. The noise of the traffic began to pound in her ears. Erica then answered in a low voice, "Okay you win, but no singing whilst I am driving, or I might lose control of the car and crash."

Dylan shook his head, "Look Erica, if you put it like that there is no way I am going to sing."

Erica believed his words and reached over and turned on the radio. The song being played was *Take it Easy* by the Eagles. Dylan sat back and closed his eyes as Erica relaxed her hands upon the steering wheel. She then pressed down on the gas pedal as a red Corvette Convertible was hanging onto her tail. The car overtook her as she breathed a sigh of relief. Erica turned to Dylan, "Babe, can you please navigate if I get lost?"

Dylan removed his designer shades and spoke, 'Okay Erica, follow this road for about four miles. When you get to a set of lights turn left."

Erica smiled, "Alright."

Dylan laughed, "No left."

Dylan opened his window letting in a cool breeze. Another classic song began to play on the radio, Sonny and Cher, *I Got You Babe*. Dylan hesitated and then broke out in song, 'I got you babe'.

Erica could see some mountains in the distance. Dylan began to sweat furiously. He opened his window a little wider letting in more cool air. Suddenly raindrops began bouncing on the window screen. Dylan laughed and spoke, "No, it's not my singing."

"I know it's just a shower, that's how I know it's not you're singing." Erica slowed down and turned left.

Dylan smiled, "Okay babe, another few miles and take a right alongside all those old buildings. Remember that old guy Conrad?"

"Yeah, I remember, wasn't he the drugs dealer that got shot five times last year near here?"

"Yeah, I suppose he got what was coming to him. What goes around comes around, that's the old saying."

"What about us Dylan, ain't we going to commit murder?"

"No Erica, I see it this way, these old guys are coffin dodgers, the time is ticking against them. I see us on a mission from God. We are going to put them out of their misery and lay their poor souls to rest in peace."

Erica continued to drive, lost in deep thought. She then turned to Dylan, "My God, you're so right. You have convinced me, Dylan; I am but an angel sent from heaven."

Dylan nodded his head then spoke with confidence, "Yes, now you are getting into the swing of things."

"Okay Dylan, how close are we?"

"Oh Erica, take the next right and then carry-on driving for another four miles."

Erica suddenly had a negative thought to share, "Oh Dylan, what happens if the old guy is on vacation?"

Dylan shook his head, "No, what are the odds on that happening? Henry has no family or kin folk. The guy is a total recluse."

Erica apologised and then spoke in a low voice, "You're right, it's just me being paranoid." Erica put her foot down on the gas pedal as the sun broke through the clouds and began to shine once more in all its glory.

Dylan gazed out of his window at the various large mansions. Dylan's mind whispered, 'peace, money and tranquillity.' Dylan could not believe the size of some of the properties. He turned to Erica wide eyed and spoke, "Slow down a bit, Erica, and take in some of the sights. My God, look at the size of that swimming pool over there – the rich have got it made."

"You're right, Dylan, we drive an old car and live in a rented apartment. How sad is that? Compared to this it's a different world."

Dylan laughed, "Yeah, but it's a world we are about to break into. Look, Erica, we are here. That is the mansion, 5 Glen Rose. Pull over outside the place. Right, we need to be fast; I need to be out of the picture as soon as possible."

Erica pulled over and parked outside the mansion. Dylan jumped out. He opened the bonnet and quickly disconnected the battery leads with the aid of a small spanner. He quickly closed the bonnet and was soon on his way.

Chapter 8

After a short wait Erica removed her shades, placing them in the glove compartment. She then got out of the car and scanned all around. It was so peaceful and quiet with the colourful shrubs and the swaying palm trees. She then turned her attention to 5 Glen Rose. There was a large garden and sitting in the garden there was a motionless man. Erica opened a large metal gate and walked along the driveway to where the old man was sitting. Erica looked at the mansion – it was very impressive and well maintained. Its colour was brilliant white.

Erica heard a voice in her head telling her she was an actress 'I can pull this off. I can pull this off' she whispered. A couple of minutes later she was standing next to Henry. The old guy had dozed off after he had done some gardening.

Erica took a deep breath and said, "Hello" in a low voice.

Again, she said, "Hello."

After the third attempt Henry opened his eyes. Stood before him he saw a beautiful angel, not something he had seen for a while.

Erica looked back at Henry and saw a craggy faced, bleary eyed old man. He was wearing a blue T-shirt and green short pants. He had long skinny legs. On his feet he wore brown leather sandals.

Erica displayed her best smile. She then spoke in a low, soft voice, "Hi, good sir, my car has just broken down outside your beautiful mansion."

Henry slowly got to his feet and said, "My name is Henry and yours, my dear?"

"Oh, my name is Erica."

"Such an unusual name. You stand here whilst I collect my box of tools. Oh, and don't worry, you're in safe hands. I used to be a mechanic and restorer of old vintage automobiles."

Erica laughed and said, "Oh that's what I drive."

Henry also began to laugh. It had been a while since he had witnessed laugher. Henry collected his toolbox from his garage. He walked over to Erica with a warm smile. He turned to her and said, "I probably won't be needing these. I've got a feeling it's going to be something straightforward."

Erica smiled and said, "Why thank you, kind sir. My car is just outside your gate."

Henry laughed and said, "Okay Erica, lead the way."

A couple of minutes later and they were both standing next to Erica's car. Henry popped open the bonnet.

Straight away he noticed the car battery leads had come away. Henry put them back. He reached for a spanner and quickly tightened the nuts. He said, "Okay Erica, your car should start now. My, it's strange the way they just came off."

Erica smiled and said, "Thank you, Henry. I will try to start it up."

Erica climbed into the car and placed the key into the ignition and the car started up first time. Henry looked at Erica, she reminded him of his late wife who was as beautiful.

Erica then turned off the car and turned her attention to Henry, "My sir, you're such a kind-hearted gentleman."

Henry was a lonely old man and could not believe he had the company of a beautiful young lady.

Erica kept her usual composure and then spoke in a low voice, "There is one more favour I must ask of you."

Henry laughed, "Ask away."

"Okay, I'm in need of a toilet."

Henry was an old school gentleman. He would never refuse a damsel in distress, "Okay my dear, it's this way. Your car should be safe. There are not many people who venture around these parts."

Erica nodded in agreement and then followed Henry up to the mansion. The door was already open. Henry walked inside and then turned to Erica, "Okay, do come in, it's straight up the stairs, the first room on the right."

Erica smiled and said, "Thank you Henry." She then walked to the top of the stairs. The mansion was decorated to perfection. It was so clean and tidy.

When Erica got to the top of the stairs she stopped, gazing at an oil painting of a beautiful woman. Her mind whispered, 'this must be Henry's late wife, long flowing blonde hair and crystal blue eyes, such a fair complexioned woman'. Erica then located the toilet. Her mind once more began to whisper, 'My, that lady in the painting looks a bit like me.' She entered the bathroom, closing the door behind her. After she had used the toilet, she stood in front of the mirror. She adjusted her hair. Erica then reached over and flushed the toilet. She then washed her hands, once more glancing into the mirror and then she was on her way, slowly walking down the stairs.

Henry stood at the bottom of the stairs. He gazed up at Erica mesmerised by her beauty. Erica was soon standing next to Henry, not knowing what to expect next.

Henry invited Erica to join him in the dining area for a tea or coffee. Erica's mind whispered, 'the old guy has taken the bait.' She spoke in her new polite voice, "Why thank you Henry, may I please have a white coffee with one sugar?"

Henry laughed, "Why yes, follow me this way, just make yourself at home."

Erica followed Henry into the dining room. The room was large and filled with old paintings and antiques. In the centre of the room sat an old oak table complete with six antique chairs. The interior was light blue in colour with a white ceiling. Henry pointed to a picture of his late wife. His eyes then looked miserable in their perplexity. His heart was pounding. He then spoke, "Oh how I miss my late wife. She was so beautiful." Henry then turned his attention to Erica, "You don't mind me saying she looked a bit like you."

Erica was an actress, she was playing the role of a leading lady and answered in a low voice, "Why thank you Henry, you're right, your late wife was exceptionally beautiful. May I take a seat?"

Henry regained his composure, "Why certainly, Erica, sit anywhere you like."

Erica sat down at the head of the table as Henry ventured into the kitchen. Erica admired the layout of the room. She had never seen such valuable antiques sitting in display cabinets and on shelves. Erica closed her eyes, oh such peace and tranquillity, an environment she was not used to.

Suddenly Henry appeared with a large tray filled with plates on which cakes, biscuits and sandwiches sat. Henry placed them onto the table and turned to Erica, "Here we go, help yourself, my dear, whilst I fetch your coffee."

Erica acknowledged his kindness and spoke in a friendly voice, "Why thank you, Henry."

Henry smiled as he returned to the kitchen. After a brief second, he had returned with two cups of coffee. He placed one next to Erica and then sat down.

"Thank you, Henry, these sandwiches are truly divine." She was hungry and helped herself to another sandwich. Henry also picked up a sandwich and began eating it. Erica sipped her filtered coffee, my it tasted good. Erica helped herself to an apple cake, it tasted so good. Erica turned to Henry and spoke in a low voice, "These apple cakes, are they home-made?"

Henry nodded and then spoke, "Yes, I made them earlier, I must have known you were coming."

They laughed and then Henry turned his attention full onto Erica and spoke in a confident voice, "I crave conversation. I don't get to talk much as I have no kin and around here, my, it's so quiet and peaceful. Anyway, can you please tell me a bit about yourself?"

"Well, it's such a long story."

Henry shook his head, "Oh forgive me. Have you somewhere you need to be?"

Erica's mind whispered, 'You're an actress, act like one.'

"No, I've got nowhere to go. I am the same as you. I have no kin. I have worked in a Care Home and a theatre, both times being made redundant. My ex-partner – he had the role of Count Dracula, but he became obsessed with devil worship, biting a neighbour on the neck. He attacked two policemen and is now locked up for a long time. I believe he went completely crazy and was sectioned. Unknown to me, he had spent all our savings, the rent was not paid on our apartment, so I am now left homeless. All I have left in this world is that old car."

Henry felt sorry for Erica, "Oh, such a sad story." He put on a concerned face and spoke, "What happened to your parents?"

Erica took a deep breath and then spoke in a low voice, "My parents – my father was a salesman, his name was Bobby. My mother, her name was Mary. They went on a journey and never returned. I sat at home worrying about them. I remember a knock on the door. Instead of my parents it was two Police Officers. My, the news was so hard. I broke down in tears. They explained to me an oil tanker crashed into them. They simply had no chance, it exploded. I didn't identify the bodies as there was nothing left, but memories."

Erica began to shed a tear. The story was so sad, Henry also began to cry. Erica wiped away her tears and spoke, "Sorry, I am so sorry."

Henry reached inside his pocked and then produced a packet of tissues. He handed some to Erica, compassion was the order of the day. Henry's eyes were filled with sorrow as he spoke, "Erica, that was such a story. I am all alone with three spare bedrooms. You stay here if you want. I must admit I could do with the company, someone to talk to."

Erica's mind whispered, 'mission completed.' She then wiped her eyes once more and spoke, "Why thank you Henry, you're such a kind-hearted man."

Henry smiled and said, "What about all your belongings?"

Erica shrugged her shoulders and then spoke, "Oh, I had to leave because he became violent. He informed me he was going to drink my blood. I then knew it was time to run, so I left my belongings behind me."

Henry showed interest and began to ask questions. "How long ago was this then?"

Erica knew what to say, after all she was an actress, "Oh, it was last week. I stayed in a cheap motel and ate as little as possible to save what money I have left."

"Oh, I think he is better off locked up where he cannot harm anybody – what was his name?"

Erica was a quick thinker and answered straight away "His name is Damian."

Henry smiled, "Oh that must have been an omen."

Erica laughed, "You're right, he was a bit of a beast."

Henry asked Erica if she required more coffee. He was intoxicated by her beauty – such an engaging smile. Erica smiled and said, "Yes please, that would be nice."

Henry stood up and ventured into the kitchen. Minutes later he returned with two cups of coffee. He placed one of the cups next to Erica. She responded with a warm "Thank you."

Henry sat down, "Okay Erica I suppose it's my turn to do some talking. My wife's name was Alice. I was married for thirty-two years. My wife was a model and painter. She had many talents. She could sing. She even spoke several languages. I met her on a cruise ship. I still remember her getting up to sing. Her voice was utterly amazing, as was her beauty. The only problem was she had a weak heart, the same condition as me. I went to fetch a new automobile and when I returned, I found her dead at the bottom of the stairs. Such a tragic ending to a talented lady. She was 66 years of age. It happened four years ago. One thing we both had in common was a lack of kin, both being an only child. We tried, but never had children. I did mention adoption, but we just didn't get around to it. I was busy restoring vintage cars whilst Alice was busy painting. All of the paintings in this mansion were painted by my late wife."

Erica sipped some coffee and then spoke, "She sounded like a lovely lady."

Henry nodded in agreement, "Yes, she was the best and the last."

Erica's mind whispered 'Oh yes'. She then made an enquiry, "And the mansion, how do you keep it so clean?"

"Oh, that's easy Erica, I employ a cleaner. She visits me once a week. My, she is priceless, such a hard worker.

Have you finished your coffee? I had better show you to your room. You just pick out which one you prefer."

Erica nodded in agreement. She followed Henry. His legs were old, but still in good working order. Erica followed him up the stairs. He then turned to Erica, "I believe this is the best bedroom. It is the largest. It belonged to my lovely wife. She had such imagination. She used to call this room her wonderland – Alice in Wonderland."

Henry opened the door. The room was decorated in white, gold and light blue. It was amazing with a large four poster bed, a large walk-in wardrobe, an en-suite and a bookshelf. Henry smiled, "It was the room my wife called her chill out room. She sat on the bed reading books for hours, it is so peaceful around here, no noise, just peace and tranquillity."

Erica was mesmerised at the beauty of the room. She turned to Henry and spoke, "Thank you for taking pity on me kind sir."

"Look, think nothing of it. Oh, your car, I'd better move it inside my driveway. Have you got the key?"

"Oh, thank you Henry, I have the key right here." Erica reached inside her pocket and then produced the keys to the car. She handed them to Henry. He took them in his hand and spoke, "Okay, I will leave them downstairs. You have been through so much. I will not disturb you. Sit here and read a book and I will see you in the morning."

Erica nodded in confirmation and then spoke, "Thank you once again, Henry."

With that, Henry left the room and made his way to Erica's car. Erica breathed a sigh of relief. The hard part was over. She sat on the bed; it was so comfortable. She then stood up and looked through all the books. One caught her eye, a thriller called 'Payback Time'. She picked it up and then sat on the bed reading it. After half an hour she began to feel tired. She removed her clothes and got into bed and fell into a deep sleep. She dreamt of Dylan betraying her when she was a lot older with a younger, beautiful woman.

Chapter 9

Dylan was now with his two brothers, Ralph and Eddie. Some called them the Bad Ass Brothers. Ralph was six foot four with huge biceps, the sort of guy you would not mess with. He had long black hair tied in a ponytail.

His other brother, Eddie, was shorter, but just as mean, with tattoos embroidered across his neck. He had a barbaric complexion and loved to fire automatic weapons of any sort. He loved killing and would not hesitate. His motto was shoot first and ask questions later.

The two of them worked on and off for an Italian gangster by the name of Big Tony Franco. Dylan sat watching the television with his brothers. Eddie turned to Dylan, "So where did you say your beautiful girlfriend was?"

"Oh, we are so short of money so she's working away."

Eddie shook his head, "No brother of mine is going to struggle like that. Do you want to make some serious money?"

Dylan did not want to go down the road of crime unless he had to. He shrugged his shoulders and spoke, "What would I have to do?"

Ralph laughed, "Oh not much, just drive me and your brother around when we ask you to. Look, you are my brother, nothing would happen to you. Me and Eddie wouldn't allow anything to happen to you, ain't that right, Eddie?"

His big brother Eddie flexed his huge biceps and said, "He's right, Dylan, no-one fucks with us. We are, after all, the Bad Ass Brothers."

Eddie smiled, "Okay, little brother, what do you say? We will soon have lots of money coming your way."

Dylan had no choice, he could not rely on Erica; if she failed, they would be bankrupt in no time. He simply had no choice and turned to his brothers and said, "Yes, okay, I don't mind driving. I m a good driver."

"Okay, we have got a black convertible motor, it's fast and reliable, but first we want you to meet Big Tony Franco, we work for him. He will want to meet you. The guy is simply old school, no-one works for him unless he gets to meet you."

Dylan agreed, "So when will I meet him?"

"Straight away, as in now. He's been expecting us to bring you over."

Dylan was now confused, "But how did you know?"

Eddie laughed and said, "Well, little brother, as soon as you showed up without your pretty girlfriend, we knew you must be in some sort of trouble, or desperate for cash, so we contacted Big Tony just in case you needed work. The guy is a star, he will pay you up front to be our driver."

Dylan shook his head, "You mean it's all so simple?"

Eddie laughed, "Yeah, it's so simple, money for nothing and your kicks for free."

Ralph began to think, then spoke, "Ain't that the name of a song?"

Eddie answered, "Yeah, I think it is. Now what's the name of the group?"

Eddie and Ralph sat scratching their heads in confusion and then Dylan spoke up.

"I believe it was Dire Straits."

Eddie laughed and turned to Ralph, "Yeah, big brother. Our little brother knows his music."

Eddie then changed the subject, "Anyway Dylan, you still an actor? You had such a bloody role; one I could get my teeth into."

Dylan shook his head, "You know, why does everyone take the piss out of me?"

Eddie laughed, "Brother, you can count on it."

Ralph laughed out loud and said, "Soon the Count will be counting out lots of money."

Dylan also began to laugh, after all his brothers were doing him a big favour. They were only joking.

Eddie stood up, "Okay, I'll take him to the Dive Bar. Ralph, you call Big Tony and tell him we are on the way."

"Okay, Dylan, let's go over to garlic and cheese land. I'll drive as I know where it is."

Dylan followed his brother out of the apartment and to the awaiting car. Eddie opened the car door as they both climbed in. The streets were gloomy and dark. The light began to fade rapidly. Dylan got into the automobile quickly. He could hear screams and shouts that echoed all around.

Eddie put the key in the ignition and put his foot on the gas pedal, pulling off slowly. The car was suddenly thrown into a bleak silence until Eddie spoke, "Okay, it's a few blocks away. Remember you are an actor. Stay cool at all times."

Dylan's eyes began to show fear. Anxiety twisted his face. His mind whispered, 'My God, I am about to meet up with a top gangster. What do I say?'

Suddenly Eddie spoke again, "Remember, watch what you say, just speak when you are spoken to. He is only going to see if you're on his level."

Dylan shook his head in confusion and spoke, "Okay, what level might we be talking about?"

Eddie announced triumphantly, "Oh, you know, level, or should I say proof of devotion. He just hates informers. Look I know you are not an informer, after all you are my little brother, but Big Tony do not take no chances. Do not worry none, he did the same with me and Ralph. He will just ask a few questions and give you some money and that is about it. You will be in and out of there in no time."

Eddie took a sharp left and then a sharp right. Dylan looked at the dark streets. He could see gutter punks fighting and ladies of the night soliciting. This was truly low life land.

Eddie pulled over suddenly. "Okay, this is the Dive Bar, Big Tony's hangout. You go in, tell the guy on the door you are Eddie and Ralph's brother, and he will take you to Big Tony Franco. Look, don't worry, you can trust these guys."

Dylan got out of the automobile and gradually ventured over to the Dive Bar's entrance. Eddie's words continued to ring in his mind, he is just going to ask some questions.

Dylan arrived at the door. A giant of a man opened it and looked down at Dylan. He then spoke with a soft Italian accent, "Hi, you must be Dylan, Eddie and Ralph had told me you're their smart younger brother."

Dylan nodded his head in agreement and then spoke, "Yes, that's me."

"Nice to meet you. My name is Mario." He then extended his hand in friendship. They shook hands as Dylan walked into the Dive Bar. Dylan followed Mario into the run-down Dive Bar. It was dark and damp and filled with strange looking old guys talking about the good old days.

Mario stopped, "Okay that's the door to the room. Just knock three times and enter. Tony is waiting for you."

Dylan put on a brave face. He hesitated for a brief second. His mind then whispered, 'show no fear, you're an actor.' With that, he knocked three times on the door. He then opened it. Inside was a room, the walls were brown. It looked dirty. Dylan could see men smoking cigars surrounded by beer and whisky glasses. There was a card game in progress. Each man had his own pot of money. The table they all sat on was long. Dylan walked towards the big guy at the head of the table. It was Big Tony. And then there was silence as Big Tony spoke as he gazed into Dylan's eyes, "Hey, you must be Eddie and Ralph's kid brother. It's Dylan, isn't it?"

Dylan put on a false smile and introduced himself.

"Okay, Dylan, have a seat and a beer."

Dylan sat down next to Big Tony; his heart was pounding. He gazed around at some of the men who were bathed in sweat. He then counted how many men there were. Big Tony was at the head of the table and then four men on one side and four on the other.

Dylan sat down as Joey Fingers handed him a beer. Dylan smiled and said, "Thank you."

Tony was a giant, imposing man with a shrivelled complexion and dark sinister eyes. His head was bald, and he was dressed in a black polo shirt. An eerie silence engulfed the room until Big Tony Spoke, "Okay, my friend, we are going to play a little game. Your brothers informed me you are the brains of the family. You're an actor is that so?"

Dylan nodded and then spoke, "At present I am a redundant actor."

Big Tony laughed and then spoke in a deep voice, "Okay, be honest with me, what part did you play?"

Dylan's mind whispered 'Stay cool, you're an actor'. After a brief delay, Dylan answered, "Oh, I played the part of a vampire."

Big Tony laughed out loud and then spoke in a deep voice, "That's what I admire, honesty. You Goddamn blood sucker."

And then a sudden eruption of laughter echoed all around the room. Big Tony looked into Dylan's eyes and said, "Okay, Count Dylan, it's not blood you are after, it's dollars and I have lots of them I can afford to give away to whoever I please and you my friend need some dollars. Let us talk some more. Did you know I knew your father, Stevie and your mother, Crystal? Do I make myself clear?"

Dylan nodded, his mind again whispered, 'Stay cool.'

Big Tony then continued to talk in his usual deep voice, "You were a young boy when your parents were killed. Your father owned a boat which he loved dearly. It was his pride and joy. Benjamin the Jew wanted to use the boat for his cocaine smuggling. When your father said no, he hired men to plant a bomb on it. The boat exploded killing both your parents."

Dylan remembered his older brother Ralph telling him his mother and father died in an accident.

Big Tony shook his head, "I know, such a tragic loss. Ralph told you it was an accident as he could not come to terms with the fact that Benjamin the Jew had killed them. Ralph came to me for help. I want you to know your parents died instantaneously. It was a big bomb. I sent out men to find out exactly who carried out this evil crime. The evidence pointed to Benjamin the Jew. He hired two killers to plant the bomb."

Dylan scanned his memory and then spoke, "Yes, I remember, it was a beautiful day for going out in the boat. My parents asked me to go with them, but I had promised my friend George that I would go with him to the fair."

Big Tony smiled and said, "Well my friend, you had a lucky escape. As I was saying, your brother Ralph came to me looking for help. I fixed him up with a bag of guns and a list of the men that had anything to do with the murder of your parents. He swore vengeance and killed each one of the criminals with a comforting sense of fulfilment. He left the Jew to the last and made him swallow the bags of cocaine before filling him full of lead. I saw the potential of him and his brother Eddie and put them on the pay roll. Since that day they have been loyal servants. That brings me to you, look around you, I have eight men, all of them have a nickname awarded to them for one reason or another. I have five hundred dollars; I will make it one thousand for you to walk out with. All you must do is guess the reason for any of their nicknames. Do you want to play?"

Dylan hesitated and then said, "Yes, I'll play."

Chapter 10

Big Tony grinned and then said, "The guy sitting closest to you is Joey Fingers. Can you tell me why?"

Dylan gazed at Joey – he had a big boned frame and a strange looking forehead. Dylan noticed Joey had large hands. He then turned to Big Tony and spoke. "Is it because he has large fingers?"

The room once more erupted with laugher. Big Tony shook his head and said, "Okay, that's enough. You are wrong, Dylan, too timid. The reason he is called Joey Fingers is because he has hands in lots of deals and if you cross him, he removes your finger. Okay, the guy sitting next to Joey is The Cleaner."

Dylan looked at the skinny short man complete with thick black curly hair and grey sideburns. Dylan then turned to Big Tony and said, "I believe he is called The Cleaner as he gets rid of the dead bodies and disposes of any evidence."

Big Tony burst into laughter as did the rest of the men. Big Tony shook his head in disbelief and then said in a deep voice, "No, you got it all wrong. We call him The

Cleaner because that is what he does. Now and again, we let him join us in a few card games until we have taken all his money off him." Dylan gazed at The Cleaner, who just sat there grinning.

Big Tony then pointed to Beno Capone and said, "His nickname is Beno Capone."

Dylan gazed at the third guy. His face was very tanned, wrinkled like a walnut. He took a puff of his cigar. Dylan looked at his nicotine-stained hands. Beno Capone; Dylan thought – why on earth would he be nicknamed Beno Capone? Dylan shook his head, "I'm sorry, Tony, I haven't got a clue."

Big Tony smiled and then spoke, "I know kid, it's a hard one. His name is Beno, we nicknamed him Beno Capone because he was convinced he was public enemy number one. Do you understand?"

Dylan laughed and said, "Yeah, okay, you got me."

Big Tony replied, "Remember, you want the thousand dollars. You have got to get one out of the last five. Okay, next to Beno Capone is The Tree. Any idea why he is nicknamed The Tree? And I do not want you to be shy, just say what you think."

Dylan looked over at The Tree. He had a hideous head and glaring eyes. Dylan could see the madness in his eyes. Dylan's mind whispered, 'That guy's barking mad.' Dylan turned to Big Tony and said, "Is he called The Tree because he is barking mad?"

Big Tony could not believe hie ears. The Tree took it personally and said, "Hey man, I ain't barking mad". He then shouted as the room burst into laughter. Dylan could not help himself; he also began to laugh.

Big Tony shouted, "No, he is The Tree, he isn't barking mad, or is that debatable? The reason he got the nickname 'The Tree' is because in the early days he was always talking about branching out, if you know what I mean. Okay, sitting opposite The Tree is Mr Lucky Legs. Any idea why?"

Dylan looked at Mr Lucky Legs. He had disproportionately long legs. A gaunt looking man with a strange complexion. Dylan thought hard, why Lucky legs? Dylan's mind whispered, 'Perhaps he always escapes trouble with the use of his long legs.'

Big Tony became inpatient and spoke, "Okay, what do you reckon?"

Dylan looked hard at Mr Lucky Legs and said, "Okay, I believe he is called Mr Lucky Legs because he always escapes the law."

Big Tony laughed, "No, no, don't mention that word – it's a dirty word. Your brothers informed me you were a smart kid. I believe you got it all wrong again. He is called Mr Lucky Legs because he took three bullets to his legs, and everyone was a flesh wound. His legs proved lucky, thus we nicknamed him Mr Lucky Legs".

Big Tony turned his attention to his hoods and said, "Okay, Dylan hasn't got one right. In fact, he is useless. Five gone, three to go. Any bets?"

Suddenly, all eight began betting against Dylan getting one right. Big Tony smiled and said, "Okay are you all finished betting. How much is now in the pot?" Joey Fingers counted the money. Each of the hoods had put in one hundred dollars. Big Tony laughed, "Okay, I still have confidence in the kid and will match the pot. Okay, game on. Now we are playing for real money. Look at the guy sitting next to Mr Lucky Legs – his nickname is The Model. Can you tell me why that is so?"

Dylan looked at The Model. He thought my God, this guy is ugly. He had a pointed nose and chin and a weather-beaten face. Dylan looked at The Model and spoke, "My God, they just get harder."

The hoods looked at each other. This was going to be easy money.

Big Tony began sweating furiously. He did not like losing a bet. He then spoke with firmness in his voice, "Come on, we haven't got all night."

Dylan looked at The Model and said the first thing that entered his head, "Is it because he ain't no model?"

Everyone burst out into laughter except for The Model. He stood up and said, "Hey, I am a good-looking guy ain't I?"

Big Tony shouted over to The Model, "Look, sit down you ugly bastard."

Again, the room erupted into laughter. Big Tony raised his voice once more, "Okay, that was a hard one.

No-one ever gets this right. Believe it or not he is called The Model because this guy is so fussy, he only dates models."

Dylan knew the odds were now stacked against him, only two to go.

Big Tony looked to Dylan and spoke, "Look, concentrate, two to go. I am going to eight hundred dollars. If I lose, you lose. Okay, the next is Caesar. Any idea why he is called Caesar?"

Dylan looked at Caesar, he was unlike the rest of the hoods. He had fair hair and was middle-aged with a close-fitting jacket and prominent shoulders. Dylan knew all of this was a lost cause. He then had an idea. He turned to Big Tony and said, "Okay, I reckon he is called Caesar as his Christian name is Julius."

Big Tony looked to Dylan and said "What, you are saying, Julius Caesar?"

Dylan nodded. All the hoods began to laugh. Joey Fingers laughed and then spoke to Beno Capone, "The money is in the bag. This guy is useless."

Dylan then overheard the remark, he took a deep breath, he knew he had to get the last one. He knew the reaction of the hoods; he was wrong again.

Big Tony shook his head and then turned to Dylan, "No, kid, the reason we call him Caesar is because he used to work in Caesar's Palace. Okay Dylan, one to go. Look at the money. All those dollars, all here awaiting you. Come on, prove all these guys wrong. They are all laughing at you. Don't you want to wipe the smiles off their faces? Just get the next question right." Big Tony turned to Joey Fingers and said, "Pour this guy a whisky. My, he needs to wake up his brain cells." The hoods all laughed as Joey Fingers poured Dylan a glass of whisky. He handed it to Dylan.

Big Tony smiled and spoke in a calm voice, "Look, I want to stimulate those brain cells of yours. I want you to down the whisky in one."

Dylan just did what he was told. He downed the whisky in one and then began to cough. Joey Fingers laughed and then spoke, "Last chance kid." He then turned to Big Tony and spoke. "Any chance of us all raising the pot? I am willing to put in another fifty dollars."

Big Tony laughed, "Okay, all of you put in another fifty dollars, it doesn't matter to me, it's only money."

All the hoods put in another fifty dollars. Big Tony laughed and said, "Okay the pot is now one thousand two hundred dollars, is that correct?" Joey Fingers nodded his head in agreement. Big Tony stood up and made a speech, "Okay friends, this is the moment of truth. Who is going to take the pot, me or you? Is Dylan going to walk out of here with one thousand dollars? Right, everyone, silence as we put this poor guy to the final question." Tony then sat down and turned his attention to Dylan and said, "Okay, what do you reckon? The last nickname is Mickey. Take a good look at Mickey."

Dylan looked at Mickey, he knew he had to get this right. He gazed into Mickey's eyes. His mind whispered, 'My God his eyes are wide and of the deepest blue. Other than that, he was average. Dylan scanned his memory – Mickey Blue Eyes, that movie. He looked all around; all eyes were focused on him. Big Tony looked at Dylan and said, "Okay, times up, have you an answer?"

Dylan smiled and said, "Yeah, I reckon I have the correct answer."

Big Tony smiled and said, "Okay, fire away."

"The answer" Dylan said, "Is Mickey Blue Eyes".

Everyone looked at each other in disbelief. Big Tony roared with laughter and then the room did the same. Big Tony said, "Shit kid, you did it. We called him Mickey after the movie, his eyes are so blue." Tony put out a hand of friendship and said, "Now we shake hands, kid."

Dylan shook Big Tony's hand – he had large hands with a tight grip. Big Tony then turned to the rest of the hoods and spoke in a commanding voice, "Okay you lot, no bad blood, he played the game and won. how I don't know, but all shake his hand as he is now one of us. Remember he is Ralph and Eddie's kid brother." All the hoods shook Dylan's hand, they knew it could have gone any way. The kid just had a lucky guess.

Big Tony turned to Joey Fingers and said, "What the fuck, I am feeling generous – the pot, bag it up and give it all to the kid. That was first class entertainment. I have never seen it go to the wire before."

Joey Fingers picked up the money off the table and put it into a bag. Big Tony smiled and said, "Okay, Dylan, it's been a pleasure doing business with you. Tomorrow night you will drive for me and your brothers on a little job. Welcome to the family."

Big Tony embraced Dylan. He then turned to Joey and said, "Okay, escort Dylan off the premises and make sure he isn't robbed."

Joey Fingers nodded in agreement. He then escorted Dylan to the exit and handed him the bag. He then spoke, "Okay kid, you earned this fair and square, spend it wisely. See you soon."

Dylan said goodbye and then walked over to his awaiting brother. He opened the passenger side door and got in. Eddie turned to Dylan and said, "My, you were gone a while. How was Big Tony? Is everything okay?"

Dylan smiled and said, "Yeah, me and him got on like a house on fire."

Eddie laughed and said, "Let me be the judge of that – how much you got in the bag?"

Dylan smiled and said, "You guess."

Eddie had an idea, "I know, you got seven hundred dollars as Big Tony was feeling generous."

Dylan shook his head and said in a calm voice, "No you can double that, I've got one thousand two hundred dollars in this bag."

Eddie looked at the bag in disbelief and said, "Shit, Big Tony must have loved you." Eddie then pulled off into the night.

Chapter 11

Erica continued to dream about Dylan. Could she trust him when she was older, and her good looks had faded? Suddenly, Erica heard several knocks on the bedroom door and then a familiar voice. It was Henry, he spoke in a quiet voice. "Hello Erica, I have prepared some breakfast. Would you like some?"

Erica opened her eyes and said, "Yes, thank you, Henry. I shall get dressed and be with you in a few minutes". Henry smiled and then made his way downstairs. Erica sat up and then got out of bed and stretched with a yawn. She quickly got dressed, she then made her way to the bathroom. Erica opened a cupboard; it was filled with cosmetics, deodorants and hairbrushes. Erica washed her face, brushed her hair and applied some makeup. She then made her way down the stairs and entered the dining room. Henry had prepared breakfast. Erica looked at the table, there was two cups of coffee, toast and a cooked breakfast.

Erica smiled and said, "Why thank you. Henry, the breakfast looks lovely".

Henry laughed and said, "it's not every morning I cook a breakfast for a beautiful young lady". Erica sat down and began to eat her breakfast, minutes later the plates were empty. Henry cleared away all the plates onto a tray.

Erica turned to Henry and asked him if he needed any assistance.

He replied "No" and removed the plates into the kitchen. He returned with two ice cold glasses of pure orange juice. He handed one to Erica, she thanked him and began to drink it. Henry turned to Erica, his face filled with excitement; he then spoke in a calm voice "Oh I have something to show you, follow me to my garage".

Erica nodded in agreement and followed Henry outside. The sun shone in all its glory.

Henry opened his garage with a key to reveal an old rare Cadillac. Erica's eyes lit up, she turned to Henry and said, "My God it's a rare, vintage Cadillac".

Henry smiled and said "Yes, what a motor; I used to restore rare, vintage automobiles, I made a lot of money. I sometimes wish I could turn back the clock. I have a heart condition; the doctor said if I take all my medication each day then I would be just fine. The worst thing about my condition is they took away my driving license, so my prize Cadillac has sat there ever since. Once a week, I just start it up and sit behind the wheel and reminisce. I want you to make an old man happy and take me out for a spin in my old automobile. The town is about ten miles away."

Erica smiled and said "I ain't the world's greatest driver and this car is in mint condition, it must be worth a lot of money."

Henry shook his head "money means nothing to me, not anymore. "Look I have the key here, Erica".

She knew she had to do this to make an old man happy. A thought flashed through her brain, maybe one day this car could be hers. She turned to Henry and said, "Okay I'll drive, as long as you navigate".

Henry laughed and said "Ok", whilst handing her the keys to the Cadillac.

Erica opened the car door and slowly climbed in, it felt good. Henry got into the passenger side. Erica put the keys into the ignition; a brief delay and then the car started up.

Henry then got out and said "Ok, you drive out of the garage, and I will lock the garage up after you". Erica accelerated slowly until she was clear of the garage. Henry then closed the garage door and locked it up.

Henry felt reborn again, he could not believe his luck. Henry opened the passenger door and climbed in once more. He gave Erica directions and she gently pulled off towards the town.

She could not believe she was driving a vintage Cadillac after years of driving a rust bucket. Henry reached over and turned on the radio, Roy Orbison was playing 'Pretty Woman', which Henry found all so fitting to his situation.

Henry turned to Erica and said, "Oh, don't worry, I ain't going to sing".

Erica could not believe her ears, her mind whispered, 'Why on earth did he say that?'

A left turn, then a right and then two more miles and they arrived at their destination. Erica noticed a parking space; it was all too quiet, like a ghost town after she parked up.

Henry said to her "Over there is a store that might interest you; a ladies' fashion store. Let's face it, you need some new clothes. You go in there and pick out what you want, it doesn't matter about the price; money is not an issue".

Erica could not believe her ears and thanked Henry and together they got out of the Cadillac. Erica locked the door and then turned to Henry and said, "Are you sure?"

Henry nodded and said "The shop is just over there. Pick out all the clothes you want, and I will be over there in ten minutes to pay for them".

Erica agreed and walked over to the store. She entered whilst Henry visited a Men's store. Erica felt like a kid in a candy store as she filled her basket with new clothes, she had never purchased before, such fun, fashionable clothes. Suddenly, Henry appeared and accompanied Erica to the till and paid for the clothes.

A middle-aged woman on the till said to Erica, "Is that your Granddaddy? Or your sugar-daddy?" Henry did not hear the conversation.

Erica became irate and then exclaimed in an angry tone "You mind your own business and keep your comments to yourself! The man in question is my future husband and he is filthy rich". The woman on the till turned red and looked away.

Henry then turned around and said, "Is everything ok?"

Erica smiled and said "Yes, everything is just fine". She then embraced Henry and kissed him on the cheek. The woman on the till looked on with a shade of horror. She had thick, curly hair and a very pale complexion. Henry was confused and unable to speak. Erica then held his hand as they left the store.

Henry felt a warm glow inside, he turned to Erica and said, "Can I take you for a coffee and pie?"

Erica gazed into Henry's eyes and said "Yes, this has been the happiest day of my life and you Sir have made it all possible".

Henry laughed and then spoke in a low voice, "As long as you are happy then so am I".

The sky outside was overcast. Erica felt a cool breeze on her face as they ventured across to their car. Erica opened the boot, and they placed the bags inside. Suddenly, the heavens open with a few raindrops and then a heavy down pour. It became heavier and heavier. Henry suggested escaping the rain, so they both got into the Cadillac.

Henry turned to Erica and said, "One thing I don't like is getting wet".

Erica replied, "I dislike the rain also".

Henry turned to Erica and said, "Ok that's decided then, let us just go home. Got plenty of Pie and Coffee back there.

Erica put the key in the ignition and started up the car. She turned on the window wipers and they were on their way home.

Erica turned to Henry and spoke in a confident voice, "Soon be back home, I love this automobile".

The roads were clear, and the rain had now stopped. Erica turned into the driveway and was soon back at the garage. Erica pulled up as Henry got out and opened the door. Erica drove in, she parked the automobile and then got out of the Cadillac as Henry got out the bags closing the boot behind him. He then handed Erica her bags. Erica thanked Henry once more. Henry smiled as they proceeded into the mansion.

After Henry had opened the door, Henry turned around and said to Erica, "Ok, you pop upstairs and put your clothes in your room, and I will make you a coffee and cut some pie".

Erica agreed and went upstairs and put the bags onto the bed. She got the clothes out of the bag and put them into the wardrobe. She then ventured downstairs as Henry poured the coffee and after cutting two slices of pie and placing them onto plates. Erica sat down in the dining area and Henry soon joined her with a tray of coffee and pie. Henry handed Erica blueberry pie and then a cup of coffee. Henry ate his pie and began to yawn.

After eating her pie, Erica smiled and said, "My, that pie was good. Are you feeling tired? It's been a busy day".

Henry yawned once more and said, "Yes, it's been nice. Do you mind if I catch up on some much-needed beauty sleep?"

Erica smiled and said, "It's ok. I will go and read a book until I fall asleep".

Henry stood up and yawned once more and then said, "Better clear the plates and cups away first".

Erica laughed and said, "No let me, you go and catch up on your beauty sleep".

Henry agreed and then made his way upstairs to his bedroom, Erica tidied up and then made her way upstairs to her bedroom. Erica got undressed. She then put on her nightgown and lay on her bed. Her eyes began to close. Erica then fell into a deep sleep, she dreamt of the past.

Chapter 12

Dylan's brothers Eddie and Ralph, she met them in a bar when she first started dating Dylan. A couple of jerks upset her; before Dylan could react, they took over the situation and beat the couple of jerks up to a pulp.

Dylan meanwhile sat in a room chatting to his brothers. It was dark and dirty, the way his brothers liked it.

Eddie lit up a cigarette. He then poured himself a glass of whisky and then spoke in a deep voice, "Brothers, we have had some fine times together. Remember that time when you had a bit of a gambling addiction and you owed money to the Harlem hatchet? Man, you were frightened when he put the word out on the street that he was going to cut your hands off. I visited him with good intentions; he just wouldn't listen to reason, so I shot him dead. My, they were fun days; he was such a big guy I must have emptied a full clip into that guy, and he just kept on talking shit".

Ralph interrupted shaking his head, he then spoke in a deep gravelly voice. "No, I remember it wasn't a full clip. The guy raised his hatchet and you shot him in the shoulder you then shot him three times in the chest, and he fell to his knees. He cursed you calling you a 'motherfucker' again and again, so you shot him in the head. I reckon that five was bullets".

Eddie agreed. He then began to laugh and said "Yeah, the Hatchet man finally acknowledged he was dead with that final bullet to his head. I also remember that t-shirt he wore, it had a large five on the front of it. So, five bullets, five minutes to kill him and it took me five minutes to find his secret stash of money, it was under his mattress, and believe it or not the total sum was five grand, and all of this occurred on the 5th of November. "It suddenly gave a new meaning to the phrase 'give me five'".

Dylan sat listening to the story. His brother lifted his glass and drank some more whisky.

Dylan then asked a question of his brother, "Are you sure about the date?"

Eddie laughed and said, "Ok smart ass, what was the date?"

"I remember it was the 4th of July. I swore from that day on I would never gamble again".

Eddie laughed once more and said, "Yeah, I remember how you turned your attention to the ladies and slept with Billy Bad Blood's wife. He put a contract out on you, I know because he said 'No one sleeps with my wife and lives'. The sad ass offered me several hundred dollars to whack my own brother. I explained we were related, and he begged forgiveness. One thing about Billy, he wasn't completely stupid. I told him his wife had slept with several men, so he had me take care of her. I spoke to her, she wouldn't listen, so I made her disappear".

Dylan shook his head in shame and disbelief, he then said, "The trouble I have caused in the past, I am like a bad luck charm. I had forgotten all about daisy and her disappearance, I could had been the death of you".

Dylan gazed at his brothers tattoos and then spoke in a low voice "Have any of you got any new tattoos?"

Ralph replied, "Yes but it's a bit of a beast ain't it".

Ralph turned to Eddie who then stood up and lifted his shirt to reveal a tattoo of the Devil on his chest. Underneath the tattoo was the number of the beast, three large sixes.

Dylan gazed at the tattoo in total shock. He then spoke in a heightened voice, "My God that is bad".

Eddie pulled a face and said, "No, it's the Devil".

Ralph laughed and then said, "I reckon this is one bad ass tattoo".

Ralph then sat back down and poured himself another whisky. He then turned to Dylan and said, "Let me tell you something; ever since I had this tattoo done,

I have been shot at and the bullets have avoided me like the plague. I am the ultimate bad ass; no one or nothing fucks with me. We dwell amongst the decay of the day the creatures of the night, our code is a modest one kill or be killed. Shoot and ask questions later. The death is done and there is magic in the air. Ever since picking up my first semi-automatic pistol I reckon I have killed over fifty men, may I add with the aid of Eddie, we simply lost count. Is that not so, dear brother?"

Eddie and I have got a plan, we have the money stashed away and once we reach a cool one million, we are going to move away from this lifestyle, live somewhere quiet maybe Mexico or Canada, a place where nobody knows our kick ass past. We have been so lucky we are all alive but eventually everyone's luck runs out".

Dylan nodded in agreement. He then said, "I reckon money is everything. It's what makes the world go around. me and Erica plan on moving to the Caribbean once we have made enough money from our mercy killings".

Eddie gazed into his brother's eyes and then spoke with great interest, "Okay, can me and Ralph help you out with anything? This killing thing must run in the family. Okay Brother tell me more about these mercy killings".

Dylan knew he could trust his brothers, so he told them everything.

Eddie smiled and then said, "Brother, it's a great way to make money". He then turned to Ralph and said, "What do you reckon?"

"Yeah, you could pass as a broad and we could muscle in on this operation. You could dress up in drag and I could call you Edna". Eddie picked up a cushion and hit Ralph over the head with it. They all began to laugh out loud.

Eddie then put on a serious face and spoke with firmness in his voice, "It's time for our business. Dylan, you are our driver, we are going to deliver some goods and you will drive us to the docks. Do you remember the way?"

Dylan replied, "Yes, I have been there lots of times".

Eddie gazed into Dylan's eyes and spoke in a deep voice, "You are only the driver. Do I make myself clear? Whatever happens you don't panic, you stay cool like when you met Big Tony. Do you understand, little brother?"

Dylan nodded and said, "Don't worry, I won't let you down".

Eddie took a deep breath and finished off his drink. He then turned to Ralph and said, "Ok, you ready for this?"

Ralph smiled. He then stood up stretching and closed his eyes for a brief second and said, "Yeah, as ever, I am ready to kick some ass".

Eddie stood up and then put on his favourite black leather jacket. Eddie and Ralph always dressed in black. Eddie then handed Dylan the keys to the automobile, and they all left the apartment together.

It was dark outside; the urban community was now in full swing. As they walked towards the automobile the noise echoed in their ears.

Dylan looked at the automobile's registration plate, he never noticed earlier it had a message, 'BAD ASS 66'.

Eddie smiled and said, "Yeah, the street knows our automobile, no one dares to touch it. I believe they respect our property, or we dispose of them which is fine by me".

Dylan felt a sudden draught of cold air run down his spine. He gazed up at the stars shining bright, livid with wrath.

Dylan opened the automobile door and all three brothers got in.

Dylan noticed a disagreeable, damp smell. He then put the keys into the ignition and started up the engine.

He then pulled off towards the docks. The streets were dark and gloomy. Dylan drove, pressing his foot down on the gas pedal and then changed up to a higher gear.

Suddenly, the silence was interrupted by Eddie. He instructed Dylan to ease of the gas and said, "We ain't in any hurry". Eddie had such firmness in his voice.

Wild eyed and noticeably confident, Dylan continued to drive, he knew he had to stay cool as his brother had stated.

Once more the silence was broken by Eddie, he said, "OK, Dylan, pull over next to that old warehouse".

Dylan did what his brother said and pulled over next to the old warehouse, then the automobile came to a halt.

Eddie then turned to Dylan and said, "Ok, we are going to do this. Remember, don't move from the automobile and be ready to drive away very fast".

Dylan nodded in agreement.

Eddie and Ralph got out of the automobile, Eddie reached inside his pocket for his spare set of keys, he then opened the boot and then reached inside and opened up a large black holdall filled with weapons. Eddie picked out an Uzi automatic complete with a silencer attached to it. Ralph then picked out a hand full of grenades, he then carefully placed them into his pockets. Ralph then picked out two semi-automatic pistols complete with silencers attached. Eddie then picked up a briefcase containing half a million dollars, this was to be a drug deal.

Eddie turned to his brother and spoke with a sense of repulsion, "I hate dealing with the Russians, all I want to do is shoot them".

Ralph had a macabre vision of the two of them killing several Russians and began to blink and frown, and then pure madness, he was such a sinister sight. A born killer.

Without hesitation he spoke in a deep, calm, cold voice, "Ok, let's kill them all. I hate Russians also".

Dylan sat in the automobile. He looked on as his brother shut the boot and he could see the black briefcase and the weapons. His heart began to pound. He sat rooted with fear as his brothers made their way to the entrance of the old warehouse.

Inside stood two Russian gangsters. As soon as they made eye contact, Ralph and Eddie opened fire, killing them both without mercy. They stepped over the dead bodies and continued on their way, killing anyone who stood before them. The body count just multiplied.

A crack of a shotgun and Ralph was hit in his shoulder. A wild cry of anger as Eddie sprayed bullets towards the Russian gangsters. Ralph also continued to fire until several Russian gangsters lay dead.

Ralph looked around with death cold eyes. Suddenly, his anger rose, and he shouted, "God damn Russians!" as blood began to pour from his wound.

This was a cold, dark heartless place complete with an unmistakable stench of death.

Eddie remained calm, he turned to his brother and said, "Ok, apply pressure on that wound; don't want you bleeding all over my automobile".

Ralph laughed and then applied pressure to the wound.

Eddie scanned all around the room and noticed a big, black shoulder bag filled with bags of white powder. Eddie walked over to the bag which was open, and he could see the cocaine. He zipped up the bag and placed it over his shoulder. Eddie took a deep breath and then said, "Let's get the hell out of this place".

Ralph agreed with a nod of his head and they both left the room. Ralph reached inside his pockets and produced the hand grenades. He turned and pulled out the pins and then tossed them into the room where the dead Russians gangsters lay dead. They both began to run.

Dylan sat in the car with the engine running. Suddenly, his brothers appeared from the dark shadows and then a large explosion. Anxiety twisted Dylan's face; panic fears began to flutter in his mind as the brothers got into the car. As soon as the doors closed, Dylan put his foot on the gas pedal.

Dylan looked in his rear mirror, he could see the flames. Faster and faster he drove, until the flames were out of sight.

Ralph sat with his eyes closed applying pressure to his shoulder wound.

Eddie turned to Dylan and said, "Ok you can slow down now".

They could hear sirens from the police and emergency services rushing to the scene and then another explosion.

Dylan remained calm and continued to drive.

Ralph opened his eyes and spoke with a shade of impatience in his voice, "What are we going to do about my shoulder?"

Eddie reached inside his pocket, produced his mobile phone and made a call. After a brief delay, he got through to Doctor Damian. The doctor answered and Eddie became livid as his eyelids flickered spasmodically. He erupted like a volcano, "Look I don't care if its late, my brother has taken a bullet to his shoulder, you know the address, you better come over or it will be you taking a bullet!"

The doctor understood and then asked what was in it for him.

"Ok, Doc, agreed usual fee and I'll throw in a bag of white candy as you have a sweet tooth".

The doctor agreed and hung up.

Ralph turned to Eddie; he was now sweating furiously, his face reddened with rage. Before he could say anything, Eddie said, "Everything is okay, the Doc is coming over to fix you up". Ralph took a deep breath and slowly began to calm down.

Dylan soon had them all back at the apartment. He parked up the automobile, they then all got out and made their way to the apartment. Eddie carried all the bags, he entered the apartment and then placed them onto a table, he then lit up a cigarette.

Dylan turned to his brother Eddie and began to yawn. After all, it had been an eventful night. Eddie told Dylan to get some shut eye whilst he took care of Ralph until the Doctor arrived. Suddenly there was a knock on the front door. Ralph laughed, putting on a brave face. He then said, "Look, the Doc is here".

Eddie smiled, "Ok, Dylan, what are you waiting for? Through that door, your bed is on the left".

Dylan did as he was told, and he entered the room and was soon in bed.

Eddie answered the door. Stood there was Doctor Damian. He was of average height and build, fair haired and wore golden framed round glasses. In his hand he carried a repair kit.

Eddie smiled and escorted the doctor to his brother.

The doctor removed Ralph's shirt and got to work patching him up whilst Eddie placed money and white candy into a bag, after all the doctor was supplying a valuable service and deserved his cut.

Doc Damian was a fast operator. A wound like this was routine for he had worked for ten years fixing up wounded criminals and was recruited by Big Tony as hospitals were out of the question.

Eddie turned to the doctor and said, "Is everything ok?"

Doc Damian smiled and spoke in a low, calm voice, "Yes, the bullet went straight through, no nerve damage. I've stitched up the wound and the bleeding has stopped; Ralph just needs to take it easy for a week or so. Does he need any pain killers?"

Eddie laughed and said, "No, he's got me". Eddie then handed the bag to the doctor, they both thanked him, and he was on his way.

Ralph sat thinking, he then turned to his brother with an expression of horror.

Eddie looked into his brother's eyes and spoke, "I know what you're thinking, maybe we shouldn't have killed all those Russians".

"That wasn't our orders. Big Tony is going to be pissed off with us, but then again it's our word against theirs and they ain't going to be saying anything as they are all brown bread".

"What will we tell Big Tony? One of the Russians pulled out a gun and shot you in the shoulder, so we took care of the situation and shot back and accidentally wiped them all out?"

"It was us or them".

Ralph forced a smile and said, "My you have got it all worked out, haven't you? The brains of the outfit".

Eddie laughed and said, "Ok now it's time to recharge our batteries. Bedtime, after all it's been a long night".

Ralph agreed and after a yawn he walked through a door into his bedroom.

Eddie finished off his drink and did the same. Silence at last, he thought.

Chapter 13

Erica awoke to the sounds of singing birds. She got out of bed and gazed into the garden; it was so fertile with a variety of colourful flowers.

She then looked up into the sky at the strange cloud formations and then the sun made a welcomed appearance.

The window was slightly open, and Erica felt a cool breeze run down her spine.

She then heard a noise and a familiar voice. It was Henry, he asked her to join him for breakfast. She agreed and she then opened a wardrobe door. She gazed inside at Henry's poor departed wife's clothes.

She noticed a golden silk dressing gown; she took it out and put it on.

The soft silk upon her skin felt good, her mind whispered, 'a perfect fit'.

She then entered the bathroom and had a quick wash. She then entered the dining area.

Henry gazed at Erica, he could not believe his eyes, it was as if he had seen a ghost. Memories of his late wife flooded back to him. He remembered purchasing the silk dressing gown whilst visiting Japan, whilst they were on vacation.

Erica smiled and said, "I hope you don't mind me wearing this lovely dressing gown".

Henry laughed and then said, "It fits you perfectly, for a brief minute I could see my late wife standing before me".

Erica then mentioned how she was awoken by beautiful singing birds.

Erica sat down and ate some breakfast after they had both finished Henry handed Erica a jewellery box.

Henry smiled and then said, "I want you to have this; it belonged to my late wife".

Erica smiled and then in a soft voice she said, "Thank you Henry".

A brief delay and then Erica opened the jewellery box, it was filled with gold and silver rings, bracelets and earrings. Erica's eyes lit up as she reached inside for a certain ring that appealed to her eye, it was a diamond cluster ring.

Erica picked it up and then placed it on her wedding ring finger. She then turned to Henry and said, "Look, it's a perfect fit".

Henry could not believe his eyes. After all, it was his late wife's wedding ring, maybe it was a sign.

Henry gazed into Erica's beautiful eyes and said, "It was my late wife's wedding ring, it's such a shame, I wish I had met you when I was younger".

Erica shook her head. She smiled and then spoke in a low voice "Age means nothing to me, it's what is inside here that counts".

Erica held her hand on her heart and then continued to talk, "Kindness, peace and solitude is what I crave most of all".

Erica then picked out a silver crucifix, she then turned to Henry and said, "Can you help me with this?"

Her mind whispered 'the finishing touch'. Henry stood up and helped put on the necklace. Erica thanked Henry; she then stood up and kissed him on the cheek. Henry was so happy and could not believe his good fortune. After all, he had now found a princess. Henry looked at Erica. He tried to speak but struggled to get his words out, his mind whispered, 'ask her the question', so he did as panic fears fluttered his mind.

Before he could finish his sentence, Erica embraced him and said, "The answer is yes if it is only a low-key wedding, just the two of us".

Henry could not believe what had just happened. He then spoke triumphantly that he 'knew just the place to tie the knot'.

Henry gazed into Erica's dazzling eyes and said, "Are you sure? After all I am old enough to be your grandaddy".

Erica kissed Henry on the cheek and then said, "I hope we have many happy years together, you're such a kind-hearted man".

Henry then had an idea. He then said, "I still have my late wife's wedding dress. Would you honour her memory and wear it?"

Erica agreed and then said, "This is all like a fairy tale come true".

Henry laughed. He then said, "Which one, Beauty and the Beast?"

Erica laughed and spoke in a low voice, "No, you're like a knight in shining armour. Can I try on the wedding dress?"

Henry replied, "Why yes, follow me upstairs and I will get it for you".

Erica followed Henry upstairs to the spare bedroom.

He opened the wardrobe and got out a white silk and cotton wedding dress. Erica's mind whispered, 'My, this is so easy'.

Henry handed her the wedding dress. Erica smiled. She then said, "Can we get married as soon as possible?"

Henry smiled, "Alright, you try on the dress whilst I make a phone call to book us in".

Henry was an old romantic fool and was putty in the hands of Erica.

Henry took a deep breath and said, "You make me feel twenty years younger".

He then left to make the phone call whilst Erica tried on the dress. It was a perfect fit. She investigated the mirror and laughed to herself.

A few minutes later Henry reappeared. He then informed Erica that they were to be married in the morning. Erica could not believe how smooth things were going.

She turned to the mirror and then to Henry and said, "Look at the dress, it's a perfect fit, this is my destiny".

Henry looked at Erica and could see his late wife on their wedding day.

Erica knew this was all going a little fast.

Henry then said, "You haven't asked where we are to be married".

Erica smiled and said, "I trust your judgement, I bet it's nice".

Henry laughed and said, "Can you take me into town? The reverend wants to meet us and has informed me he wants his money up front. The reason he said was because sometimes he arranges flowers and music and of course his valuable time and couples simply don't turn up."

Erica shook her head, "My, Henry, that's terrible, we better go see him hadn't we. Just give me five minutes to get into that new dress you bought me".

Henry smiled and left the room. He then walked downstairs and made himself a coffee.

Erica picked out some clean clothes and then entered the bathroom and had a quick wash. She then got dressed, a brush of her hair and she was making her downstairs.

Henry stood at the bottom of the stairs, he gazed at Erica and rubbed his eyes. He then made a comment on the dress, "My God you look like a million dollars. That dress fits you like a glove and it's my favourite colour; pale blue. I have driven the Cadillac out of the garage and locked the door. Maybe I should drive; I've took my medication".

Erica smiled and said, "No. Imagine if the police pulled us over, it ain't worth the risk".

Henry agreed with Erica, they both got into the Cadillac and Erica pulled off slowly heading towards the town.

The sun was replaced by clouds, minutes later it returned.

Erica looked in her rear mirror and could see an old car moving closer and closer behind her, it was full of local punks. Erica turned to Henry and said, "Oh my God, don't look back but we've got a car full of Hillbillies behind us".

The guy driving wore a black vest, he had tattoos on his arms, black greasy hair and a scar down his right cheek.

He began to hit his horn and shout, "Move over; I want to meet you and your Grand-Daddy".

His friends all laughed.

He then shouted, "Lovely lady, you're driving me crazy".

Erica put her foot down on the gas pedal as did the car of Hillbillies in pursuit and then a welcome sound of a siren. It was the local sheriff. The Hillbillies overtook Erica as did the Sheriff in hot pursuit of the Hillbillies.

Erica slowed down and took a deep breath.

Henry had his hands on his heart, he shook his head and said, "My God, imagine if I hadn't listened to you and I had drove, anything could have happened. God damn Hillbillies. I blame all that interbreeding, they grow up in poverty, no education, confused, with no sense of wrong-doing. But I have to say you are a real diamond, you remained so cool. I never heard what they were shouting but I heard that annoying horn that Hillbilly was hitting".

Erica opened her window a bit and felt a draught of cold air suddenly run down her spine.

Henry turned on the radio. Elvis was playing, and Henry could not believe the song that was being played, it was 'all shook up'.

Erica began to drive into the town, the noise was still pounding in her ears, the Hillbillies left her bewildered. She now had an uneasy feeling. She then turned to Henry and said, "Ok, where about is the place?"

Henry regained his composure and said, "It's just a bit further up on the right. Do you see that white building? The Chapel of Elvis".

Erica burst into laughter, her mind whispered, 'This can't be real'.

Henry also laughed and then said, "I am a big fan of Elvis, got all his albums".

Erica laughed and said, "I bet you have".

"What a singer".

She then pulled over and they both got out of the Cadillac. Erica gazed at the Chapel of Elvis; it was a magnificent structure painted white to perfection. They both entered the building and were greeted by the Pastor Eddie Elvis which did seem fitting. He was larger than life, wearing a white costume, like the one Elvis wore. He wore an Elvis wig and even spoke like the King.

He began to talk fluently in a heightened voice, "Ok honey, in the Chapel of Elvis age means nothing, it's all about love".

He then turned to Henry and said, "You got the payment, five hundred dollars, the fee for a quicky. It's all above board, I supply the flowers. You said on the telephone there will be no guests, me and God shall be watching over you and your beautiful bride, and I shall be the witness to this match made in heaven. All of this means I shall sign the marriage certificate, and may I have a choice of Elvis song good sir?"

Henry looked to Erica and said, "Have you got a favourite Elvis song?"

Erica stood motionless, she then looked to Henry with a fixed expression and said, "My late mother had a favourite Elvis song; I think it was 'Peggy Sue'."

Eddie Elvis put his hands over his face, shook his head and then put his hands in the air. The reverend then spoke in a heightened voice, "What you just said is a sin in the Chapel of Elvis. Wrong song; the singer of 'Peggy Sue' was of course Buddy Holly. I don't know today's generation".

Erica shook her head and said, "Oh, I am so sorry - my mind - I just went blank and I said the wrong song. I meant to say 'Love Me Do'."

Eddie could not believe his ears. He began to frown then roared with laughter, as did Henry. Erica stood confused with why they were both laughing. Eddie Elvis then spoke once more in a heightened voice, "Oh, such blasphemous language from such a little lady. We have gone from Buddy Holly to across the pond to Liverpool.

I do recall that their song 'Love Me Do' was sung by none other than the Beatles. I reckon you need some help, my dear, and yes that was another song by the Beatles. May I add, Henry, please take control of this delicate situation and pick out an Elvis song."

Henry, without hesitation, said "How about 'crying in the Chapel?'"

Eddie Elvis nodded his head. He then said, "Yeah, I reckon that song is romantic, more like laughing in the Chapel."

Erica knew she had made a complete fool of herself and kept quiet. Erica stood gazing at the various pictures of Elvis hung on the walls of the Chapel.

Henry paid Eddie Elvis. He then walked over to Erica and said, "You okay? That sure was funny. You're not offended, are you?"

Erica shook her head and then replied, "No, not at all. I guess I just made a complete fool of myself but that happens to all of us." Henry agreed. Erica took hold of his hand and they then left like two young lovers.

Chapter 14

Henry stopped. He then turned to Erica and said, "Do you fancy pie and coffee? I promised you the café is just over there." Henry pointed to an old café.

Erica didn't want to go but what could she say? After all, the old man only had a short time left on Earth. Erica put on a false smile and then spoke, "Yes, Henry, let's go." Henry and Erica crossed the road hand in hand. Erica was aware of the funny looks they were getting from people passing by. Erica gazed up and down; the title of the café was 'Café Cool'. Erica then followed Henry inside the café.

Henry sat down and then Erica sat opposite him. A waitress soon appeared; she was definitely local stock. Erica knew this to be the case as soon as she opened her mouth and said, "Okay pops, what are you and your daughter having?" Henry picked up the menu and then spoke, "No, she ain't my daughter. Can we start off with two coffees." He turned to Erica and said, "What pie you having?" Erica replied saying the first thing that came into her head "I will have the Hillbilly Pie."

Henry sat looking confused, as did the waitress. She then looked down at Erica and spoke in a heightened voice, "What sort of pie is that? There are no cannibals here; we don't eat our own."

Erica smiled and then said, "No, I meant to say Blueberry Pie."

The waitress shrugged her shoulders and pulled a face. She was in her late thirties and of Hillbilly stock, ugly and uneducated.

Henry looked up at the waitress and said, "I will have the Blueberry Pie." The waitress rolled her eyes and walked away, shaking her head. Henry was captured by Erica's beautiful eyes.

Erica in return looked at Henry, her mind whispered 'look at that shrivelled complexion and them bags under his eyes'. Erica once more put on a false smile.

Henry shook his head. He then spoke in a low voice, "Is everything okay, Hillbilly Pie?"

Erica shook her head, slightly bewildered by what had occurred on the eve of their wedding. She then replied, "Must have been those guys in the Dodge. I must be in some sort of shock." Erica could hear the waitress talking to a customer. "That there woman just asked me for a Hillbilly Pie." The customer sat alone drinking coffee. She had ginger curly hair and a crooked nose. She had a think then spoke, "Oh yes, you are from good Hillbilly stock as I am good looking and intelligent." The waitress nodded in agreement and then carried on serving customers. She then turned her attention to

Henry and Erica and poured them some coffee. She then placed two small Blueberry Pies on the table. The waitress made a sly comment, "Enjoy your Hillbilly Pie, lady. Its good looking and intelligent."

Erica burst out into laughter as the waitress walked away. Erica then turned to Henry and said, "Can you believe that woman, a Hillbilly, good looking and intelligent. I beg to differ - more like check in the mirror, mutant."

Henry took a deep breath and said, "Okay, let's just forgive and forget all about the Hillbilly thing. I know they pissed you off, as did they with me but this is meant to be a happy occasion; we are to be married in the morning."

Erica smiled then spoke, "Oh I am sorry." She then began to eat her Blueberry Pie. Erica looked to Henry and said, "My, this pie is really good." Henry agreed with a nod of his head. Erica closed her eyes for a second. She then opened them and finished off her coffee.

Henry smiled and then said, "Okay, you all finished? I will pay the bill and we shall be on our way."

Erica stood up as Henry asked for the bill. He paid the bill and then they both left the café. They walked back to the Cadillac as the sun shone in all its glory. Erica opened the door. She then noticed how hot it was inside. She opened the car windows to cool the inside. Erica and Henry both got in and Erica pulled off slowly.

Her mind whispered 'the day of judgement will soon be upon you my old friend' but how on Earth could she contact Dylan as Henry was with her all the time. Erica continued to drive, her mind once more whispered. She then had an idea - the garden - what if Henry was to fall asleep in the garden? After all, that is how they first met him.

As they reached their destination, Erica turned to Henry. She could not believe her luck, Henry had nodded off. Erica slowly pulled the Cadillac into the driveway; she needed him to stay asleep. Erica parked the Cadillac up. As she did, Henry opened up his tired eyes. Erica turned to Henry with an expression of horror; she then said, "My, you look so tired. Go and have a quick power nap whilst I sit in the garden and listen to the birds singing."

Henry yawned as he got out of the Cadillac. He then turned to Erica and said, "You don't mind, do you? I need to be at my best tomorrow morning. I will do as you say and have a good nap. I will have a bath after my nap; that might make me feel better. Say hello to the birds for me."

Erica laughed and then spoke in a heightened voice, "Okay, I will". Erica parked the car in the garage and locked the door. Erica then sat in the garden listening to the birds singing. After five minutes Erica mind whispered 'it's now time to contact Dylan'. Erica quietly slipped into the house. She stood and absorbed the silence. She then walked over to the phone. She only had a few sets of digits to remember in her life, one of them was Dylan's phone number. Erica then called

Dylan and awaited a reply. Erica informed Dylan all about the good news. "I am to be married in the morning; it's heart attack time. I will leave this back door open for you to get in. Remember the costume and the fake blood; we will give poor old Henry the shock of his life."

Dylan shook his head as he sat down in a quiet bar as his brothers played pool. Dylan then said, "My, you a cold-hearted woman."

Erica replied, "Yeah, warm on the outside and cold on the inside. I reckon it's being with you for all those years."

Dylan laughed and said, "Yeah, thanks a lot for that. Anyway, how rich is the old guy? I can't believe this is going to be so easy."

Erica thought she heard a noise and then said, "Okay, got to go. See you tomorrow." Erica then put the phone down. A minute later Henry appeared. Erica moved swiftly into the kitchen and poured herself a cold drink.

Henry entered the kitchen and spoke, "I could have sworn I heard you talking to someone."

Erica had no fear of detection; after all she was an actress. Erica put on a sad face and then spoke, "Oh, I was just telling my late parents about my wedding tomorrow. Do you ever see and talk to your late wife?"

Henry smiled and replied, "Yes, of course I do. Tomorrow is a big occasion. Oh, that reminds me;

I must talk to my doctor. Eventually, you're going to require us to share a bed and perform a couple of duties together. I need to get me some Viagra; it's been a long time but I am sure you will be able to help me out in that department."

Erica could not believe her ears. She put on a false smile and nodded as her mind whispered 'over my dead body'. Such a sense of horror panic fears fluttered her mind. Her imagination then got the better of her. What if Dylan didn't turn up? She would have to do the job herself.

Henry walked over to the phone and made a call to his doctor as Erica returned to the garden in a state of shock. Erica now just wanted this nightmare over with. She sat down on a seat, her mind then whispered 'do not lapse from your immoral code; you have to pull this off. Just think of the money, the mansion and that beautiful Cadillac'.

Henry finished off his phone call and then joined Erica in the garden. He sat next to her and said, "Oh, I just couldn't sleep properly. I am so excited about tomorrow. Is everything okay? You seem a little quiet. It wasn't my comments back there about us sleeping together, after all I am a lot older than you. I know it will take time but you, my dear, have enough time for both of us."

Erica took hold of Henry's hand and spoke, "You're right, it will take time, but we will get there eventually."

Henry gazed into Erica's eyes and smiled. He then said, "Oh how I love you."

Erica put on a false smile and then spoke in a low voice, "I love you also, Henry. Have you any champagne for tomorrow?"

"Oh, Eddie Elvis promised me a bottle of the best bubbly on completion of the wedding."

Erica laughed. she then said, "Why Henry, have you thought of everything? Are you okay to drink it? What about your medication?"

Henry laughed. He then replied, "Well, my doctor said I could have one glass but not to overindulge. He is a good doctor and has been for over twenty years. I don't know what I would do without him; he's always there at the end of the line ready to lend some advice. He asked me about you."

Erica's mind whispered 'I never saw that one coming'. Erica took a deep breath and then said, "What did the doctor say?"

Henry replied, "Oh, you won't be offended, will you?"

Erica shook her head and replied, "No, Henry, tell all?"

Henry then replied, "The doctor said 'are you sure she isn't a gold digger?' He asked me for your name so he could do some checks. I told him to mind his own god dam business. I also said I was a very good judge character, and you had a heart of gold and you ain't no digger."

Erica smiled and then said, "Good. I bet that put him straight. Thank you for being such a good judge of character." Henry closed his eyes for a minute. He then began to yawn. Erica laughed and then she began to yawn. Erica then said, "I reckon we both need to catch up on our beauty sleep, all nice refreshed for tomorrow." Henry agreed. They booth stood up and made their way back to the mansion. Erica kissed Henry on the cheek and then said goodnight. Erica then walked upstairs to her bedroom. The day had been long and very eventful. Erica rubbed her eyes. She got undressed, lay on the bed and fell asleep.

Chapter 15

Dylan sat with his brothers in their apartment drinking whisky. Ralph turned to Dylan and said, "So tomorrow is the big day; your Erica is a fast operator. Let's get this straight; you're going to turn up, she is going to leave the back door open; you sneak in and give that old guy the shock of his life dressed as a vampire. The big mansion and all his money then becomes Erica's and yours."

Dylan laughed and then said, "Yeah, you make it sound so God dam easy."

Ralph laughed then spoke in a heightened voice, "That's because it is so God dam easy. You pair could kill another one or two old guys and end up wealthier than us and look at the amount of killing we have done; it's the work of pure genius. Who was it that first thought of this idea? This sort of thing must run in the family."

Dylan nodded his head in agreement and then suddenly there was a loud knock on the front door. Eddie and Ralph reached for their semi-automatic weapons.

Eddie turned to Dylan and spoke in a heightened voice, "You stay put." Eddie then opened the door to find

Joey Fingers stood before him. Eddie looked into Joey's eyes and then spoke, "Step inside." Joey did as he was asked whilst Eddie shut the front door. Dylan had an uneasy feeling his heart began to pound, panic fears fluttered his mind. Eddie and Ralph remained calm. Eddie then did the talking. "Okay, Joey, why are you here?"

Joey replied, "Big Tony wants a word with you guys."

Eddie shook his head. He then spoke in a heightened voice, "I sent a message on what went on. Those Russian bastards opened fire on us, we fired back in self-defence. We did the right thing; we got the drugs and the money."

Joey looked into Eddie's eyes and then spoke, "I know what you are saying but it's not like the old days anymore. Those Russians hold some heavy muscle; they are real mean mother fuckers."

Eddie laughed. He then said, "So are we as they found out to their cost."

Joey continued to speak, "Look, Big Tony wants to speak to you in private."

Eddie looked into Joey's eyes, anxiety twisted his face. he thought of his moral responsibilities. He then spoke, "Dylan ain't going, he's done nothing wrong; he was just the driver."

Joey shook his head and then spoke in a heightened voice, "Look, Big Tony gave that kid a lot of money; he wants to speak to him also. Look, it won't take long."

Ralph smiled and then said, "Look you guys, Joey is right; let's go and hear what Big Tony has to say".

Joey then said, "Look, I have my automobile parked outside. I will take you there and return you."

Eddie took a deep breath and then spoke in a heightened voice, "Let's just do it."

Dylan had a vivid imagination and loved watching gangster movies. He had a macabre vision of all of them getting wacked.

Eddie turned to Dylan and said, "You look scared shitless; are you alright?"

Dylan shook his head. He then replied, "Let's just get this thing over with."

Eddie collected the bags they then all left the apartment and got into Joey's silver automobile. Joey then started it up and hit the gas pedal and drove towards their destination. The streets were dark and sinister gunshots, shouts and screams echoed in Dylan's ears. His mind whispered 'I am scared shitless'.

They soon arrived at Big Tony's place. Joey parked up and they all got out. Two hoods stood guard outside the club. Joey spoke to them, and they opened the door. They then all entered. On the inside stood several hoods armed to the teeth. Eddie and Ralph knew something wasn't right. Joey took them to Big Tony's office. Big Tony sat at the head of the table. Big Tony stood up as Eddie placed the bags on the table front of him and Big Tony then spoke in a heightened voice, "Okay, I will make this quick as possible. Let's all sit down." All four men sat down. Big Tony then shook his head. He then continued to talk in a deep voice, "The Russian mafia are well and truly pissed you killed their men. One in particular was the son of an ex-KGB officer. He has over a thousand men, all trained killers and they want your blood or compensation. I am afraid this time you have gone too far; I cannot protect you; they have informed me they will wipe out all of my family if I interfere with their plans."

Ralph reflected a sense of doom; his mind whispered 'endgame'.

Eddie then became irate. He then spoke in a heighted voice, "So what were we meant to do, get shot and die without a fight? Those bastards shot Ralph in the shoulder."

Big Tony nodded his head. He then spoke in a heightened voice, "I know. Doctor Damian told me how he treated the wound. Okay, I want you to listen carefully to what I have to say; let me start off with how much money have you two collected over the years, it may save all of your lives. The Russians want over five million dollars compensation the deadline is two days and then, my friends, they put a contract out on each of your heads. They informed me they will hire the best and will not stop until the job is done. Do I make myself clear?"

Eddie's anger erupted like a volcano. He shouted, "God damn those Russians! Why the fuck did they let them in our country in the first place?"

Big Tony replied, "You're right. Everything was controlled until they came over. They have money and plenty of muscle and they have cold hearts, no morale code."

Ralph then spoke in a heightened voice, "What do you suggest we do?"

Big Tony replied, "Well, the choice is yours; you pay up or disappear off the face of the Earth. The Russians have said they will hunt you down like dogs."

Eddie turned to Big Tony and said, "What happens next if we pay up? What's to stop them killing us anyway?"

Big Tony replied, "You're right; nothing. They hold all the cards, they have double my men, maybe even triple; it's a war I cannot win. Brothers, go home and sleep on it and give me the answer tomorrow. Right, I have now finished. You have two days I said. They replied they wanted to put the fear of God into you."

Ralph turned to Eddie and said, "Shit, they going to wipe all three of us out."

Eddie turned to Big Tony and said, "Okay we will think over what you said and let you know tomorrow." all three brothers said goodbye to Big Tony and left his office. Joey escorted them to his automobile and took them back to their apartment in silence.

Ralph turned to Eddie and said, "What the fuck are we going to do?"

Eddie replied, "We are all going to sleep, and, in the morning, we are going to help our brother out with his little task. That mansion is out of the way; no-one would look for us there."

Ralph laughed and then said, "Goodnight, sleep tight, don't let the Russian bed bugs bite." They all laughed and then made their way to their beds.

The following morning Erica awoke. She found it hard sleeping knowing she was to play a vital role in the murder of an old man. Erica stretched out her arms and then the usual knock on the door, the last before everything went to plan. Erica then heard a familiar voice, "Hello Erica, are you awake?" Before he could open the door Erica replied, "Yes, I am just getting out of bed; be down in a couple of minutes."

Henry said, "Oh good. I have done you some coffee and breakfast."

Erica got out of bed and put on the silk dressing gown. She then entered the bathroom. A quick wash and she was walking downstairs. Erica could hear music as she entered the dining room. Breakfast was all laid out for her; she thanked Henry then sat down to eat it.

Henry gazed into Erica's eyes and said, "Oh, I got Elvis playing in the background." 'Love me Tender' was playing. Henry then continued to speak, "I got all his records. Oh, I have to ask this question before it is too late; are you sure you want to marry an old man like me?"

Erica's mind whispered 'yes, right'. she said, "Without a doubt, yes I want to marry you."

Henry smiled and then spoke, "You're like an angel; I have had a lifetime of witnessing good and evil."

Erica sat confused she then said, "Where have you witnessed evil?"

Henry shook his head then replied, "Oh it's a long story, one I promised not to tell. I gave my word to a creature of darkness." Henry shook his head. He then had a macabre vision of extreme terror horror beyond imagination. Henry closed his eyes and then opened them. He then regained his composure.

Erica felt his fear and said, "You're right. There is good and evil everywhere but today we just don't care as we are to be married."

Henry began to smile and said, "Okay this is it. You go upstairs and get ready, I'll tidy up here."

Erica nodded in agreement and then made her way to the bathroom. She got into the shower; the warm water felt good on her naked body. Erica washed her hair and then turned off the shower and dried herself off with a towel.

Henry washed the dishes. He remembered his late wife and how she died in a dark heartless place at the hands of a barbaric creature. Henry's mind whispered 'forget the evil look, to the light. Erica is the light; she will help me forget my inner demons'. Henry then went upstairs to his room to get ready

Erica had finished in the bathroom and was now putting on her wedding dress. Erica applied some makeup. She then fixed her hair and was now ready.

Henry got dressed in a light blue suit and white shirt and matching tie. He then met up with Erica in the dining room. Erica had just finished off a cool glass of pure orange juice. Henry smiled and said, "Are you ready?"

Erica put on a false smile and replied, "Ready as ever I will be. Oh and Henry, may I say that suit makes you look twenty years younger."

Henry laughed and then said, "I wish, if only. Okay, may I say your dress makes you look like a princess. Okay, let us be on our way."

They left the mansion and got into the Cadillac. Erica started it up as Henry opened the garage door. The weather outside was cloudy and overcast. Erica drove out of the garage and Henry locked the door. She hadn't left it open. Erica turned to Henry and said, "Have you the ring?"

Henry replied, "Yes." Henry gazed into Erica's eyes and said, "Don't tell me, I can tell by your face you have forgotten something, haven't you?"

Erica had an idea. She then replied, "Yes, I have forgotten my lucky charm. I will dash back inside the

mansion and get it. You wait here, I won't be long."
Erica got out of the Cadillac and opened the front door.
She then walked to the backdoor and unlocked it. Erica
then went to her jewellery box and picked out a bracelet;
this would be her lucky charm. She put it on and then
returned to Henry. she got back into the Cadillac

Henry smiled and then said, "Okay, let me see your
lucky charm." Erica lifted her wright wrist to reveal a
golden bracelet. Henry laughed and then spoke, "It's
the icing on the cake."

Erica laughed and then said, "The wedding cake." She
then put her foot down on the gas pedal towards the
Chapel. As Erica drove she remembered the previous
day; her mind whispered 'God dam Hillbillies and
Eddie Elvis and the fact she could not think of a single
Elvis song'. Her mind then whispered 'very soon this
will all be over'. She then put her foot down on the gas
pedal, driving faster and faster. She loved the Cadillac
and had a comforting sense of fulfilment knowing it
would soon be all hers.

Chapter 16

Several minutes had passed since she put her foot down and they had now arrived at their destination. Erica parked outside the Chapel of Elvis. The dollar signs began floating in her mind; later she would have everything. They both got out of the Cadillac. Erica then locked the doors. She then walked over to Henry and then placed her hand in his. Erica then spoke, "Come on, let's get this over with."

Henry nodded his head in agreement. They then entered the Chapel and were greeted by Eddie Elvis. He then spoke in a high pitched voice, "Hi, you all. Are you both ready for this? In the Chapel of Elvis, you are truly under the eyes of our Lord. Say Amen." Henry and Erica did as requested and said 'Amen'. Eddie Elvis then spoke once more in a heightened voice, "Enter with love and peace in your hearts and souls. Follow me and set your spirits free."

Erica and Henry followed Eddie Elvis to the alter. In the background music was playing by none other than Elvis. Henry's mind whispered 'what a song'.

Eddie Elvis stood before them. He then spoke in a deep voice, "Okay, let us begin. We are all gathered to witness the marriage of this beautiful couple in the eyes of the Lord. Henry Jones, will you love, cherish, honour and enjoy this beautiful young lady? Erica Thompson, will you do the same?"

Erica could not believe her ears and just said "Okay, I agree."

Henry then spoke, "Yes, I also agree."

Eddie Elvis then spoke once more in a deep voice, "Henry my man, have you the ring?"

Henry replied, "Why yes, I sure have." Henry then got it out of his pocket.

Eddie Elvis then laughed out loud. He then spoke in a heightened voice, "Okay, you both know what to do. Now place the ring on her finger." Henry placed the gold wedding ring on Erica's finger. Eddie Elvis then shouted, "I now pronounce you man and wife. You may kiss the bride and the Lord deliver you pair from evil."

Henry kissed Erica. Her mind whispered once more 'just think of all that lovely money, mansion, and motor'. They embraced and then Eddie Elvis produced some flowers for the bride and a bottle of bubbly. He then spoke in a deep voice, "Can you both sign the marriage certificate and then its legally binding."

Erica moved fast and signed the certificate and then Henry also signed. Eddie Elvis played the requested song 'Crying in the Chapel'. Henry put the signed certificate in his pocket and then escorted his new bride away from the Chapel. Henry carried the bottle of bubbly whilst Erica carried the flowers.

The brothers arrived at the mansion. Eddie parked his automobile at the rear of the mansion. Eddie turned to Ralph and spoke in a heightened voice, "This place is amazing, pure Heaven; it's so peaceful and quiet." Eddie then turned to Dylan and said, "Okay, do you want any help? We could put some bullets in him and dispose of the body; it's easy enough."

Dylan shook his head in disbelief he then replied, "Look, this is my show. All I want you pair to do is lay low."

Eddie laughed and then spoke in a heightened voice, "You can count on it."

Dylan shook his head. His mind whispered 'everything to them is just a joke'. Dylan got out of the automobile with a bag in his hand containing his costume. Dylan then entered the mansion through the back door. He then walked upstairs into the bathroom. He gazed at himself in the mirror and applied some make up. Dylan then opened his mouth and then put in his vampire teeth. He looked into the mirror and snarled. He then applied some fake blood around his mouth. Dylan was now ready to fulfil his role.

Erica and Henry got into the Cadillac. Erica announced to Henry triumphantly, "This is the best day of my life."

Henry then said, "Are you sure you don't want to do something else, maybe go for a meal or something?"

Erica smiled. Her mind whispered 'your destiny is calling'. She then replied, "Maybe later when I have got out of this wedding dress." Henry nodded in agreement as Erica put her foot down on the gas pedal. She drove faster and faster as her mind whispered 'the sooner this is over the better'. Erica kept telling herself it was but a mercy killing, put an old man out of his misery. Was that really so bad?

Henry sensed there was something wrong and said, "Erica, can you not slow down a little? You are in a bit of a hurry."

Erica turned to Henry and put on her usual false smile. Erica then said, "Okay Henry, I will slow down a little." Erica slowed down; they soon reached the mansion. Erica pulled up to the garage.

Henry turned to Erica and smiled. He then spoke, "No point in putting the motor in the garage. Let's just get out of the Cadillac."

The howl of the wind, a storm began to rage, the rain started to patter against the window screen of the Cadillac. Erica turned to Henry and said, "Where on Earth did this come from?" Erica's mind whispered 'perfect, straight out of a horror movie. This ought to frighten the old man'. Erica was an actress, she knew she had a part to play. Erica turned to Henry, her eyes and mind became more and more sinister. She then spoke, "My God, this reminds me of those old vampire movies I used to watch."

Henry reflected a shade of terror; his bottom lip began to tremble. Past memories returned to him. Henry's heart was pounding.

Erica knew he was frightened; it was now time. She then spoke in a cold weary voice, "Come on, Henry, let's get inside out of these uncomfortable clothes."

It was now pouring down with rain. Erica and Henry got out of the Cadillac. Erica picked up the flowers as Henry picked up the champagne. They then made a dash to the front door. In the distance they could hear the echo of thunder and lightning. They entered the mansion. Henry shut the door and took a deep breath.

Erica turned to Henry and said, "I need to get out of this dress." She turned and went upstairs. Henry shook his head in disbelief at the change in weather.

Dylan stepped out from the bathroom and saw Erica. He whispered, "I am here my dear, fancy a bite?" Erica shook her head as she entered the bathroom. Dylan grabbed hold of her arm squeezing it tight. Erica pushed Dylan. He then spoke in an angry voice, "Look, we got to make this look real. Have some fake blood." Dylan opened up a small tube containing fake blood. Dylan then smeared it onto Erica's neck. Dylan then began to twist Erica's arm. She then screamed.

Henry's heart began to pound; a thought flashed through his brain. Henry stood rooted with fear as a wailing choking scream echoed all around. She then shouted the word 'vampire'. Henry knew it was his duty to protect his wife. Henry rushed into the kitchen, he reached inside a draw and then produced a knife. Henry took a deep breath and then slowly walked towards the stairs. Henry began to shake as he made his way towards the stairs. Henry soon reached the top of the stairs. He gazed towards the bathroom; there lay Erica on the floor, motionless, blood pouring from her neck. Henry then heard thunder and lightning; the mansion began to shake. All of a sudden Dylan appeared. Henry's mind was paralysed by the hideous sight. Henry started exhaling and shaking, his speech was slurred. He dropped the knife, his eyes were wild terror. He gazed at the mysterious stranger with death cold eyes. Henry was sweating furiously, his eye lids flickered spasmodically. He held his chest and then fell backwards; this proved fatal. Henry died instantly.

Dylan laughed as Erica got to her feet. He then said, "My God, that old guy took a while to die and what was with the knife?"

Erica shook her head. All of a sudden her anger rose. She then spoke in a loud angry voice, "God damn, you have you no respect for the dead."

Dylan took a deep breath and then replied, "I am sorry. I will now get the hell out of here. All you need to do is clean up the kitchen and fake blood off your neck and put the knife back in the kitchen and call for an ambulance in that order."

Erica was still angry. She looked down at Henry's motionless body. She then picked up the knife. Erica and Dylan walked downstairs. Erica placed the knife back in the drawer as Dylan changed out of his costume. He then left the mansion. Erica wiped the fake blood from her neck. She then called for an ambulance. She informed the operator her husband Henry had fallen over after having a massive heart attack. The operator asked if she had checked his pulse. Erica remembered calm and then spoke and said, "Yes, there is no pulse." Erica gave the operator the address and then hung up. Erica dashed upstairs. She stepped over Henry's lifeless body. She then entered the bedroom and quickly changed her clothes. Erica then remembered the marriage certificate was in Henry's pocket.

All of a sudden, a large bang on the front door; it was the emergency services. Erica stepped over Henry's body once more and then rushed downstairs. She opened the front door. She was greeted by a tall man with a handsome face. He then spoke with firmness in his voice, "Hello, my name is Peter. I believe your husband Henry has suffered a massive heart attack."

Erica wiped a fake tear from her left eye and then replied, "Yes, he fell backward and died instantly. I checked his pulse; he was stone dead."

Peter shook his head. He then spoke in a heightened voice, "Okay, where is the body?"

Erica replied, "The body is upstairs."

Peter walked upstairs with Erica. He then examined the body. A second paramedic entered through the front door with a first aid kit. He dashed through the house. Upstairs, Peter then said to his buddy "There is nothing we can do, it's his age. Look at the poor guy's face - what do you reckon?"

The second paramedic, Leo, was a lot older. He then replied, "Look at the anxiety; his face is twisted. I reckon the heart attack was brought on by extreme terror." Leo's mind whispered 'something wasn't right'. A brief glance at Erica; with a sense of compulsion, he turned to Peter and said, "Are you thinking what I am thinking?"

Peter nodded and said, "Yeah, let's get this poor old guy to the morgue. The coroner's examination, that's what this guy needs."

Erica watched as they removed the body. Erica was an actress; she knew she had to perform. She pinched herself and put on a miserable face. She then shed another tear. Erica followed them downstairs. she then turned to Peter and said, "Oh, I will miss my Henry; he was such a kind man."

Peter's mind whispered 'gold digger'. She then explained the marriage certificate was in Henry's pocket. Peter put on a false smile and then said, "Alright, I will get it for you. The poor old guy must have had a lot of money."

Erica looked at Peter with a contemptuous smile. Her mind whispered 'stay cool'.

Peter reached inside Henry's pocket. He then took hold of the marriage certificate and handed it to Erica. Peter then informed her all about the coroner examination. peter then put on a false smile and said, "Oh, and another thing, a detective will be around shortly to ask you some routine questions." He announced this triumphantly. He stood awaiting some sort of response.

Erica just nodded in confirmation. Her mind whispered 'from now on coolness is the key to unlock all of Henry's money'.

Peter turned to Leo and said, "Okay, lets wrap this up." The two paramedics placed the corpse of Henry into the ambulance. Peter then said, "The cold hearted bitch; I reckon she somehow frightened the old guy to death." Leo agreed with a nod of his head. They then left the scene of the crime.

Erica shut the front door, marriage certificate in hand. She placed it down on a table and then made herself a coffee. Five minutes later another knock on the door, it was detective Murphy; he was a bright young detective, fair haired with a face of cool ivory, under his arm a brown briefcase. The detective knocked twice more. Erica then opened the door. The detective introduced himself and displayed his badge. Erica invited him into the mansion. The detective followed Erica inside. He shut the front door behind him.

Detective Murphy spoke with firmness in his voice, "Okay, this is purely routine. I am here to make a few notes on what went on and to box off a simple investigation."

Erica displayed a sad face and said, "I still feel a bit shaken and dazed. Would you like a coffee?"

Detective Murphy replied, "Yes, okay, and may I say you have nothing to worry about. Just answer the questions to the best of your knowledge. Do I make myself clear?"

Erica nodded her head and then proceeded to make two cups of coffee. Erica then spoke in a heightened voice, "Milk and sugar?"

Detective Murphy replied, "Oh, just milk, I am sweet enough."

Erica's mind whispered 'what a jack arse; this guy makes me sick but I must remain cool at all times'. Erica then completed her task and placed the coffee cup next to where the detective sat. He took a sip of the coffee and then opened up the brown briefcase. He removed some paperwork and a pen. The detective was dressed in a dark tailored suit. The detective began to talk in a heightened voice, "Okay, I will fill in an investigation sheet. I want you to tell me in your own words what went on leading up to the death of Henry. I believe you pair just got married; I must admit the age difference does baffle me." The detective looked at Erica with a fixed expression. He sat with pen and paper at hand awaiting a response.

Erica's mind whispered 'you're an actress for God's sake, act'. Erica smiled and then spoke, "Oh, let me start from the beginning; oh, my old car broke down and Henry was my knight in shining armour. He helped me out; he had a heart of gold and I guess our love blossomed."

the detective smiled and said, "I bet it wasn't that beautiful vintage Cadillac parked up next to the garage."

Erica shook her head and then replied, "No, it's an old banger parked up at the back of the mansion."

the detective smiled and then said, "Yeah, this place is pretty impressive, must be worth quite a few dollars. My, I wish I could afford to live here. Okay, just tell me the truth as you see it."

"We got married in the Chapel of Elvis."

the detective laughed and then spoke, "Yeah, Elvis; I grew up listening to Elvis, watching his movies. A true king. Okay, let's get back to your story."

Erica smiled and then continued, "Henry kept talking about good and evil; something bad happened to his departed wife. He had fear in his eyes as he spoke about her. He informed me he could see her and she wasn't very happy about him remarrying."

The detective made notes and then said, "Maybe a vengeful spirit. Did you see anything spooky?"

Erica took total control; after all, she was an actress. She gazed into the detective's eyes and then replied,

"There is an evil spirit in this mansion." With an expression of horror she continued to speak, "Me and Henry had just got married. We pulled up to the mansion; before we got out of the Cadillac something strange happened, it was like something out of a horror movie. A howl of wind, a storm started to range; the rain started to patter against the windows of the Cadillac. Henry reflected a shade of terror; we heard the echo of thunder and lightning, he began to hold his heart. I told him to calm down; we dashed inside out of the rain. He informed me everywhere he looked he could see his late wife's face and she was very pissed. Henry informed me he needed to go to the bathroom. He dashed upstairs as I made him a coffee. I heard him talking to someone in a heightened voice, his words still echo in my mind. He kept saying 'leave me alone'. A draught of air suddenly ran down the detective's spine as Erica's continued her story. "Henry cried out 'God help me' and then cold air and silence. I rushed upstairs and found his dead body. He had no pulse."

The detective finished writing. He took a deep breath and then said, "Shit, what a story; the poor old guy. Maybe he should have gone to a priest; it sure sounds like the work of a vengeful spirit."

Erica nodded and then said, "Henry did say she died a really horrible death but would not go into detail."

The detective then said, "Sounds like you did all you could, so sad."

Erica shed a tear. She then said, "Henry's heart attack proved fatal; he died instantly."

The detective's voice perked with curiosity as he asked a question: "I must admit you are rather cool; you ever worked as an actress?"

Erica reflected a shade of terror. Her mind whispered 'prove it, jerk'. She then replied in a cool voice, "Maybe one day I might have lessons."

The detective smiled and said, "What you need is a priest to bless this place."

Erica then spoke in a low voice, "I will take your advice and get a priest just in case."

The detective finished off his coffee and put his papers back into his case. The detective then spoke, "My conclusion is something bad did happen to his poor departed wife and marrying you triggered a of a serious supernatural event, being visited by his departed wife on his honeymoon triggered of a massive heart attack. I will finish off the report when I get the coroner's report. I may contact you or I may not; all you need to do now is arrange a decent send off, by that I mean funeral."

Erica agreed. He shook Erica's hand and she then escorted him out of the mansion. Erica's mind whispered 'that was easy'. She then made herself another coffee. All of a sudden, a knock on the front door. Erica walked over to the front door and opened it. Stood before her was a familiar face; it was Dylan. Erica looked into his eyes and said, "My God, that was quick. You wasted no time, did you?"

Dylan smiled then replied, "Well, you know me, babe. Was it all cool with the detective? I bet he was putty in your hand. I watched him come and go from behind the hedge."

Erica nodded her head and then spoke in a heightened voice, "Yes, everything is cool. The detective reckoned poor old Henry was having visions of his poor departed wife and that is what caused his heart attack. The detective believed every word I said; like you said, he was putty in my hand."

Dylan laughed and then spoke, "You are a work of art, a rare masterpiece like the Mona Lisa."

Erica shook her head and then said, "Yeah and you are like a massive bull full of shit."

Dylan knew how to piss her off. He believed he had it down to a fine art. Conscious of her annoyance he then said, "Are you having a coffee?"

Erica shook her head. Her mind admitted defeat. She looked into Dylan's eyes and said, "Are you staying the night?"

Dylan laughed and then replied, "Yes, you can count on it."

Erica began to laugh. She then made Dylan a cup of coffee.

Chapter 17

Dylan's brothers' time had ran out. They returned to their apartment to get their money out of the safe. As they pulled up an almighty explosion as a bomb ripped through their apartment. Eddie turned to Ralph and shouted, My God its started, they never even gave us a chance to get our money."

Ralph gazed all around and then spoke in a deep heightened voice, "Alright, they must be watching us. The money would have helped us escape the country. We have to go into hiding." Ralph picked up his mobile phone and called his younger brother.

Dylan sat drinking his coffee on the same seat the detective was sitting on. Dylan's mobile phone rang out, he answered it straight away and listened carefully to what Ralph had to say. Dylan then invited them in. Erica asked Dylan who was calling; Dylan hung up and replied it was his brother Ralph. "My brothers need somewhere to lie low for a short while."

Erica's eyes began to shine with livid wrath, anxiety began to twist her face. She then spoke in a heightened voice, "My God, no, this is my mansion. I don't want them staying here."

Dylan could not believe his ears. He gazed into Erica's eyes and said, "Look, this mansion belongs to the both of us. We killed that old man and don't forget it. There are plenty of bedrooms, they just need a roof over their heads for a while. Don't worry, I will have a word with them; they won't misbehave, that I do promise."

Erica calmed down and said, "What happens if that detective or anyone else calls round?"

Dylan replied, "Don't worry, we will all hide upstairs. Imagine what the neighbours would think!"

Erica shook her head and replied, "What neighbours?"

Dylan replied, "Exactly, we got none."

Erica's mind whispered 'what about Henry's money?' She then turned to Dylan and said, "Let's go through the old man's documents and find out where all his money is."

Dylan smiled and then said, "That's my girl, good thinking. Let's try his bedroom." Erica agreed and they both walked upstairs to bedroom. They both entered the room. On the wall hung a picture of his late wife. Erica removed it off the wall and placed it into a wardrobe. The room was full of vintage items and furniture, including a very old record player. They searched and searched until Erica found all of the documents and an envelope full of dollars.

Dylan's eyes lit up. He said, "Here, let me relieve you that I can count it out." Erica handed the envelope to

Dylan. He then sat on the bed. He opened the envelope and counted out the fifty dollar bills. He then said, "One, two, three, I love to count."

Erica shook her head and said, "Grow up you muppet."

Dylan disagreed and then spoke, "No, that was Sesame Street."

Erica shook her head and then continued to search. Erica then found the envelope; written on the front 'investment'. Erica's mind whispered 'bingo'. She opened it up and began to read the document, an investment of ninety thousand dollars. Her mind whispered once more 'this money is mine all mine'.

Dylan finished counting the money and then turned to Erica and said, "Eight hundred and fifty dollars; that ought to keep us in food and beer for a while. Dylan gazed at Erica and then said, "What is that letter in your hand?"

Erica replied, "Oh nothing; it's about his late wife. It reads he had a lot of bad investments; all of his money was invested in this beautiful mansion."

Dylan shook his head and said, "Oh that is a shame. You wouldn't be holding out on poor Dylan, would you?"

Erica shook her head. She then quickly put the paperwork back in the drawer before Dylan could react. All of a sudden Dylan's mobile rang, it was Ralph. He asked for directions to the mansion once more and then hung up.

Erica looked into Dylan's eyes and said, "Was that your brother?"

Dylan replied, "Yes, they are on their way."

As soon as he finished his sentence a loud knock on the front door echoed all around them Erica turned to Dylan and said, "I will answer the door, you stay here." Erica laughed and rushed downstairs. She opened the front door and was greeted by Ralph and Eddie. They entered the mansion. Eddie put a brave face on and then spoke in a heightened voice, "Thank fuck you pulled this off; I guess the old guy is brown bread and all of this is now yours."

Dylan nodded as Erica shut the front door. She then decided to keep out of sight. She walked upstairs and entered Henry's bedroom. She removed the envelope containing the document and then entered her bedroom and hid them under the mattress. Erica sat on top of the bed; she then reached for the envelope, opened it once more and began to read it. On the letter was the solicitor's number.

The brothers sat down and Dylan made coffee. Eddie turned to Dylan, he handed him a cup of coffee then said, "That fucking Cadillac is awesome. I need to get my automobile out of sight in that garage; the Russians are looking for my motor. Those bastards blew up our apartment; all of our money was inside in a safe. We have lost everything, you know what I mean?"

Dylan nodded his head and then replied, "So what are you going to do?"

Eddie replied, "Well to start with we got to lay low here until we got ourselves some real [money?], the more the merrier. That's where you come in. What happened to the money Big Tony gave you? Let's face it, that old guy must have left Erica some serious dollars."

Dylan then said, "Okay, I got the money Big Tony gave me. The old guy left an envelope with eight hundred and fifty dollars in it."

Eddie shook his head and then spoke in heightened voice, "No way, man. Look at the size of this place - more like hundreds of thousands."

Dylan became confused. He then said, "But Erica said all of his money was invested into the mansion."

Eddie shook his head. He then spoke in a deep voice, "Well, brother, you got to ask yourself do you trust her? I know I wouldn't, not with that sort of money. where did she find the papers telling her all the money was invested in the mansion?"

Dylan replied, "Oh, Erica said it was in the man's bedroom drawer."

Eddie laughed. He then said, "Okay, that will be my bedroom. We need as much cash as possible to get out of the country. Does Erica know about the Russians? Remember one thing, we must all stick together or they will pick us off one by one. did I make myself clear?

Dylan replied, "Erica doesn't know anything. I reckon we pull off one more job whilst you two lay low."

Eddie lit up a cigarette and said, "Got any beer or jack Daniels in the mansion?"

Dylan smiled and then said, "I will take a look in the dining room." Dylan walked over to the dining room. He searched until he found an old dusty bottle of whisky and a bottle of French brandy. Dylan lifted up the bottles and then took them back to his brothers.

Ralph took a look at the bottles and laughed. He then said, "My God, you got some spirits salvaged from the titanic."

Eddie laughed and then said, "Yeah, I got a sinking feeling."

Dylan reached for three glasses. He poured out the whiskey. Eddie picked up a glass and then had a sip. He coughed and then said, "My God, that is strong stuff. How long has it been there?"

Dylan and Ralph took a sip and coughed. Dylan laughed out loud. He shook his head and then said, "It tastes just like cough medicine."

Eddie laughed. He then spoke in a heightened voice, "Maybe we should stick with the French brandy."

Dylan read the label on the bottle of French brandy. He then said, "Napoleon."

Eddie looked confused. He then spoke, "Who was that guy Napoleon?"

Dylan replied, "I remember doing a history lesson about this guy; he was a French version of Hitler. He met up with an English guy called Wellington who gave him the boot in the Battle of Waterloo."

Eddie scratched his head. He then said, "Are you sure you just haven't made that all up?"

Dylan replied, "It's all true. Back in those days the Brits ruled the world, real bad asses. I reckon our ancestors may have been British."

Ralph took another sip. He coughed and said, "My God, this is rocket fuel. About the British thing, maybe that was the case who knows? If we don't find some serious dollars I don't think we will be alive long enough to find out. Remember what Big Tony said; those Russians are well and truly pissed and will not stop until all three of us are dead. I reckon even if we had paid them our money they would have still had us killed."

Eddie stood up. He then poured his whiskey down the sink. He then poured himself a brandy. He took a sip and said, "Guys, that's a lot better; I reckon that whisky is bad stuff, must be cheap and nasty brand."

Dylan and Ralph followed Eddie's lead pouring their whisky down the sink. They then poured themselves a brandy. Ralph took a sip, a thought then entered his mind. He turned to Dylan and said, "Do the Germans make brandy?"

Dylan shook his head and then replied, "No, they are famous for their sausages and getting their arses kicked in two world wars. That is the reason they lack in sense of humour department. I remember a friend of mine who went on holiday to Spain; he said he got up early every morning but couldn't get a sunbed on account of the hotel being full of Germans. They were the master race of the sunbeds."

Ralph smiled. He then spoke in a heightened voice. "Spain; been there once on a job. We were the muscle needed to deliver some merchandise after our task was completed in Majorca, and my did it rain, we visited Bar Papis and watched a great indie/rock duo. After the brilliant entertainment, we went to the karaoke bar and met Andy, the king of the karaoke. He brought us some Jack Daniels and then explained he was from a small town called Ellesmere port but was now living in Scotland. Later on, we met up with his drinking buddies, Dave and Carl, we all walked from bar to bar singing in the rain. Andy was a true diamond geezer, my those were the days."

Eddie turned to Dylan and said, "I reckon it's time to go to bed. Show me my room."

Ralph then said, "Okay, I will have the other room."

Eddie looked to a black holdall in the corner of the room. He then said, "The money Big Tony gave you is in the black bag over there?"

Dylan replied, "Yes, it's safe in there."

Eddie then said, "We got one month to lie low tops and then we get out of this country. I fancy the Caribbean."

Dylan and Ralph agreed with Eddie. "The money from selling this fine property would get us there and help us live happily ever after; no more crime, just sitting in the sun sipping on ice cold beer." They then all said goodnight to each other and then walked upstairs to their rooms.

Dylan entered Erica's room. She was fast asleep; it had been a long eventful day. Dylan yawned then got into bed and fell fast asleep.

The following morning Erica awoke. She turned over and saw Dylan fast asleep in the bed with her. Erica crept out of bed. she put on a silk dressing gown, hidden in the pocket the letter. She made her way downstairs. She walked over to the phone. All three brothers were fast asleep. Erica picked up the phone and phoned the financial adviser. A few minutes later he answered. his name was Charlie. Erica explained her situation as she saw it. She married Henry, he had a massive heart attack and was now deceased and she wanted all the money.

Charlie could not believe his ears. He was in his fifties, of medium height and build, complete with blue eyes and light brown hair. Charlie ended the conversation by explaining to Erica they would have to meet so she could provide the marriage certificate and papers would have to be signed before she could get her hands on the money.

Erica agreed and they arranged to meet up the following day. Erica hung up. She then noticed a calendar on it, a reminder the cleaner was coming. 'My God' her mind whispered. 'What about the brothers?' Panic fears fluttered her mind as she made her way to the kitchen. She made herself a cup of coffee.

Erica gazed outside. It was dull, damp and dismal. Erica closed her eyes embracing the solitude and silence until it was broken with a knock on the door. Her mind whispered, 'great, the brothers were still fast asleep in bed'. Erica answered the door and explained the situation. Erica then said, "Sorry, but with Henry gone I can do all the cleaning myself." The cleaner stood before Erica, finding all she had said really hard to believe. Erica then said, "Are you owed any money?" The cleaner shook her head. Erica smiled and then spoke in a heightened voice, "Okay, if I ever require your services soon, I will call you." Erica then shut the front door leaving the cleaner confused and upset.

Suddenly Dylan appeared, blinking and yawning. He then said, "Who was that at the front door?"

Erica replied, "Oh, that was the cleaning lady. I explained to her Henry was no longer with us and I had no need for her services."

Dylan laughed and then said, "So that means from now on you're going to be doing all the cleaning."

Erica shook her head. She then said, "Look, you make a mess and you tidy it up. That is the way it's going to be around here, so you make sure you have words with your chuckle brothers."

All of a sudden Ralph and Eddie appeared. Eddie began to laugh. He then said, "I woke up and could smell that there fine coffee. Anyway, who are these chuckle brothers you are referring to? Ralph and me and you are right; me and Ralph do like a good chuckle."

Ralph smiled. He then spoke in a heightened voice, "Okay, I am starving. What are you going to be cooking for breakfast?"

Erica bit her lip, anxiety twisted her face. Her mind whispered, 'stay cool'. She then replied in a low voice, "Oh, how about sausage and eggs and I shall make us all a nice cup of coffee."

Ralph shrugged his shoulders and then said, "Sounds good to me."

The brothers all sat around the kitchen table as Erica made the coffee. She knew exactly how they liked it. Erica handed them their coffee. Erica then stood gazing at the brothers.

Ralph looked at Erica and then spoke in a heightened voice, "What about the sausage and eggs?"

Erica laughed. She then replied, "I was only joking. The poor old guy had a heart condition; no sausages, just egg."

Ralph smiled and then said, "My, I love your sense of humour. I guess sausage is off the menu. In that case eggs sound okay."

Erica laughed and then spoke, "Alright, eggs fried or poached?"

Ralph smiled. He then said, "I reckon she should settle for the healthy option. I will have mine poached. What do you reckon, guys?" All three brothers agreed so poached it was. Erica reached inside a cupboard and produced a large pan designed for poaching eggs. Erica opened a box of eggs and continued with the task in hand. Erica completed the breakfast. She buttered some bread and then handed out the food on expensive plates. Erica then sat next to Dylan. They then all began to eat.

Eddie turned to Erica and said, "My compliments to the chef. Has anyone ever said you do a mighty wicked egg?"

They all began to laugh. Ralph then spoke in a heightened voice, "Okay, Erica, the food and drink provisions are they looking good?"

Erica replied, "I must admit they are not good but there is a supermarket in town. I reckon we will need supplies now there are four mouths to feed."

Ralph then spoke in a heightened voice, "I reckon you pair go to the supermarket as we are going to be here for a while. I reckon we make a list. What do you want, Eddie?"

Eddie laughed and then replied, "I reckon you should start off with some paper and a pen."

Erica stood up. She then reached inside a drawer and produced a pen and paper. Erica handed them to Ralph. He smiled and then said, "Now we are in business. We need milk, bread, burgers and not forgetting pizzas - all part of a stable diet and most of all we need lots of beer and Jack Daniels."

Dylan then spoke in a heightened voice, "Okay, how many Jacks?"

Ralph lit up a cigarette. "Well, for starters every bottle they got in the supermarket and you don't need to get us cigarettes as we have plenty in our boot. We got ourselves a good deal on smokes off Joey fingers; his mates robbed a warehouse full of cigarettes."

Erica turned to Dylan and said, "Okay, I will go upstairs and have a quick wash and change my clothes." Dylan nodded in agreement. As Erica made her way upstairs, she listened as the laughter of the brothers echoed all around the mansion. Erica had a quick wash and then changed her clothes. She stood looking at herself in the mirror.

Suddenly Dylan appeared. He stood before he and gazed into her eyes. He then said, "I am so sorry about all that has gone on. Are you really pissed off with me?"

Erica put are arms around Dylan. She then kissed him tenderly. Erica smiled. She then said, "Look at us; we got a mansion to sell, a Cadillac and we got some money. I reckon if we did one more job, we could settle down in the Caribbean and never have to work again. Sun, sea and ...?" Erica awaited Dylan's reply.

Dylan hesitated and then replied, "Oh, okay, the sooner the better."

Erica kissed Dylan once more and then a thought began to echo again and again in her mind: 'poor Henry, is he in Heaven looking down on her? Dylan and Erica then left the mansion to go to the supermarket whilst Eddie and Ralph sat playing cards. Erica did the shopping and then returned to the mansion. It was now late in the evening. Erica yawned as she and Dylan carried the shopping bags into the mansion. The two brothers continued to play cards. Erica turned to Dylan and said, "Alright, you put away the shopping whilst I fix us a coffee."

Dylan smiled and said, "Alright, make it a strong one."

Erica walked past Eddie and Ralph and made herself and Dylan two strong coffees.

Ralph turned to Dylan and said, "You got the beer and Jack?"

Dylan replied, "Yeah, I got your order right here." Dylan placed the beer and bottles of Jack Daniels onto the table.

Erica sipped her coffee and then once more began to yawn. She turned to Dylan. "Okay, I am taking my coffee upstairs. I am going to finish off my book. Okay, goodnight, everybody." The brothers all said goodnight as she left the room and made her way to her bedroom. Erica got into her nighty then sat reading her book. It was such a good read. She then said to herself, "My God, how on earth did the author think of that?" The book was entitled 'Five Fives Beyond Imagination', one of the greatest stories ever written. She continued to read faster and faster whilst sipping her coffee. Erica then slowly lay down and drifted into a deep sleep.

Chapter 18

The following day the brothers had become more and more of a pain in the arse. Dirty dishes in the sink, cigarette butts on the table, along with discarded rubbish. The slobs were completely out of control. Erica turned to the brothers and then her anger erupted like a volcano. She knocked the rubbish off the table. She then began shouting in a loud voice, "Look, you pair, I ain't here to clean up after you pair of slobs. Either clean up or clear off."

A few seconds of silence and then Ralph turned to Eddie and said, "Do you reckon she is serious? After all, we wouldn't be here if she hadn't had that old guy bumped off."

Erica knew she couldn't win in an argument with these couple of bad ass brothers. She knew somehow she had to get all three brothers out of the mansion as the solicitor was due to arrive in one hour's time. Erica then had an idea. She turned to Dylan and said, "Look, love, can you take your brothers out for a spin in the Cadillac? That way I can give this place a good clean in peace."

Dylan smiled. He turned to his brothers and said, "Ralph and Eddie, is that okay with you? We could do with getting a bit of fresh air."

Ralph stood up and then spoke in a heightened voice, "Okay. Eddie, let's do this. Let's give this place a good make over. After all, eventually we will need to sell this for further capital. Okay, Erica, you're right, no more slobs after this. We will turn over a new leaf from now on. Me and Eddie will clean up any mess we make. Okay?"

Eddie smiled and then said, "She is right, we need to stretch our legs and get us some fresh air." All three brothers then left the mansion. Dylan drove the Cadillac as all three drove off to the nearest town.

Erica moved fast clearing up all the mess the brothers had left. The time flew by and then a knock on the door. It was Charlie. Erica rushed to the front door and invited him in.

Charlie smiled. His mind whispered, 'my, she is young and very pretty'. Charlie had with him a briefcase. He was dressed in a brown suit and matching brown shoes.

Erica smiled and then said, "Would you like a drink?"

Charlie replied, "No thank you, dear. I got me a busy day ahead of me. I need to get all of this boxed off as soon as possible. Henry is to be buried tomorrow, next to his late wife in the old cemetery just before town. I believe the time of the burial is ten in the morning. Shall you be attending?"

Erica shook her head and then replied, "No, I don't like graveyards; oh, such sad places."

Charlie knew she was just a gold digger. He opened his briefcase and then said "Okay, have you the papers and your marriage certificate?" and then said, "All of this seems in order." Charlie then produced some documents and said, "Right, this should be over in no time. Just sign each of these documents and the money is yours as Henry has no kin other than you, his wife."

Erica smiled as she took hold of the documents. Charlie smiled and then said, "Alright, I as with Henry will look after your money."

Erica shook her head. She then said, "Look, I need that money now."

Charlie gazed into her eyes in disbelief. He then said, "Alright, it's now your money. Have you your bank details so I can forward the sum into your account?"

Erica then produced a purse. She opened it up and got out a bank card. She then informed Charlie her bank details. Charlie took down the details and then said, "This will take five working days as I will have to make all of the arrangements. Is that okay?"

Erica smiled and then replied, "Yes, I understand."

Charlie then spoke in a heightened voice, "I must be on my way; such a busy day. Oh, before I go - you definitely want all of the money going into this account?"

Erica replied, "Yes. As I have pointed out, I need all the money I can get."

Charlie then made his way out of the mansion. He said goodbye but his mind whispered 'bitch'.

Erica closed the door behind her. She made herself a pizza. Ten minutes later a knock on the door - it was Dylan and his brothers; they had been in town, stretched their legs and now returned. Erica opened the door and was greeted by a bunch of flowers.

Dylan then said, "Here you are, babe, flowers for a beautiful flower." Ralph and Eddie began to laugh as Dylan handed Erica the flowers. She smiled and said, "Why thank you, kind sir."

All three brothers entered the room. Ralph then spoke in a heightened voice, "My God, something smells mighty nice."

Erica laughed and then said, "Oh, I put in that giant pizza. You arrived just in time; I reckon it must be cooked now."

Dylan said, "Look, you sit down. I will make us all coffee and calve up that pizza." Erica nodded in agreement. The brothers sat down as Erica put the flowers in a vase. Dylan got the pizza out of the oven. He then cut it into four pieces and put them onto plates. Erica sat down. She liked the idea of someone else doing the work. Dylan handed everyone a plate containing a slice of pizza. He then made everyone a cup of coffee.

Ralph then said, "My, this is looking good. We are all going to take it in turns to tidy up and cook. Today is Dylan's turn; tomorrow its mine, then Eddie, then back to you, Erica. Does that sound fair?"

Erica smiled. She then spoke, "The old man is getting buried tomorrow in a cemetery on the outskirts of town. I may pay him a visit later on after he is six feet under, just to pay my respects."

Ralph then spoke in a deep voice, "Alright, you do that. Is it alright if us brothers all play poker and have a beer or two? I promise there will be no mess."

It was now getting late. Erica finished off her pizza and then said, "Okay, I am off that damn book. I always fall asleep." The brothers laughed as Erica made her way up to the bathroom. Erica had a shower and then dried herself. She remembered she had placed the brown envelope under her pillow. She entered the bedroom. She then hid the envelope under the bed. After all, Dylan wouldn't think of looking there. She sat reading her book as the brothers played cards until the early hours. Erica was now in bed fast asleep. Dylan got into bed; as soon as his head hit the pillow he was asleep.

Erica got up the following day. She made her way downstairs to the kitchen. Erica made herself a coffee and decided to cook breakfast for everyone, sausages, bacon, eggs and beans. Ten minutes later she had finished cooking the breakfast. Erica then walked upstairs and announced she had cooked breakfast. Very slowly all three brothers made their way to the table.

Ralph spoke in a heightened voice, "That looks good, I'm starving." They all sat down and began to eat.

Erica smiled and then said, "I know it wasn't my turn but what's the point in cooking for one?"

Eddie then spoke in a heightened voice, "Leave all the pots and pans, I will wash up."

Erica finished off her breakfast and then left the table. She then announced she was going to have a shower, get dressed and visit the cemetery. Erica then walked upstairs. She then entered the bathroom and had a shower. Erica then got dressed.

Erica made her way downstairs. All three brothers sat in the living room listening to music, just chilling out. Erica shouted, "Okay, see you later, guys." She then left the mansion and made her way to the Cadillac. Erica opened the car door then she got in and started it up. She then drove slowly towards the cemetery.

Erica drove along as her life flashed before her, the good and the bad memories of the past. Erica gazed at the strange cloud formations in the distant sky and then a sign the cemetery was two miles ahead. Erica continued to drive, thinking 'shall I visit Henry's grave and say a prayer for forgiveness?'

Erica soon reached her destination, a small, very old deserted cemetery. Erica parked her Cadillac. Erica made her way to the entrance. She opened an old iron gate and then all of a sudden an old lady appeared.

A rush of cold air ran down Erica's spine as the old lady gazed at her, complete with haggard face and rotten teeth.

the old lady spoke in a deep voice, "Hello, I work here looking after the graves of the departed - well most of them. Is there anyone you are seeking? I know this place like the back of my hand."

Erica gazed into her death cold eyes and replied, "I am here to visit Henry Jones. Could you point me in the right direction?"

The old lady then said, "Henry Jones, a new edition to the cemetery. How were you related? No-one appeared at his funeral. He was buried next to his wife. I know the both of them; many moons ago she died a horrible death in Transylvania. I believe if you go looking for something you find it." She then shook her head and spoke in a quiet voice, "Oh, don't mind me. People say I'm mad and should mind my own business. The grave is over there – you can't miss it; the new one with fresh flowers."

Erica nodded her head and said, "Thank you." She then moved quickly towards the grave. The old lady then disappeared out of the cemetery. Erica continued to walk until she reached Henry's grave. The cemetery had an eerie feeling to it, an atmosphere of death and decay. Erica gazed all around at all the old stones; some dated back to the eighteenth century, most of which were in a poor state. The fresh flowers on Henry's grave began to die.

Chapter 19

Erica closed her eyes and whispered a prayer. All of a sudden, dark clouds appeared over the cemetery. Erica opened her eyes, panic fears fluttered her mind as a sudden breeze ran down her spine. Darkness fell upon the old cemetery.

Erica felt a presence and then an old man appeared. He had a pale face, grey hair and blood-shot eyes. He was dressed in black. Erica began to shake with fear as he moved closer and closer. He then spoke with a strange accent, "Hello, do not fear an old man that is all alone in a dark world. My name is Cradual. I was born in Romania. I moved over to this beautiful country years ago. I am here to pay my respects to my friend Henry. I haven't seen him for years. I feared he had passed away. He is at peace with his wife. Henry and his wife visited Romania; they were rich tourists. His wife pleaded with Henry to go to Transylvania to investigate the legend of Count Dracula. I met up with them and had a taxi pick them up and take them to an old sixteenth century castle, its name I forget. It's been such a long time but what I do remember - the taxi driver, I informed him to take them back to town as it was getting late. The taxi driver decided to drive them back through the forest. There he pulled over and robbed them. He then left them at the mercy of the forest. All of a sudden, a beast appeared from the shadows. Henry fell, banging his head. His poor wife was not so lucky; she suffered several bites from the beast. I ordered a search party which located the two of them. They were both rushed to hospital. Henry recovered but his wife died later. She had lost a lot of blood. Henry later changed from grief to revenge. He paid local hunters a lot of money to hunt down the beast at the cost of three men; an eye for an eye. I visited Henry and informed him how sorry I was as it was my wife; she went crazy as some women do. She attacked some people just like an animal and then simply disappeared without trace. Henry and his wife were so unlucky to fall upon her at her worst; the full moon drove her even more crazy. I explained to Henry with medicine I could put a stop to future attacks. Why on earth should other tourists suffer such a cruel fate? After all, blood is thicker than water. Anyway, back to the story. Henry wanted to do the right thing as I saw it, so he introduced me to his brother, Oliver. Oh, such a noble name! He delivered the medicine in a lorry and dropped off the supplies. I paid him and then he drove back through the old forest. I am afraid luck was not on his side; he had a puncture. As he attempted to change the wheel, he met up with a hungry pack of wolves. I found what was left of him the following day, bones and a shoe. The forest can be such an unforgiving place; he never stood a chance and that concludes my story. I owe this man a dept of gratitude and one day I shall repay him."

Erica felt a cold chill run down her spine. She then said, "I am confused; Henry is dead. How can you repay him?"

Cradual smiled and then replied, "Yes you are right. Maybe my words are somewhat mixed up; it must be my age. I, like Henry, am cursed with a weak heart. I have no family and often worry what shall become of all my riches when I pass away. I do not believe I have long left on this Earth. Did you love Henry? There was such an age gap between the two of you. Could you love again? I believe it is your destiny to remarry and live happily ever after".

Erica thought for a moment. her mind whispered 'this could be the last hit and then retirement in a climate of peace and tranquillity'. Erica then spoke in a confident voice. "Maybe you are right. It would be nice to live happily after with a man of my dreams."

Cradual began to laugh out loud. He then said, "Oh, life can be such a nightmare for some and heaven for others. I have enjoyed your company. Maybe we could meet up again sometime in the future. I could show you around my mansion; would you like that? It is not far from here".

Erica agreed to meet Cradual the following evening. He then handed her a card with his name and address on it. Erica read out the address; she then noticed something in the title on the card. Erica then said, "My God, it says here you are a Count. Are you a real Count?"

Cradual replied "Yes, a title handed down through the generations. Back in Romania I owned lots of properties including an old castle. I have a chest from the sixteenth century filled with gold and silver; it must be worth millions. One day I shall show you."

Erica placed the card in her pocket. All of a sudden she began to sneeze again and again. She closed her eyes and seconds later Erica recovered her composure. Erica gazed all around, the Count had simply disappeared.

The dark clouds had now passed beyond the cemetery and were now replaced by a clear blue sky. Erica could not believe what had just happened; the Count had simply disappeared without trace. Erica stood in silence and said goodbye to Henry. She then left the cemetery and walked back to her Cadillac. She opened the door and got in. She started it up and then drove off towards the mansion. Erica tuned on the radio and then sat in disbelief as Elvis 'Love Me Tender' played. The words rang out in her ears; memories of Henry flashed in her mind. Suddenly, she began to curse; "Shut the fuck up" she shouted again and again. She then turned to another station playing 'River Mountain High' by Tina turner. Erica began to talk to herself: "My God, I will be glad when this is all over."

Erica was soon back at the mansion. She pulled into the driveway and was greeted by Dylan. He stood before her smiling. Erica parked up and then got out of the Cadillac. She then approached Dylan. Before she could speak Dylan said "Is everything okay?"

Erica replied, "My God, you would not believe what just happened to me; it was so scary. I met an old friend of Henry's, an old rich guy who claims he has millions in gold and silver."

Dylan smiled and then said, "My, that sounds like my kind of guy. Oh, and carry on with the story. Fancy going inside? I will pour us a nice, chilled drink."

Erica nodded her head in agreement and then they both entered the mansion. Erica looked all around; the mansion was clean and tidy. The brothers had kept their word and tided up any mess they had made. Erica smiled and then said, "My, you guys are sure clean cut."

Ralph smiled. He then stood up and said, "Right, let me make you and lover boy a nice cup of coffee."

Dylan and Erica sat down next to Eddie. Dylan then said, "Erica met an old friend of Henry's who claims he has millions in gold and silver. She is now going to tell us all the full story of which I reckon we need to hear."

Ralph made them their coffees and then placed the cups in front of them. Dylan and Erica thanked him. She then began to tell the story. "Oh, well, it was after I left here; I visited the old cemetery to see Henry's grave. I met a strange old lady resembling a witch and she pointed me in the right direction. I stood next to Henry's grave and I said a short prayer. Suddenly a dark cloud appeared over the cemetery, a cold chill ran down my spine and the next minute I was shocked to see an old guy standing next to me dressed all in black, a pale face and blood-shot eyes - a real creepy old guy. He then spoke and told me a story; he said his name was Count Cradual. Back home in Romania he said he owned lots of properties, including a castle. He then explained Henry and his wife visited Romania because they were interested in the legend of Count Dracula. They visited a castle but on the way back the taxi driver robbed them and then left them to the mercy of the forest. The Count told me his wife went mad and attacked Henry's wife and bit her several times. Henry fell to the ground knocking himself out cold. A search party found them. His wife died later from her horrific injuries."

Ralph shook his head in disbelief. He then spoke in a heightened voice, "Wait there - I have been killing people for years; I don't believe a woman could kill another woman with bites unless she wasn't a woman. Let's face it, if he is a Count, she must have been a Countess. Shit, this all sounds like something out of a horror movie. Anyway, sorry for the interruption; carry on with the horror story."

Erica took a deep breath and then continued with the story. "Okay, what happened next? Oh, I remember. Well, the next bit doesn't make much sense whatsoever. The Count said Henry wanted revenge and hired some local hunters to hunt down his wife's killer at the cost of three of them dead."

Ralph shook his head. He then interrupted once more and spoke in a deep voice, "Shit, no way could one lady kill three armed hunters; unbelievable. Eddie, what do you reckon?"

Eddie replied, "I reckon the old guy is making the whole thing up. The story sounds like some sort of classic fairy tale. Is there more to this story?"

Erica took a sip of coffee and then replied, "The Count said he needed medicine, so Henry introduced the Count to his brother Oliver. He delivered the medicine in a truck but after delivering it he drove through a dark forest. He had a blowout; he pulled over and whilst fixing on the spare tyre he was attacked by a hungry pack of wolves and eaten. Poor Henry was heartbroken. The Count also said he didn't have long to go on this Earth; he said he had a bad heart and no-one to inherit all his wealth. The Count gave me his card and wants to show me around his mansion."

Eddie began a slow clap. Dylan and Ralph also clapped their hands. Ralph then spoke in a heightened voice, "Shit, that was some story and what a retirement plan! If this old guy has got millions, then me and Eddie want a piece of the action. We split it four ways and then head off into the sunset. Erica, you go visit the old guy and take a look at his riches; a couple of visits and then we take him out and then become rich ourselves. What is his name again?"

Erica replied, "Count Cradual. As I said, he gave me his address and wants me to visit his mansion. I also remember something strange; after our conversation I began to sneeze and closed my eyes for a few seconds.

When I opened them, he was gone, along with a dark cloud that was hanging around the cemetery. My God, it was so spooky, like something out of a horror movie."

Dylan tuned to his brothers and said, "I don't like the idea of her going to see this guy; he sounds creepy."

Ralph then spoke in a deep voice, "I reckon you ought to give the Count Dracula routine a miss this time and just put a bullet in his head."

Dylan agreed with a nod of his head. Eddie then spoke after finishing off his coffee, "Okay. Erica, you need to pay this old guy a visit and find out all about his alleged gold and silver. What you reckon, Erica - are you up for this?"

Erica replied, "Yes, if it gets me to the promised land."

Ralph stood up and spoke. "Good, then that is all settled. Tomorrow – shit, how ironic; from Count Dylan to Count Cradual." With that remark spontaneous laughter echoed all around the mansion. Ralph then said "Okay, let's all have a beer together to celebrate our last job and then we all shall retire in paradise." Ralph then entered the kitchen and returned with four opened bottles of beer. Ralph placed them onto the table and then everyone picked up a bottle. Ralph then spoke in a heightened voice, "Okay everyone, I want to make a toast to our last job. Cheers, everybody." They all raised their bottles and each of them said cheers. They all began to drink their ice-cold beer.

Dylan looked to Erica and said, "What do you reckon to the bullet to the head instead of Count Dracula routine heart attack?"

Erica closed her eyes for a brief second and then replied, "I must admit it would be less dramatic. We could dump the body and then be away with all the Count's riches and you, brother, would only be doing mercy killing putting an old guy out of his misery."

Dylan had a sip of his beer. Panic fears began to flutter his mind; he then spoke, "Do you want me to come with you when you visit that spooky old guy? I could just hide in the back of the Cadillac, just in case."

Erica put on a brave face and then said, "Look, don't worry about me. Remember, I am a seasoned actress; no old guy could ever get one over me."

Dylan laughed and then spoke, "yeah, it's the same with us young guys. Let's face it, we don't stand a chance, come to think of it. That old guy will be putty in your hands." Erica laughed. She then nodded her head in agreement.

Ralph finished off his beer and was soon back in the kitchen. He picked up several more bottles of beer and then returned to the others. He then spoke in a heightened voice, "Okay, help yourselves." Ralph sat down next to Dylan and then turned on a radio. Playing was 'Paint It Black' by The Rolling Stones. Dylan stood up with Erica and began to dance.

Ralph turned to Eddie and spoke in a deep voice, "Okay, what do you reckon to all that has happened?"

Eddie replied, "I say all of this is mighty strange, Erica meeting that old guy that just happens to have a stash of millions in gold and silver. It's so unreal."

Ralph then spoke, "I reckon we take the shotguns and fill the old Count full of lead. We then take everything of value and maybe torch the place. I remember the Albanians - we sure put an end to them with our shotguns. Oh, such a high body count and it just got higher and higher. I reckon we must have killed about ten of them."

Eddie laughed out loud. He then said, "That was one fine day for blood and guts. Albanians, dumb mother fuckers, we caught them out with the element of surprise and they all fell like dominoes. That big guy - the almighty meat head - I had to finish him off with my semi-automatic pistol. Two bullets in the head and he was brown bread. Do you remember that bit?"

Ralph replied, "Yeah, but what is up with you always wasting our ammo? one bullet would have been quite sufficient. I reckon without the element of surprise we wouldn't have stood a chance. Most of them never had time to pick up their weapons; it was pure extermination, but they all deserved to die. The big man put out a contract on them because they were filthy animals, and all needed putting down. As I see it, we were acting as vets and might I say the operation was a complete success."

Eddie agreed with a nod of his head and then panic fears fluttered his mind. His left hand began to shake. He then spoke in a low voice, "Shit, the Russians are a completely different ball game. I reckon they will be searching for us, no stone unturned, until they find us and kill us."

Ralph laughed and then spoke in a deep voice, "So what? We all got to die sometime. As long as we got our guns at the ready we stand a chance. We can't have those mother fuckers sneaking up on us. I see this place as a safe house; no one knows we are here. The Russians know nothing of Erica and this mansion, do they?"

Eddie replied, "You're right; must be getting all paranoid in my old age. What you reckon, bro?"

Ralph replied, "We kill the old guy and rob him. We move the riches here for a bit longer. The Russians will be watching all the airports; maybe we shall hire a boat load, it up with money and get the hell out of here. Does that sound like a good idea?"

Eddie smiled and then replied, "My, Ralph, I always said you were the brains of the outfit. It's a great idea; you are right, the Russians will have men looking out for us in all the airports."

Dylan and Erica sat hand in hand listening to the music. Blondie was playing 'Heart of Glass'. Dylan smiled whilst gazing into Erica's eyes. He then spoke, "My God, this song is sort of ironic; a heart of glass, he done us proud. Look at us now, enjoying his lifestyle in this beautiful mansion."

Erica finished off her beer and then said, "Oh, I suppose so but poor Henry was such a sweet soul, a kind-hearted man. I reckon he still had a few years left in him."

Dylan finished off his beer and then said, "Yeah, you're right but you must admit the old guy had a real good life. I reckon everyone would love to live as long as Henry."

Erica shook her head as memories played again in her mind of his happy, smiling face. Erica took a deep breath and then said, "Don't you think his life was sort of tragic? He lost his wife and brother in such a place. I wonder if all the Count told me was the truth; he did say he got his words mixed up and some of the things he said just didn't add up. I reckon it's an old age issue. The Count looked like death warmed up, if you know what I mean."

Dylan smiled and then stood up. He then said, "I know something – it's well past my bed time and it's a big date for you tomorrow, a date with our destiny."

Erica stood up as Dylan said goodnight to his brothers. They then made their way to the bedroom.

Ralph turned to Eddie and then spoke in a heightened voice, "Don't they make a lovely couple? I reckon they are in love. What do you reckon?"

Eddie replied, "I agree. They have been together for quite a while. They have got a lot in common, a match made in heaven. I must admit I will be glad when all of this is over and we are all in paradise. I can see the palm trees, the golden sand and the blue ocean. Imagination, brother, it's the only way forward."

Ralph laughed out loud and then spoke in a heightened voice, "You're right, a man with imagination can go a long way - the power to think beyond the realms of his dreams. Do you know what helps me dream and do?"

Eddie gazed into his brother's eyes and then replied, "Oh, I believe it's a Jack Daniels before I go to bed, a nightcap to help with the dreams. You having one, bro?"

Ralph laughed and then replied, "You know me; I never say no to a nightcap." Ralph stood up and then collected two glasses and a bottle of Jack Daniels. He placed them onto the table. He then removed the lid and poured the whisky into the glasses. Ralph than sat down and said, "Cheers, brother."

Eddie sipped his whisky and he then turned to Ralph. "That hit the spot; I never get tired of the taste."

Ralph sipped his whisky and then spoke, "You're right, I can't get enough of the stuff." A few minutes later and both glasses were empty. Ralph filled the glasses once more.

Eddie began to have negative thoughts. He turned to Ralph and said, "Do you reckon we will make it to paradise?"

Ralph blinked and then replied, "Look, brother, positivity; we have got this far haven't we? Imagine all the times we could have been killed - talk about a cat with nine lives. We, my brother, are indestructible. No one is going to kill us. We, between us, must have killed a lot of bad people; I mean bad people who lived by the gun and died by the gun, of which I find quite refreshing, just like my glass of Jack Daniels. Anything to add to that, brother?"

Eddie took another sip of his whisky and then replied, "Yeah, you're right. We have killed a lot of bad people. Oh, what about that woman who got caught in the crossfire with the Mexicans?"

Ralph began to yawn. He then replied, "Simple; in the wrong place at the wrong time. I guess she was kind of unlucky. Anyway, wasn't she related to the Mexicans?"

Eddie replied, "I guess so. Doesn't that make it kind of right?"

Ralph replied, "Yeah, we were there to take out Mexicans and she, my friend, was in fact a Mexican. Male or female, the Mexicans were who we got paid to shoot. Anyway, I took a bullet to the leg, did I not? Okay, it was only a flesh wound; I remember you calling me 'the walking wounded' but by the grace of God we got out of that situation as we always do. Lady luck likes to shine on me and you."

Eddie had memories and visions of the past, all the close calls he and Ralph had escaped from. Eddie then said, "We have been a couple of cold-blooded killers for a long time now. We have been lucky; most don't last in the killing game. Remember big Joe Johnson?"

Ralph replied, "Yeah, the poor guy never stood a chance. Poor guy had his brains blown out by a sniper, just like J. F. Kennedy, he never saw the bullet coming. Okay, Eddie, do you remember Frank the Crank?"

Eddie smiled and then replied, "Yeah, one big car bomb - there was nothing left of the guy. He went out for a few beers, he left the bar, got into his car and bang! The bomb also took out the front of the bar. I remember glass flying everywhere. I jumped out of my skin and hid under a table. Oh, such a shock to the system. I remember Frank's happy, smiling face before he left the bar - such a bad way to go."

Ralph shook his head and then spoke in a heightened voice, "At least it was quick. I would rather be blown up than suffer a slow death. Okay, that's enough chit chat; I reckon it's late and we both need to catch up on our beauty sleep." They both finished off their drinks and then went to bed.

Chapter 20

The following morning Erica and Dylan were up bright and early. Erica had a shower and then sat in the garden drinking a coffee. Golden rays of sunshine beat down on her as she shaded her eyes from the sun. Suddenly, Dylan appeared. He walked over and sat next to Erica. She smiled and then said, "Isn't it peaceful and quiet here. No wonder Henry used to sit out here for hours on end. What do you reckon about the place?"

Dylan replied, "If we were not going to paradise this would be a mighty fine place to live. I reckon we are much too young; I crave adventure, I want to see the world and never work again. Do you agree?"

Erica smiled and then replied, "Yeah, you're right; I want to see the world. All we need is this old fool's gold and silver." A thought flashed through her mind. She already had Henry's money. It was all on a need-to-know basis and Dylan and co did not need to know. Erica then said, "After this I never want to work again. Maybe one day we could get married and have children. What do you reckon on that?"

Dylan laughed and then said, "Well, it seems like a good idea - married on the sand in paradise and we live happily ever after; beautiful, like a dream come true."

Erica laughed to herself and then said, "I wonder what ever happened to your mate, William? Do you reckon he ever met anyone special?"

Dylan laughed and then replied to Erica, "special needs."

Erica shook her head and then said, "No, don't be like that. William was so sweet; he deserves to meet the right girl, someone beautiful like me." Suddenly it all went quiet, there was no reply from Dylan. Erica gazed into Dylan's eyes and then said, "Say something. Do you agree or disagree?"

Dylan laughed and then replied, "Whatever you say, babe."

Erica closed her eyes. She then drifted away back to the cemetery; she was walking in the sunshine towards Henry's grave when suddenly it was pitch black. She stumbled and fell to the ground. She picked herself up, only to see a rabid beast stood before her. She then jumped out of her seat.

Dylan took hold of Erica's arms. He then embraced her and said, "Are you okay?"

Erica opened her eyes wide and replied, "Oh, I was just daydreaming."

Dylan laughed and then said, "Are you sure it wasn't a daymare? You jumped out of your seat; must have been something scary. What was it?"

Erica shook her head and then replied, "Oh, it was nothing; just a vision of that scary cemetery." Dylan laughed as Erica kissed him on the cheek.

Suddenly Ralph and Eddie appeared. Ralph approached Dylan and then spoke in a heightened voice, "Okay, brother, can you and your lovely sweetheart go get some more supplies from the local supermarket as we are running low on basic supplies. Bro, I even made a shopping list." Ralph handed Dylan the shopping list and two hundred dollars.

Dylan smiled and then said, "Okay, I understand you and Eddie are not to be seen as the Russians are looking out for you?"

Ralph yawned and then replied, "Yeah, they are looking for three brothers, not a young couple; you know what I mean?"

Dylan turned to Erica and whispered, "You driving, babe?"

Erica replied, "Yeah, let's go and do a shop." Erica and Dylan walked over to the Cadillac, then they both got in and drove towards the supermarket. Dylan turned on the radio and Journey 'Don't Stop Believing' was playing. Dylan began to sing out loud 'shadows searching in the night, streetlights hiding in the night' and then the guitar. Dylan then shouted, "Yeah, what a song; us Americans have always had the best music."

Erica shook her head and then turned off the radio. Dylan began to sulk; his mind whispered 'why?' Suddenly, his anger rose. He then spoke in a heightened voice, "God damn you! What is wrong with me enjoying myself?"

Erica then replied as she pressed down on the gas pedal, "Don't insult my intelligence. You know you can't sing; why can't you just listen to the music without singing? And yes, you are right, America has always had the best sounds. Okay, I will turn the radio back on if you promise not to sing."

Dylan nodded in agreement as Erica turned the radio back on. the song playing was by a group called Heart, the song 'Alone'. Dylan smiled and then said, "Oh, I love this woman's voice; such energy, but I ain't going to sing as I will just spoil the song. Is that alright?"

Erica replied, "Yes, now you are learning. I have suffered for years, Dylan, you just cannot sing."

Dylan was speechless. He sat gazing at Erica, she possessed such appealing beauty. She wore a white, silk dress and matching white shoes. The radiant sun shone down in all its glory as they arrived at the supermarket. Erica parked in the car park and then they both got out and walked over to the supermarket. Dylan got a trolley. He then smiled and said, "It's a nice day for a shop."

Erica smiled as they walked into the supermarket. Dylan believed he and Erica were perfection; he gazed at the locals in disbelief. His mind whispered 'my God, look at this variety of inbred, ugly, damn right uneducated people'. He then said, "My God, this place is full of Hillbillies and mutants."

A local Hillbilly overheard Dylan's comments. He then called over two friends. He had tattoos embroidered across his neck and a large square forehead. His friends, one of them had long hair tied in a ponytail whilst the other had dark circles under his eyes and a very shrivelled complexion. The leader informed his fellow Hillbillies what Dylan had said. Suddenly, they moved closer, gathering around Dylan and Erica. The leader introduced himself. "Hi, my name is Jacob. I believe you two are not from around these parts. We ain't mutants and we certainly ain't no gold diggers." He gazed into Erica's eyes with a sinister expression. Erica stood motionless, frozen with fear. Jacob then spoke in a deep voice, "Well, look at you, little Miss; how old is Henry? Is he still alive? I guess not. Word gets around here quick; he's dead and you got all his money. Want to share some of it with us and we won't inform our Hillbilly sheriff you are the black widow woman, a real man eater."

Dylan expressed annoyance; with an expression of horror he began to shout, "Fuck you, Hillbilly!" Again and again he shouted, until a giant imposing man arrived on the scene. It was the store manager; he then spoke in a heightened voice, "I just heard me some blasphemous language. Jacob, what is going on? You know I won't allow any trouble in my supermarket."

Jacob shook his head. He then talked in a heightened voice, "Oh, I am sorry Mr. Asdaport, but this joker here reckons our supermarket is full of mutants."

Mr. Asdaport turned to Dylan and then spoke in a heightened voice, "Is this true, boy?"

Erica stood silent; her mind whispered 'oh my God'.

Panic fears fluttered Dylan's mind; anxiety twisted his face as he replied, "Look, it was just a joke."

Mr. Asdaport looked down on Dylan. He was complete, with massive biceps and bulged shoulders. He then spoke, "Say sorry, pay for any groceries and then get out of my store and don't return. Do I make myself clear, boy?"

Dylan looked up at Mr. Asdaport with a fixed expression and then replied, "I am sorry." Perspiration began to leak from his forehead, his heart was pounding.

Suddenly Jacob began to speak with a comforting sense of fulfilment. "Boy, now leave our store and don't come back. Remember, we know where you live as poor old Henry rots in his grave."

Erica reflected a shade of terror and then her anger erupted like a volcano. With wild strength she stepped forward and slapped Jacob across the face. Dylan also joined in; he punched Jacob to the left side of his temple. He fell to the ground. The big man pulled them all apart. He then shouted with firmness in his voice, "Get the fuck out of my store right now."

Dylan and Erica rushed to the exit and then into the awaiting Cadillac. They both jumped into the vehicle as the Hillbillies followed, shouting rude words. Erica could not believe what just happened. Her face was reddened with rage as she drove off away from the supermarket. Dylan was conscious of her annoyance; he began blinking and frowning. After some hesitation he spoke, "Shit, we got no groceries." The words 'man-eater' kept ringing in Erica's ears. Dylan turned on the radio. Playing was Daryl Hall and John Oats, the song 'Man Eater'. Erica grew hysterical. She pulled over, turning the radio off. Her eyelids flickered spasmodically. Uncharacteristically, Erica began to weep hysterically.

Dylan put his arm around her and then spoke in a low voice, "I know all of this is my fault, me and my big mouth; and shit, what odds would you give me on that song being played when I turned on the radio?"

Erica regained her composure. She wiped away her tears and then said, "We got to do this last job and then get the fuck out of this mutant town."

Dylan began to laugh out loud. He then said, "So you do agree it's full of mutants."

Erica put on a brave face and then reached for her sunglasses. She put them on and then started up the Cadillac. She then hit the gas pedal. They soon arrived back at the mansion.

Eddie and Ralph sat awaiting their return. Erica parked up and they then both got out. Ralph automatically knew something wasn't right by their body language. He and Eddie walked towards them. Ralph then spoke in a heightened voice, "Tell me everything; what just took place?"

Dylan shook his head and then replied, "Shit, it was the Hillbillies. I said something as a joke that the supermarket was full of mutants. One of them overheard my comment. Soon after, there were three of them, they insulted Erica again and again."

Ralph became angry. He took a deep breath and then spoke in a heightened voice, "Okay, Erica, take off the shades." He could see she had been crying. With a homicidal look he shouted "Eddie, get the shotguns. We are going to pay this supermarket a visit."

Dylan expressed annoyance. He then shouted, "Wait a minute, what about the Russians?"

Ralph shook his head. He then replied, "Shit, you're right; they will be looking out for such reckless behaviour. If we go in guns blazing there could be a massive body count and the Russians could put two and two together and then come here looking for us and that is the last thing we need." Ralph began to think and then spoke, "Okay, a solution is the good old internet. We get our goods delivered. Okay, I am on to it, you two go inside and take a couple of chill pills."

Dylan and Erica went inside the mansion and sat down together. Erica rubbed her eyes. Her mind was crying out in pain; the words of the Hillbillies began to ring out in her ears: 'man eater' 'gold digger' and 'black widow'.

Dylan looked to Erica and said, "What are you thinking?"

Erica took a deep breath and then replied, "We need to get out of this place, far away from Hillbilly land. My God, these people are such backward, uneducated scum bags."

Dylan agreed with a nod of his head. He then spoke his mind. "Yeah, I reckon they're all interbred. My God, they are damn right ugly; that one with the square head and the scar on his nose - he looked like something out of that movie 'The Hills Have Eyes'."

Erica began to see the funny side and then burst out into laughter. She then spoke in a low voice, "Yeah, that one with the tattoos - I am sure one of them was a helicopter, the other a woman riding a whale. I reckon they should be round up and shot and put out of their misery."

Dylan laughed. He then spoke, "Yeah, and that slap was mighty impressive. He wasn't expecting that you could have knocked him off his feet."

Erica laughed. She then said, "That guy deserved it, calling me all those names. That big guy soon stepped in after you hit the Hillbilly. Let's face it, we were outnumbered; those Hillbillies may have been carrying blades."

Dylan laughed. He then said, "That guy Jacob, he really smelt rancid. I reckon he was a cannibal."

Erica once more began to laugh and then silence as the weather began to change. The howl of the wind and then the rain started to patter on the window, a storm began to rage fiercely. Ralph and Eddie entered the mansion in a hurry. Ralph then spoke in a heightened voice, "Shit, did you see that dark cloud and then the heavens opened."

A draught of cold air suddenly ran down Erica's spine, a strong shudder and then a macabre vision of the Count gazing at her through a window. Frowning in confusion, she then stood up and pointed at the window. She then shouted, "Shit, did any of you see that face in the window?"

All three brothers turned and looked towards the window Erica was pointing at. Suddenly the cloud began to move away. Erica stood mesmerised as the light returned and the sun shone in all its glory. Ralph then spoke in a heightened voice, "Shit, that was spooky. Erica, what did you see in the window?"

Erica replied, "Oh, maybe it was just a shadow. I thought I saw the face of the Count; must be my imagination. My God, I can't believe I have a date to go to that creepy old guy's mansion."

Dylan became concerned for Erica. Her eyes looked miserable in their perplexity. He then spoke in a low voice, "Look, once more are you sure you want to go through with this? That old guy sure put a lot of fear into you."

Erica took a deep breath and then spoke, "Look, I have no choice – remember paradise, even if I must walk through hell first."

Ralph laughed and then spoke, "That's the spirit. All you must do is get the old guy to share his secret of where his treasures are and later, we will do the rest and may I add, clean up the mess. What is the Count's address?"

Erica picked up her bag and then reached inside it. She then produced a card. Erica read the card. She then replied, "Oh my, even the address sounds spooky. It's called 'Blackheart Lane'. I reckon we ought to Google it."

Ralph agreed. He then picked up his laptop from the table. He plugged it in and then turned it on. Ralph then searched for the property. When he found it, he began to talk in a heightened voice, "Okay, look at the size of this place! it's in the middle of nowhere; no neighbours - that is good, no one will hear the crack of our shotguns. I am going to fill this guy so full of lead; I haven't met him, but I don't like creepy old guys." Ralph zoomed in closer, gazing at the mansion.

Dylan then said, "Look at it; it's like something out of a horror movie, some sort of Gothic, must have been there for hundreds of years."

Erica then said, "I got the satnav on my phone, I should be able to find it. Okay, guys, I am going to be leaving soon as time is moving so fast."

Ralph produced a small handgun from his inside pocket. He then said, "I don't trust this creepy old guy. This is going in your handbag. Use it if he tries anything." Ralph gazed into Erica's eyes and then continued to talk in a heightened voice, "Look, put it in your handbag. Do I make myself clear?"

Erica nodded in agreement as Ralph placed it into her handbag. Erica put on a brave face and then said, "Okay, I am going to have a quick wash and change into a princess, but you guys remember one thing - if I ain't back by midnight, come find me guns blazing."

They all agreed as Erica went upstairs to change her clothes and have a quick wash. Dylan sat down. He turned to Ralph and then spoke in a low voice, "I can't wait until this is all over and we are all sitting in the sand drinking cocktails, my vision of the perfect paradise."

Eddie went into the kitchen. He then returned with bottles of beer. They all sat around the table drinking as Erica appeared in a silver dress. She looked stunning; she picked up her handbag and then said, "Okay, guys, wish me luck."

Chapter 21

The brothers all laughed as Erica left the mansion. She got into her Cadillac. Erica gazed at her mobile phone; she then remembered Henry's money and checked her bank account. The money was there awaiting her. Erica smiled, her mind whispered 'if something goes wrong and the brothers get whacked, this was her back up money'. She then turned on the satnav and put in the postcode. Erica looked to the radio and after a minute of hesitation she turned it on. The radio was playing a popular song 'Thriller' by Michael Jackson. Erica shook her head and then quickly turned it off. Erica then mumbled, "Shit, of all the songs that could have been playing that was the one I did not need to listen to'. Erica then started up the Cadillac and hit the gas pedal.

As she got closer and closer to the destination, the light begins to fade rapidly. Erica turned her lights on; she could see the mountains in the distance and then a voice: 'turn left'. Erica turned left and then drove along a dirt track surrounded by trees. Five minutes later she had arrived at her destination, Blackheart Lane. She parked the Cadillac and then got out. She felt a cold chill run down her spine. Erica scanned all around the wind-swept trees and then walked towards the front door. She could hear the rustle of dead leaves. She gazed up as the stars shone bright, livid with wrath. It was horror beyond imagination.

Anxiety twisted her face as she knocked twice on the front door. Suddenly it opened by itself. After some hesitation, Erica entered the old mansion. Erica gazed at every shadow and then a disagreeable damp smell. She began to sneeze and closed her eyes for a brief second. When she opened her eyes, the Count stood before her. Erica reflected a shade of terror; she stood motionless frozen with fear.

The Count was dressed in black. His face was extremely shrivelled, complete with dark, sinister bloodshot eyes. The Count then spoke in a low voice, "Do not be afraid; I am sorry for my appearance, I am not a very well person. I believe I have not much time left on this earth."

Erica took a deep breath and then said, "You're right, you are very pale." Erica gazed all around the room; the furniture was all dark - the only light was a selection of candles.

The Count then said, "Follow me into the dining area." Inside the dining area was a large oak table. In the centre of the table sat more candles. Erica looked at the ancient furniture and pictures surrounding the room. The Count sat down and then pointed to a seat. The Count then spoke in a low voice, "Let us both sit down and talk for a while. I see you are but a picture of perfection, a true princess."

Erica sat down and said, "Well thank you. How old are you, if you don't mind me asking?"

The Count began to laugh. He then replied, "To be honest with you I have lost count."

Erica quickly said, "But you're sitting in your mansion, you're not lost."

The Count and Erica began to laugh. The Count then said, "You jest. Well, I like a sense of humour. Your age, I reckon - oh what am I saying? You never ask a lady her age, but may I ask if you would like a drink?"

Erica replied to the Count, "Okay, Count, a drink would be nice."

The Count stood up and then walked over to the drinks cabinet. He then opened it up and produced two wine glasses and an old bottle of red wine. He lifted them onto the table and then poured the wine into the glasses. The Count then handed one of them to Erica and then spoke in a low voice, "Here you are, my lovely." The Count then sat down and began to sip his wine.

Erica also sipped the wine. She then announced, "That is strong; it's so thick it's like drinking blood."

The Count nodded in agreement and then spoke, "Yes, my dear, the wine keeps me going. Oh, such a delicate taste! it is from an old secret recipe from many centuries ago; without it I believe I would simply fade away. Oh, did I not mention I find direct sunlight so upsetting to my weary old eyes."

Erica gazed all around. She then pointed to the pictures on the walls and said, "Are all of them ancestors of yours?" Her eyes perked with curiosity.

Erica captivated the Count's weary old eyes. He then replied, "Yes, all the way back to the fifteenth century. I rescued them from my castle as it began to burn; I believe a group of jealous locals set it on fire hoping I would burn but it was not to be - I escaped the fire. It did not spread but the damage was done and I decided to move to your fair country. I only crave peace and tranquillity; is that too much to ask for? I believe you wish the same. I sometimes listen to music; my taste is fifties and sixties music. I love Frank, Dean and Sammy, you know, of the rat pack?"

Erica reflected a shade of terror. She then replied to the Count, "My God, you have rats here?"

The Count began to laugh out loud. He then spoke, "No, I am sorry. You are much too young to remember The Rat Pack. They were a group of singers nicknamed The Rat Pack. I would certainly never entertain any rats in my domain. I know what you are thinking, I am so old-fashioned; look around you, no technology whatsoever."

Erica looked into the Count's eyes, confused. She then spoke in a low voice, "How ever do you manage all on your own?"

A tear came to the Count's left eye. He then replied in a sad voice of solitude, "It is my sanctuary. My, look at the time. Erica, you must return here a little earlier; if you come, say, one hour earlier, I shall show you all around. Oh how time flies on by! Oh and I want to say sorry, I had no fresh food in. Tomorrow I will be more prepared. Until tomorrow then."

Erica stood up. She picked up her bag and then was escorted to the front door. The Count then spoke in a low voice, "I hope I haven't put you off, I humbly apologise." The Count then yawned and carried on with the conversation. "I am so old and frail. Now be on your way and have a safe journey. Farewell, sweet maiden."

Erica nodded her head in agreement. She then rushed out of the mansion to her awaiting Cadillac. Erica could hear the howl of the wind and see dark shadows all around her. Erica opened the car door with great haste, climbed in and then started up the motor. She turned on the lights then hit the gas pedal and was soon driving down the dirt track. She was gripped by a hot flush panic; her mind was paralysed by the hideous sight of the Count. Erica turned on the radio not knowing what song to expect; the song playing was the beautiful song by the Beatles 'Yesterday'. Erica put on a false smile as she gazed ahead into the darkness.

Erica was soon back at the mansion. She parked and got out of the Cadillac. Erica then made her way to the front door. Erica reached inside her handbag to get her front door key and then noticed the small pistol had disappeared. Erica opened the door and entered, escaping the dark shadows of the night. Once inside she looked to the brothers who were sitting around the table laughing and drinking beer.

Ralph looked to Erica. He stood up and then spoke in a heightened voice, "That was quick; what happened?"

Erica sat down and then began talking fluently in a heightened voice, "Shit, that old guy is sure spooky. I arrived there and knocked on his door twice and it opened by itself. I sneezed when I entered due to the damp smell and then the old guy appeared from nowhere. His face was so pale and those eyes cold as ice. He informed me he was weak and frail; he said he hasn't got much time left on the earth. Everything in his place is ancient; he has no technology whatsoever."

Ralph smiled and then spoke in a heightened voice, "That's good. Did you take a good look around the place?"

Erica replied, "No, not really. The Count was really tired. He wants me to return tomorrow, a bit earlier so he can give me a grand tour of the place. Oh, and something else happened; the small pistol in my handbag – it simply disappeared into thin air."

Ralph sipped his beer and then spoke, "Shit, how on Earth did you lose that? Maybe that old guy took it. When we pay him a visit, we are going to be extra careful."

Erica then said, "I don't know what to say. It was in my bag when I entered the mansion, when I got back here it was missing."

Dylan then spoke, "What I don't understand, if he's so tired why won't he meet you in daylight?"

Erica replied, "Oh, he said he has a rare illness, direct sunlight affects his eyes."

Dylan laughed. He then said, "My, that is strange. Perhaps he is a fellow vampire!"

Erica shook her head and then spoke in a heightened voice, "Don't be stupid. Vampires don't exist, do they?"

Dylan replied, "What are you saying, babe, I don't exist? Come here, your perfume smells divine."

Erica shook her head then said, "There is nothing worse than a drunken Vampire, Count Beer Monster." The brothers all began to laugh. Erica said "Goodnight" and then made her way upstairs. Erica walked over to her bed, yawning several times. She got undressed then got into bed. Erica then fell into a deep sleep. She began to dream she was back in the Count's mansion; she could smell the unmistakeable stench of death. Darkness then fell upon the room, a draught of cold air suddenly ran down her spine. A door creaked and then slowly opened. Erica could see a candle lit in the other room. Erica then gradually ventured towards it, mesmerised by the glimmer of light. She began to blink and frown, anxiety twisted her face as she entered the room. Inside, a table on which the candle sat. Erica gazed all around the room; horror beyond imagination – oh, such a sinister sight - four coffins. A voice in her head whispered 'the treasure, look inside'.

Erica, uncharacteristically, after some hesitation and with a sense of compulsion, opened the first coffin. Her eyes lit up as it was full of silver antiques and coins. Erica then opened the second which was filled with gold coins. She triumphantly picked up some gold coins. She then removed the third lid, it was full of precious stones. This was oh such a pleasant dream, riches beyond her imagination! With a comforting sense of fulfilment, she removed the fourth lid. Her eyes became wild with terror; inside the fourth coffin was a creature of the night, a glaring face with death cold eyes.

Erica, with an expression of horror, turned to escape the creature. She ran from the room; her heart was now pounding, her mind was paralysed by the hideous sight. The Count then appeared before her. Erica began to run; she slipped and toppled over face first and then felt her whole body shake vigorously and then a familiar voice: "Erica, You've had a nightmare."

Dylan helped Erica out of bed, Anxiety twisted her face and she shuddered. Her right hand was clenched; she then opened her hand to reveal an old gold coin. Erica then whispered, "Shit, where did that come from? My God, I dreamt the Count had coffins filled with silver and gold coins. I remember in the dream I picked up some gold coins - this is one of them. Look at this coin, it must be hundreds of years old."

Dylan looked at it with a fixed expression. He then said, "I reckon you had some sort of out of body experience; all of this is so spooky. I just don't know what to say."

They both carried on talking until it was morning. The radiant sun shone through the window in all its glory. Dylan then whispered, "Oh, by the way, the food arrived. You have a shower whilst I fix us a nice breakfast."

Erica placed the coin in her handbag. She then had a shower whilst Dylan cooked them both breakfast. She then gazed into the mirror. Her eyelids flickered spasmodically. her eyes looked miserable in their perplexity. Her face was small and delicate. She reached for her hairdryer and brush and was soon dressed and ready for breakfast. Erica then made her way downstairs and sat at the table.

Dylan smiled and then said, "Oh, perfect timing." The table was set, coffee and breakfast at the ready. Dylan placed them in front of Erica. She began to eat as Ralph appeared. He then spoke in a heightened voice, "Very nice. I woke up and smelt the bacon; any left?"

Dylan replied, "Yeah, I reckon I did too much; over there on the worktop, some spare bacon and beans." Ralph walked over and helped himself to the food. He then sat down next to Erica. Dylan finished off drinking his coffee. He then looked to Ralph and said, "Erica had a nightmare last night. She dreamt the Count had coffins filled with treasure, gold and silver. What do you reckon?"

Ralph replied, "That don't seem like no nightmare to me."

Erica then said, "It wasn't until I opened the last coffin; inside that was a moving corpse, real scary stuff. The strange thing was Dylan woke me from the nightmare, I then found a very old gold coin in my hand. I remember picking up gold coins in the nightmare."

Ralph looked to Erica with a fixed expression. He then spoke with firmness in his voice, "You said a very old coin, can you show it to me?"

Erica nodded her head in agreement. She then walked upstairs and entered her bedroom. Erica then picked up her bag and returned downstairs.

Eddie then appeared at the table after making himself a coffee. Erica placed her bag on the table and reached inside; shock and horror as she produced the missing pistol. She then became angry and emptied the contents of her bag onto the table. the gold coin had gone. Erica stood motionless; she then started to frown in confusion. Erica then spoke in a heightened voice, "My God, what is going on? The gold coin has been replaced by the missing pistol. Maybe it's this place, must be haunted."

Ralph laughed and then said, "I don't believe in ghosts or vampires. Must be your mind playing tricks on you."

Erica shook her head then turned to Dylan and said, "You set eyes on the gold coin, didn't you?"

Dylan could not believe what had just happened. He then replied, "Look, the coin was there, the pistol wasn't. Perhaps the old guy is playing tricks on us. There can be no other explanation."

Eddie finished off his coffee. He then said, "Okay, let's just forget about all this. Erica shall visit this guy for the last time. We go in and rob him on Friday."

Dylan smiled and then said, "You can count on it but there is one problem."

Ralph looked to Dylan and said, "What is the problem?"

Dylan replied, "The date is Friday the thirteenth, plus I reckon it's going to be a full moon."

Ralph shook his head in disbelief. He then spoke in a heightened voice, "Bullshit. I don't believe in any crap like that, it just ain't happening - ghosts, vampires now Friday the thirteenth. Whatever next? The only thing I believe in is my twelve-gauge shotgun, it makes me feel invincible."

Eddie nodded his head in agreement. He then spoke, "I don't believe in aliens. Ralph's right - it's all bullshit. Ralphs, the ultimate killing weapon, my brother. Ralph has saved me lots of times; why, the guy deserves a medal! Who knows, we might even find a coffin full of medals." They all began to laugh and then they finished off their breakfasts.

Erica then spoke to the brothers. "For me this is the ultimate nightmare. I can't believe I am going back to that place - that old guy really gives me the creeps."

Ralph then spoke, "I must admit, doll, you are a brave one; just listening to your stories about this guy sends shivers through my soul. You never know, maybe this guy is into witchcraft or some sort of dark arts."

Dylan shook his head and then said, "Look, let's not go there. Look at Erica, the poor woman is frightened out of her skin. Let's just say the old guy is a freak and end it there."

Eddie laughed and then spoke, "Look, all we need to know is where he keeps his millions. Erica, meet the old guy and let him show you his treasure and I promise you us brothers will do the rest. Just remember, you're a cool actress, okay?"

Erica put on a false smile and then agreed with a nod of her head.

Ralph then turned to Dylan and spoke in a heightened voice, "Okay, when was the last time you shot a gun? I reckon we should take a drive to the forest and get some shooting practice. You never know, if that old guy has got millions in his mansion, he may have guns."

Erica shook her head and then said, "I don't think so but then again, I only entered two rooms in his mansion, and it was mighty big."

Ralph then said, "Okay, that is settled then. Erica, are you coming?"

Erica smiled and then replied, "Yeah, I wouldn't miss this for the world. I would love to learn to shoot. I only ever shot a pistol once when I was a teenager. I was a pretty good shot as far as I remember."

Ralph then disappeared into the back room. He then returned with a large, black holdall filled with shotguns and pistols, plus ammunition ready for the kill. Ralph then turned to Erica and said, "We got plenty of time. Erica, you look tired - you okay to drive?"

Erica replied, "Yeah, once this is over, I shall get plenty of catch-up sleep."

Ralph smiled. He then said, "Yeah, that's the spirit. Let's get going."

Chapter 22

All four of then left the mansion and made their way to the Cadillac. Ralph placed the holdall in the boot as they all got in. Erica then started it up and put her foot on the gas pedal and they were on their way. The weather was cloudy and overcast. Dylan sat in the front of the Cadillac; he was tempted to turn on the radio, hesitated and then he turned it on. He listened to the song and then said, "Shit, all the songs that could have been playing the song playing was 'Bad Moon Rising'."

Ralph then spoke in a heightened voice, "Yeah; I remember the movie in the eighty's - American werewolf in London."

Eddie began to sing along *"don't go out tonight, there's sure to be a fight."*

Erica then erupted like a volcano. She reached over and turned off the radio. She then shouted "Yeah, a fight with me if you don't shut the fuck up! I just want a bit of peace and quiet."

All three brothers began to laugh. Ralph then spoke in a heightened voice, "Dylan, you said she didn't like your singing; I reckon she don't like any man singing."

Erica shook her head and said, "I ain't got nothing against men singing if they can; being unable to sing must run in your family."

Ralph shrugged his shoulders and then spoke, "Okay, valid point. We ain't no singers, but I reckon if we pull this off and get the old guy's millions, we will all be singing in paradise, if you know what I mean."

They all agreed. Erica then found the perfect stop and pulled over. They all got out of the Cadillac. Ralph then opened the boot and got out his holdall containing the weapons. Ralph turned to Erica and spoke, "Okay, I will lead the way and I need to explain myself. You and Dylan need to be able to shoot in case, God forbid, anything should happen to me and Eddie. Both of you will be carrying guns; in my eyes if you got a gun, you should know how to use it. Okay, this way."

They all followed Ralph into the forest. It was quiet, dull and overcast. After walking for a couple of miles, Ralph stopped, placed his holdall onto the ground and he reached inside. He then produced various targets, some small nails and a hammer. Ralph then walked over to a tree and nailed the target to it. Ralph then turned to Erica and Dylan and said, "Okay, help yourselves to the pistols" Erica reached inside and then produced two automatic pistols. Erica then handed one to Dylan. Ralph then spoke in a heightened voice, "Okay, the safety is on. Do you both know how to shoot these pistols?" Dylan and Erica nodded their heads in agreement. Ralph and Eddie stood back as Dylan took the safety off. He then took aim and let off five rounds. Only one hit the target, the rest hit the tree. Ralph then produced a pistol. He took the safety off and opened fire on the target, six shots, every one hitting the centre of the target.

Erica could hear birds upon wing, the silence of the forest was broken. Ralph then explained why he was such a good shot. He gave them advice on improving their aim. Dylan took his advice. He took aim and fired three more shots. All three hit the target.

Ralph smiled and said, "Good. Okay, Erica, let's see if you can beat Dylan."

Erica smiled, took aim and fired four shots. They all hit the target. Erica had another go and fired. This time she hit the centre. Ralph and Eddie began to clap out loud.

Eddie then spoke, "My, Erica you sure can shoot." Eddie then lifted a shotgun out of the holdall. He stepped forward and blasted the target to pieces. Ralph laughed as Erica and Dylan looked on in shock of the power of his shotgun.

Ralph then said, "Nice one, bro. I reckon it's time to go. I must admit I feel good now I know we all can shoot. You never know when those Russians are going to turn up." Ralph then collected all the weapons and placed them back in the holdall.

Eddie gazed at the wind-swept trees as he walked towards the Cadillac. Erica rubbed her eyes; the sound of the forest echoed in her ears, strange bird sounds and then with every step the rustle of dead leaves. Ten minutes later and they were back at the Cadillac. Erica opened the door as Ralph placed the black holdall in the boot. Ralph then said, "Okay, let's get back. This shooting is such thirsty work I could murder me a coffee."

They all laughed then got into the Cadillac. Erica then started it up and hit the gas pedal. Dylan once more looked to the radio. Erica looked to Dylan and said, "Do you have to?"

Dylan replied, "Okay, if the song doesn't agree with you, I will turn it off and I promise no singing from anyone." Before Erica could agree or disagree, Dylan turned on the radio. 'Ride like the wind' was playing by Christopher Cross.

Erica smiled, turned to Dylan and said, "Okay, I like this song, this guy can sing." Erica began to think 'ride like the wind', and she then put her foot down on the gas pedal, speeding faster and faster.

Dylan began to yawn as they arrived back at the mansion. Erica parked the Cadillac and they all got out. In the sky above, dark clouds suddenly appeared and then the rain began to patter against the windows. As they entered the mansion the wind began to howl as Dylan closed the door behind him. Dylan then spoke in a heightened voice, "That was close."

Eddie laughed and said, "Bro, its only wind and rain."

Ralph marched over to the fridge and then produced bottles of beer. Erica shook her head; a thought flashed through her mind. She then spoke in a low voice, "Not for me. Anyway, Ralph, you said earlier you were going to murder a coffee not a beer. I won't be having a beer - I got me a real hot date." She then had a vision of the Count; panic fears fluttered her mind as a draught of cold air suddenly ran down her spine. She closed her eyes as Dylan put his hand on her shoulder and said, "Are you okay?" Erica opened her eyes and replied, "Oh, it's that old guy; the thought of visiting him again." Erica reflected a shade of terror.

Dylan gazed into her uneasy eyes and said, "Look, this will be the last time. Let the old guy show you where he keeps his millions and on Friday we will do the visiting and put the old guy out of his misery. Is that okay with you?"

Erica replied, "I suppose so. It's the only way we are all going to paradise."

Dylan smiled and then said, "Alright, now you sit down whilst I make you a nice coffee." Erica sat down next to Ralph and Eddie.

Ralph reached across the table for his laptop and turned it on whilst sipping his beer. He then spoke, "Look at all these bars for sale in Barbados. I have always wanted my own bar - I have even thought of a name for it 'The Royal'."

Dylan returned with Erica's coffee and placed it on the table next to Erica. She smiled and said, "Thank you."

Ralph turned his laptop around and said, "Look at this everyone; true paradise, amazing beaches - the Caribbean is the place for me. Me and Eddie had us a vacation there five years ago. We stayed at the Butterfly Hotel. The staff were so laid back and the food - I loved the garlic fish and Caribbean curry. I went swimming with the turtles. Eddie gave it a miss; tell them why, Eddie."

Eddie shook his head and then replied, "Oh, when I was young me and a friend visited New Smyrna Beach in Florida. We were swimming in the sea; my friend Carl swam ahead and was attacked by a shark. It bit his leg clean off. I tried to save him but he died later, lost too much blood. I swore from that day I would never become a meal for some hungry shark. Later, I did a bit of research and found out the place where Carl died was deemed the shark capital of the World. I then decided I would not become a meal for some hungry shark and would stick to the swimming pool. I remember that Reggie bus; I sat next to a dreadlocked Rasta - his head was bobbing up and down to the music of Bob Marley. We had two young kids taking it in turns driving. The guy driving was going a bit fast. Suddenly, a big mama stood up waving her walking stick. she then shouted to the boys "You better slow down or else!" We then slowed down to a snails pace - we found it so funny. I remember Charlie's Bar; the manager, by the end of the night, was as drunk as us - free drinks all around. The Australian Hockey team – my, they were a barrel of laughs. We both got up with them and sung 'Waltzing Matilda' then it was back to their place. That was one fun vacation."

Dylan put his hand in Erica's and said, "Just think, babe, we will soon be there in paradise."

Erica smiled and gazed through the window. The rain had stopped but it was still overcast. She finished off her coffee and then stood up and spoke, "Okay, this is it time to see the millions. I reckon the sooner I can get there the sooner I can get back with the information." It was one in the afternoon. Dylan wished her luck. Ralph then spoke in a heightened voice, "Oh, your bag - don't forget your bag." She opened it up. The small pistol was still inside the bag. her mind whispered 'ain't getting changed to meet this creepy old guy; just need to find out where he keeps his treasure'. Erica then said goodbye and left the mansion.

It was now dark and overcast. She could hear the howl of the wind as she got into the Cadillac. She then started it up and put her foot on the gas pedal. Erica drove towards her destination as the light faded rapidly. The stars began to shine bright. Livid with wrath, Erica turned on her lights. She then gazed at every shadow, her eyes looked miserable in their perplexity. She investigated her mirror, a macabre vision of the Count looked back at her. Erica sat rooted with fear – oh, such a terrified human soul. She closed her eyes for a second and then opened them. She looked once more in the mirror, her face bewildered. This was horror beyond imagination. A brief hesitation and then she turned on the radio. The Disk Jockeys were talking. Erica listened as they said "Okay, this is for all of you on a hot date tonight" They then played 'The Power of Love' by Huey Lewis and the news.

Erica put on a brave face and then began to sing along to the song.

Erica soon arrived at the Count's mansion and parked up. Erica picked up her bag and took a deep breath, a brief hesitation, then she opened the car door and stepped out. A draught of cold air suddenly ran down her spine. With an expression of pure horror she made her way to the front door.

As Erica moved closer and closer to the entrance, it suddenly began to creak as it opened itself. Erica stepped inside; once more she was standing on a cold floor, with a disagreeable damp smell of such unwholesome air. She was mesmerised by a glimmer of light in the corner of the room, six candles burning with livid wrath.

Chapter 23

The Count suddenly appeared. Erica jumped out of her skin - such a sinister sight. The Count then spoke in a heightened voice, "Oh, I am sorry. Did I scare you? Welcome once more to my humble abode. Follow me into the dining area, I have cooked some dinner."

Erica put on a brave face then nodded her head in agreement. she followed The Count into the dining area. The table was all set out for two. Erica was very nervous she gazed at the Count's glaring face and cruel smile. The Count then said, "Alright, Erica, take a seat and make yourself at home. After all, one day this could all be yours."

Erica sat and smiled; her mind whispered 'just show me where you have the millions hidden'.

The Count began to laugh as though he had read her mind. The Count then whispered, "It's so quiet around here; that is the reason I fell in love with this place - peace and tranquillity. Oh, how do you like your steak, blood red or well done?"

Erica smiled and then replied, "Well done. I must admit I do love garlic steaks."

The Count laughed out loud he then spoke in a low voice, "Oh my dear, to me garlic is a dirty word. I have never liked it; the smell I find quiet revolting but everyone to their own. Would you like a glass of wine?"

Erica replied, "Oh yes please, have you any white wine?"

The count replied, "Maybe, I am not sure. I only drink red wine." The Count ventured over to his drinks cabinet. He gazed amongst his bottles of wine and then produced an old bottle of white wine. He then removed the cork and poured the wine into a glass. He then placed it on the table next to Erica. She thanked him. The count then disappeared into his kitchen. Erica sipped the wine she then said to herself my god this wine is strong.

Erica gazed all around the room. She looked up at the cobwebs, her mind whispering 'this is like a show my late parents used to watch, the Munsters'. she then said, "Herman, come out wherever you are."

Suddenly a door opened. Once more Erica jumped out of her skin. The Count entered the room carrying a tray. He then placed it on the table. The Count then said, "Here you go, my dear, a well-done steak with fries and a spot of gravy. I, myself, only eat steak dripping with blood. I believe well done is hard for me to digest, thus I have it rare."

Erica thanked the count and after some hesitation began to eat her meal provided by the Count. Erica gazed at the dark circles under his eyes - oh such a shrivelled complexion, a dark-eyed malignant face. Erica turned away in disgust as the Count began to eat his blood-red steak. He had blood dripping from his lips matching his blood-shot eyes. The Count sat in a world of his own, eating the steak as if he hadn't eaten in days. The Count was right, the steak was dry. Erica took another sip of wine and then she felt a little dizzy. The Count poured himself another glass of red wine. He then smiled and said, "Is everything alright, Erica? Is the meal up to your standards?"

Erica replied, "Yes, thank you. This gravy - I have never tasted anything like this before. It's packed with flavour. Wherever did you buy it?"

The Count replied, "Oh, you cannot buy it. I made it myself from an old recipe dating back to my late Grandmother. She was such a divine cook. Oh, I nearly forgot - I promised you a tour of my old mansion. You may also look at my fortune."

Erica's mind whispered 'now you're talking'. Once more the Count burst out into laughter as if he had read her mind. His eye lids flickered spasmodically as he sipped his red wine. Erica finished off her meal as did the Count. He then stood up and spoke in a heightened voice, "Alright, Erica, let me escort you around my humble abode. Follow me and don't worry about the dishes." Seconds before the Count spoke her mind whispered, 'I am sure he can read my mind'. Once more the Count broke out into laughter. He then said, "Let us start in the library, I have lots of very rare books." The

Count opened the door. He then walked slowly down a corridor.

As Erica followed the count, she gazed upon the candles either side of the corridor, glowing and flickering. Erica scanned all around at the old oil paintings. Anxiety twisted her face as she stopped and stood gazing at the picture of a lady that looked like her. The Count turned around and whispered, "The picture, is it not like looking in the mirror?"

Erica could not believe her eyes; anxiety twisted her face her heart was pounding. A voice in her head whispered, 'composure: remember you're an actress'. Erica then replied, "Who on Earth is she?"

The Count replied, "She is not of this Earth. She died over three hundred years ago. Her heart was weak; she was an actress who upset a nobleman. He paid men to kill her and cut out her heart. Oh, such a sad story and yes, a pure coincidence you both look alike. My family had their revenge on him. I believe they tortured him for days and as for his men, they all died horrible deaths. I can still here their screams." Erica could not believe what she had just heard; her face was full of fear. The Count shook his head and then whispered, "Oh, what have I just said? Forgive me; sometimes I do say stupid things - I believe it's my age. Anyway, this way." The Count continued to walk. He then stopped and opened the door to the library. The Count entered the room, followed by Erica.

The library had a lot of bookshelves all full of old books. Erica gazed at the large collection of old books. The

Count picked out an old book, turned to Erica and whispered, "This was written by Rasputin - his life story. He believed he had walked the Earth from the dawn of time. If he were to die, he would simply be reborn. At the time he wrote his book, he was one of the most powerful men in Russia. His powers were well documented; he had a proven healing ability and also psychic abilities and remarkable accurate prediction. This man was born a Siberian peasant; a group of aristocrats hated him and they invited him to his own death. Rasputin knew this but went anyway. Cyanide was the most lethal poison and its effects almost instantaneous. He drank the poison wine given to him and ate cake filled with deadly cyanide. There was enough poison to kill ten men, yet there were no effects on Rasputin. The Prince then produced a pistol and shot him at point blank range in the chest. The conspirators checked his body and believed Rasputin to be dead. Suddenly, he came back to life and fought them. The conspirators beat and stabbed him. He carried on fighting and nearly escaped until he was shot again. They then tied him up and dragged his body to the icy Neva River and threw him in. Later, his body was found. An autopsy was carried out, the cause of death was drowning. He somehow managed to escape his bonds but not the icy river. I believe he is with us today, now in charge of his beloved Russia. Rasputin - the R stands for 'reborn', and you are left with 'as Putin'. I believe there is a lot of darkness hiding amongst us, if you know what I mean."

Erica thought for a while about the story the Count had told her. She then said, "You are saying Rasputin was reborn as President Putin?"

The Count replied, "Oh yes, I have studied the dark arts and have answers that are beyond your comprehension. By the way, that is no insult; you are young and naïve, whilst I am old and wise and wishful for a quick ending. Sometimes, I feel like I have roamed this Earth for centuries. Oh, such sweet history and of course horror. Let us now visit the treasure room."

Erica's eyes lit up; the word 'treasure' had oh such appeal to it. Erica followed the Count to the next room. He then reached inside his pocket and produced a key. The Count then whispered, "One cannot be too careful; this room is filled with valuables passed down through the generations." The Count opened the door and stepped inside. Erica followed the Count inside and looked to the long wooden tables. On top of the tables in the centre of the room sat an old metal safe. The Count then turned to Erica and whispered, "Feel free to look inside my treasure chests."

Erica was like a kid in a candy shop. She moved closer and opened the first chest. It was filled with jewellery. Erica was mesmerised by the quality of the gold and silver jewellery. The Count stood back and watched as she opened another chest. It was filled with gleaming priceless gems. Erica became wild eyed as she picked out some of the gems from the treasure chest. Erica turned to the Count and said, "No way; are these real?"

The Count replied, "Yes, everything in here is real."

Erica's eyes perked with curiosity as she opened the next chest. It was filled with silver and gold coins. The

Count then opened the safe and pointed to the piles of dollar notes. He then said, "They are in stacks of fifty dollar notes; I have no need for all this money. Before I depart from this Earth, I will donate it to a worthy cause back in my homeland, Romania. Do you know how much money is in there?"

Erica replied, "No, I have no idea how much is in there."

The Count then said, "One million dollars. If you were to add up all my valuables together, I reckon I am worth about ten to twenty million dollars. It is a lot of money is it not?" Erica nodded her head in agreement. The Count then said, "Shall we carry on with the tour?"

Erica began to yawn. She then spoke in a low voice, "Oh, there has been too much excitement for one day. Can we leave it for another time? I am so tired."

The Count then whispered, "If you want, you could spend the night here. I have spare rooms." Erica's mind whispered 'shit, no way'. The Count began to laugh out loud. He then said, "You're right, you're tired and must be on your way."

Erica then said, "Okay, thank you for the meal and the tour. I hope to see you tomorrow and we can finish off the tour."

The Count agreed and then escorted Erica back to the dining room. Erica looked to the table and said, "Oh, my bag I must get my bag." Erica walked over to where it sat. She then picked it up and moved quickly towards the front door. Erica could not get out of the place fast enough; her mind whispered 'mission accomplished'.

The Count stood next to Erica and said, "Alright, I must now bid you goodnight, my fair maiden." The Count then moved forward as if he was going to kiss her goodnight.

Erica moved quickly out of the Count's way. She then whispered, "Oh, such a strange person." Erica rushed out of the front door over to her Cadillac. She opened the door, started it up and put on the lights. Erica hit the gas pedal and took a deep breath. Her mind then whispered, 'stay calm; all of this will soon be over'.

Faster and faster she drove, overtaking a slow-moving vehicle. Her mind began to whisper, 'slow down'. She took notice and lifted her foot of the gas pedal. Erica then looked to the radio and turned it on. Playing was Roy Orbison 'I Drove all Night'. Erica smiled and said, "Yeah quite fitting really." She then turned up the volume and said, "I ain't driving all night." As soon as the song finished, she turned off the radio.

Erica had reached her destination and was back at the mansion. She parked the Cadillac up and turned off the lights. Erica opened her car door and then stood gazing at the stars which shone down in all their glory. Erica entered the mansion; the brothers all sat around the table playing cards.

Dylan stood up and then spoke in a heightened voice. "Erica, did everything go to play? Are you alright?"

Erica replied, "Yes, fix me up with a cold beer and I will tell you all about the old guy's millions."

Ralph and Eddie both stopped playing cards, she had their full attention. Ralph then spoke, "Okay, Erica, come and sit here and tell us more."

Dylan poured Erica a cold beer into a glass and then handed it to her. Erica sipped her beer and said, "Okay, the old guy has gold and silver coins. He has a safe filled with fifty dollar bills, a cool one million worth. He said he has no use for it and when he passes away, he will donate it all to charity back in his own country. He also has chests filled with jewellery, precious stones, gold and silver. I reckon all together he must be worth up to twenty million."

Ralph's eyes perked with curiosity. He then spoke in a heightened voice, "Okay, this is but a dream come true as we all shall be millionaires. When we get to paradise, we shall all live like kings." He then looked into Erica's eyes and said, "Oh, and a beautiful princess."

They all began to laugh. Eddie then said, "What about security?"

Erica replied, "The guy has a key to open the door and a key for the safe. He then got them out of his pocket."

Eddie laughed. He then spoke in a heightened voice, "This should be like taking candy from a child."

Erica finished off her beer and then said, "Okay, Ralph, what is the plan for tomorrow evening? We visit the old guy?"

Ralph replied to Erica, "You can be our driver. When we arrive at the mansion us three will pay the old guy a visit, we will get the keys to the safe, get the money and treasure and then I shall perform a mercy killing. We then torch the place".

Erica smiled and then said, "My, you make it all sound so easy. Could anything go wrong?"

Ralph replied, "Yeah, but that's life. Okay, the layout."

Erica replied, "Oh, I forgot to mention the library; his collection of old books must be worth millions. Did you know he has a rare book written by Rasputin?"

Dylan then said, "Wasn't he the mad monk?"

Erica replied, "Yeah, that was the guy. The room with the millions is next to the library, so all you must do is come through the front door and then into the dining area through another door, along a corridor which takes you to the library, then a door to the dosh."

Ralph laughed. He then spoke in a heightened voice, "Okay, we got a big day ahead of us tomorrow. Let us all get some shut eye." They all finished off their drinks and then ventured up to their bedrooms.

Chapter 24

Erica lay in bed. She closed her eyes and could see the Count. Her eyelids began to flicker spasmodically, her heart began to pound. She then awoke from the nightmare. She could see the woman in the picture; she had a sinister expression on her face. Suddenly, several men appeared; the nightmare then became more vivid. The men attacked her, she struggled violently, then they beat her again and again. Erica knew what was about to happen next; the Count's story - one of the men in the dream produced a knife. She watched as the man stabbed the lady in the chest. She then felt a sharp pain in her chest. She reflected a shade of terror and then light and a familiar voice.

Dylan put his arms around her and said, "Are you having another nightmare?"

Erica looked to Dylan with a fixed expression and replied, "Yes". She then began to rub her chest and said, "I felt a sharp pain in my chest, my heart was pounding." Her eyes looked miserable in their perplexity and then tears began to flow and anxiety twisted her face.

Dylan reflected a shade of terror. He began to frown in confusion, then produced a tissue and handed it to Erica. He then whispered, "Look, after tomorrow all of this will be over. That old guy will be ten feet under and we will all be living in paradise living happily ever after." Erica wiped away her tears, put a brave face on. Dylan then whispered, "Look, I will leave the light on. Just try and get some sleep - think of paradise, those lovely gold sands, me and you hand in hand in the promised land."

Erica nodded in agreement then closed her eyes, determined not to have another nightmare. Erica's thoughts changed from negative to positive sunshine, sea and sand, happy smiling faces, no more darkness.

Erica was then awoken by Dylan, who said, "Do you feel any better?"

Erica replied, "Yes, I took your advice and dreamt of paradise, me and you walking along hand in hand upon golden sand."

Dylan put his arms around Erica and then kissed her passionately on her lips. He then whispered, "I love you."

Erica then whispered, "I love you. Oh, and do you fancy cooking me some breakfast?"

Dylan closed his eyes for a second, he then opened them and replied, "Yes, I am starving; I need some sausages."

Erica laughed and then said, "So do I."

Dylan kissed her once more and then made his way to the kitchen. Erica then entered the bathroom and had a quick shower. She then got out of the shower, dried herself and got dressed. Erica investigated the mirror as she brushed her hair her, mind whispering, 'I'll be glad when all of this is over'. Erica then left the bathroom and made her way to the dining area. Sat in front of her was Dylan and his brothers, all eating breakfast. Erica turned to Dylan and said, "Where's mine?"

Ralph began to laugh and replied, "Here, I am eating it."

Erica looked to Dylan; her anger suddenly rose. Before she could open her mouth, Ralph spoke with firmness in his voice, "Look, sister, I am only joking. Yours is in the microwave."

Dylan stood up and said, "Look, I have finished mine. Have a seat whilst I heat your breakfast up." Erica nodded in agreement she then sat down.

Ralph turned to Erica and spoke, "Look, Erica, Dylan has told us all about your nightmares. Let me assure you they will soon be over, and you, my friend, will be sitting on a beach in paradise. I am a man of my word."

Erica began to smile once more. Ralph laughed then said, "Nice one, sister; a smile - that's what we all want to see."

Dylan then returned with Erica's breakfast and coffee. He placed them in front of her. Erica smiled and thanked Dylan. He then sat down. Dylan then turned to Ralph and said, "I can't wait until all of this is over with."

Eddie then stood up and said, "Does anyone fancy another coffee?"

Ralph replied, "Yeah, and put in an extra sugar; I am feeling sweet." Eddie shook his head as he made his way to the kettle.

Erica finished off her breakfast and then stood up and walked over to the window to check out the weather. Erica gazed out of the windows as the rain began to patter against the glass. Erica then heard the howl of the wind, a door creaked and then a draught of cold air suddenly ran down her spine. Erica shivered and then spoke, "My, it's bleak out there. What you reckon, Dylan?"

A brief delay and then Dylan replied, "Yeah." He stood up and walked over to the window. Dylan gazed at the wind-swept trees; a storm began to rage fiercely, dead leaves began to dance. He then had a sudden chill as the door creaked once more. Dylan then turned to Ralph and said, "I can't believe how bleak it is out there. What do you reckon, Ralph?"

A scratch of his head and then Ralph replied with his eyes closed, "This weather makes me feel like hibernating." He then yawned. Erica also began to yawn. She then rubbed her eyes. Eddie then appeared with four cups of coffee all sat on a plastic tray. Ralph turned to Eddie and said, "What kept you?"

Eddie replied, "Oh, I decided to make everyone a coffee. It's going to be a long day, so I just took my time. I also stood there for a while looking out the window. The weather is bad, there is one hell of a storm brewing out there." Eddie then handed a coffee to everyone.

Erica turned to Ralph and said, "I know what, why don't you tell us one of your stories to pass the time away."

Ralph agreed and then began to talk fluently in a heightened voice, "Oh, one story does spring to mind. I had a mate called Joe Gigolo, or better known as the Italian Stallion. He was a big boy, if you know what I mean." Erica began to laugh out loud and then suddenly spontaneous laughter ringed out all around the room. Ralph also began to laugh then said, "Right, where was I before I was rudely interrupted? Oh, I know, my ex-mate Joe the Gigolo did a few porn movies. He then started banging any woman with a pulse and then made a fatal error of judgement - he started dating Maria. Her big Mexican husband became well pissed; he found out and then put a contract on Joe. There were three attempts to kill him, and he escaped each one. Joe then came to me and begged me to have words with the big Mexican who, by the way, was called Moses. He was one basket-case motherfucker. He was a giant imposing man with a barbaric complexion and had tattoos embroidered across his whole body. Joe offered me a shit load of money to take care of the situation. You must remember, he was a friend so I naturally took the money. I met up with Moses, he informed me if I didn't shut the fuck up, I would be next. This just pissed me off big time. Moses then introduced me to a guy that had just planted a bomb in Joe's car; it was too late - Joe blew up with his custom Gigolo mobile. Imagine how pissed I was when I was given such bad news. My anger erupted like a volcano, I pulled out my semi-automatic pistol before anyone could react. I shot the two of them dead, I also killed his two bodyguards. I put three bullets in each of them. I was reddened with rage. Moses was murmuring out in pain; he then began to pray, so I did the decent thing - I put a bullet in his head. He died with a prayer on his lips. There was an unmistakable stench of death. This was a dark heartless place. I noticed a bag next to the dead bomber; inside it was another bomb. It was on a timer, so I flicked the switch and left. Later, the place blew up, as did my mate Joe the Gigolo. You could say it was his own fault, he should have kept his dick in his pants. In the end he lost everything, including his best asset. Believe me, it was a big bomb."

Erica smiled and then spoke, "Ralph, you tell some amazing stories you forgot to mention what happened to Maria, the cheating wife?"

Ralph replied, "Oh yeah, Maria - she simply disappeared of the face of the planet. I reckon Moses had her killed and buried somewhere. Her family must have been devastated, she had two beautiful daughters, real pretty like their mother but that's life in the cruel city."

Eddie then said, "I have heard that story before but every time you tell it I believe it gets so your mind whispers 'judgment'. What goes around comes around. Joe, Moses and Maria all dead. I believe in a balance the world goes around; Joe upset the balance of all this, a knock-on effect." Eddie turned to Erica and spoke, "What do you reckon?"

Erica finished off the coffee and then replied, "Yeah, I agree. Fate, or destiny, and I agree what goes around comes around but none of us in this room are angels."

Ralph turned to Erica and then spoke in a heightened voice, "Less of the blasphemous language. I have done some bad things in my life, but I have done some good. Remember the money I took off Joe? I never mentioned I was riddled with guilt, so I donated the money to the poor. I must admit, it felt good doing good. You should have seen those happy smiling faces knowing they were going to be looked after. Later, I made regular donations to that charity. I see myself as a bit of a saint, a good guy like Saint Ralph, if you like. I have told this story before, but I never mentioned what I did with the money until now."

Dylan smiled and then said, "That is one hell of a story."

Ralph nodded in agreement and then spoke, "Maybe I just donate my cut from the job to the poor." He then he pulled a funny face and said, "Okay, I am only joking; I need the money to spend in paradise. Just imagine, sea, sand and sunshine. Shit, it's so dull and overcast out there." He then turned to Erica and said, "What do you reckon? Say something constructive"

Erica sat thinking for a few seconds. She then replied, "I should be rich; I used to play the lottery- every week I would put on the same numbers. The week I changed two of my numbers they came in. I should have won a cool forty million dollars. I was so pig sick it put me off pork for life."

The brothers all looked at each other, pulling faces. They all then began to laugh out loud. Ralph then said, "Have you been telling us porkies? What do you reckon, Dylan?"

All laughter stopped as Dylan gave his reply "No, I remember her telling me this story many moons ago and she won't touch pork and that is the truth. As for the lottery, I guess she was just unlucky. I remember she got four numbers, but the pay-out was poor. Just imagine, if she had not changed those two numbers I reckon we would not be here now. Is it fate or destiny? I don't know; all I know is time is going fast, afternoon already. I reckon I'll order a pizza take out - there is a new pizza place opened in town, I got this leaflet yesterday, they deliver. What you all reckon?"

Ralph replied, "Can you order me some garlic bread?"

Dylan then said, "You can count on it. I will order four specials. Is that okay with you lot?"

Ralph laughed then said, "Make that order." Dylan made the call as Erica removed all the dishes from the table. She then took them into the kitchen and washed them.

Dylan finished his call. He then spoke in a heightened voice, "Okay, everyone, the guy said thirty minutes and the order shall arrive." Dylan turned on the radio. The news was being read out. The reporter mentioned that powerful storms were to hit the area. The reporter finished the weather report. Suddenly it began to go dark outside as a large rain cloud arrived on the scene and then the heavens opened.

Chapter 25

Erica finished washing the dishes. She could hear the howl of the wind and the heavy downfall. Erica gazed out of the window as the noise began to pound in her ears and then thunder and lightning. Erica jumped out of her skin. She reflected a shade of terror, a draught of cold air ran down her spine and she shivered through her frame. Gripped by a hot flush panic she stood motionless, frozen with fear. Erica looked through her window at every shadow, her eyelids flickered spasmodically and then a voice - it was Dylan. He whispered, "Are you okay?"

Erica replied "I think so. That last bolt of lightning made me jump. Shit, I am going to be driving in this; it's so scary, like something out of a horror movie."

Dylan scratched his head and then spoke, "Yeah, I reckon so. If you want, I will do the driving. You can be my navigator."

Erica smiled then whispered, "Thank you. There is no way I want to be driving in this storm." She then kissed Dylan on the lips.

Suddenly there was a knock on the door. Dylan answered the door, it was the Pizza delivery guy. Dylan paid him and then returned to the table. He placed the boxes of food onto the table and then said, "Okay everyone, our food's here."

Ralph ate some garlic bread and then spoke, "This garlic bread sure tastes good; what you all reckon?"

Erica replied, "Yeah, lots of lovely garlic. As for the Pizza, it's a bit cheesy. Give me a big, fat juicy steak anytime." Erica then thought back to the time when she met William the Nerd. Erica began to laugh and then said, "Dylan, do you remember that time we visited William the Nerd?"

Dylan began to laugh then replied to the story, "He told us about the girl he once dated; it was hilarious. She was called Delilah; he said she was cheating on him and he just couldn't take anymore. He said the guy was a Tom Jones tribute act, then he also said he took her to his green grass of home." They all began to laugh. Dylan then said, "My God, he didn't give up, so he met up with another girl, a French one by the name of Esmerelda, a complete yak. She turned up with her father who looked like Quasimodo. He then said 'does that name ring any bells?'" The room then erupted with laughter. Dylan then said, "Okay, we are all here laughing but the poor guy was mighty lonely. I remember he stood up and hugged me and said thank you for saving my life. I saved many a nerd from bullies; my two older brothers already had their reputations - no one messed with me. Instead of ducking, the bullies used to walk into punches. Guess how the nerds used to repay me."

Ralph smiled and then replied, "In kind?"

Dylan shook his head and then spoke in a heightened voice, "No, they paid me in Marvel comics, Superman, Spider-Man, Batman etc. I ended up with a nice collection. Later, I needed the money so I sold them to Joshua the Jew. Remember that old pawn shop? That guy well ripped me off; five hundred dollars he gave me for that collection of rare comics. Today, that collection must be worth a small fortune. That guy made pure money from ripping people off. I hope he got what was coming to him."

Ralph then spoke in a heightened voice, "You obviously never heard the news about that poor Jew, did you?"

Dylan replied, "No, I did not."

Ralph then continued with his story: "Well, a few years ago he pissed off some Muslims. He well ripped them off, so they took matters into their own hands and blew up his shop with him in it."

Erica turned to Ralph and said, "My, that was sad."

Eddie shook his head and then spoke in a heightened voice, "I got a sad story to tell. I remember a lady I met in a night club, a pretty little thing; her name was Lucy Ball. We dated but she kept asking me what I did for a living so I told her. She then started asking questions about Big Tony. Naturally, we found out all about her through a corrupt cop on his payroll by the name of Billy Bones, as he was lacking in the meat department. He informed me her nickname was Lucy Ball-breaker. Big Tony met up with me and questioned me about her. He then had her kidnapped. I knew where he was holding her; I then heard he had the Death Star flown in, a mad homicidal torture merchant - he dealt out his torture real slow, that's how he got his results. I visited her; she knew her fate. The poor girl was a mess, covered in blood and crying. She began to beg me for help. If I had helped her escape, Big Tony would have had me bumped off so I gave her a cyanide tablet. Before the Death Star could carry on with his line of work, she died. My, Big Tony was so pissed; I said I was sorry. Eventually, he let me off after I paid the Death Star's expenses and the money to the goons that kidnapped her. I even had to pay a little bonus to keep him sweet. Soon after this, Big Tony would not let this rest. He brought back the Death Star as he found out who Lucy was working for, a private detective by the name of Jack Jones. He wanted to dig some dirt on Big Tony. The motive, revenge. It seems Big Tony had killed one of his relatives by the name of Bobby Briscoe. Jack claimed he had evidence Big Tony had his relative killed, so Big Tony had his goons kidnap Jack. The Death Star kept him amused for several days but he said absolutely nothing. In the end, Big Tony had Jack Jones put down, a mercy killing amongst madness he called it."

Dylan shook his head and spoke, "Shit, we all got so many sad stories."

Ralph then stood up and said, "Anyone fancy a Jack Daniel's? By the way, you still driving Erica?"

Dylan replied before Erica could. "No, she ain't, I am. Erica is going to be my navigator."

Ralph then spoke in a heightened voice, "Okay, that's settled. You driving, you ain't drinking. The last thing we need is to be pulled over by a state trooper, with a holdall full of weapons and a drunken driver."

Dylan agreed with a nod of his head. They all finished off what food was left. Ralph then poured himself and Eddie a Jack Daniel's. He handed the drink to Eddie and said, "Okay, just the one each. I need to wash down that Pizza." Ralph downed his Jack Daniel's in one. He then turned to Dylan and spoke, "Okay, it looks a lot calmer out now. Let's all get our shit together."

Erica left the room and went upstairs. She walked into her bedroom, over to a Jewellery box that had belonged to Henry's late wife. She opened it up and picked out a large silver necklace, on the end of it was a silver cross. Erica placed it around her neck and then picked out a black jacket from within her wardrobe. Erica then made her way downstairs.

Ralph was the first to notice the silver cross. He shook his head and then spoke in a heightened voice, "My God, what on Earth is that for?"

Erica pulled a face and then replied, "Just in case."

Ralph then spoke once more in a loud voice, "You got us three brothers to protect you from a strange old guy. Do you really need that?"

Dylan interrupted and then said, "Look, leave her alone. It's only a cross for Christ's sake."

Ralph smiled and said, "It sure is. Look, I won't say another word on the subject, you wear it. Dylan, you still driving?"

Dylan replied, "Yeah. Erica shall sit in the front and give me directions to the old guy's mansion."

Ralph then said, "Okay people, let's do this. Paradise is awaiting us."

They then all left the mansion and got into the Cadillac. It had now stopped raining, but the wind still howled, the rustle of dead leaves and on view wind swept trees. The light began to fade rapidly. Dylan turned on the car lights, hit the gas pedal, then they headed towards the Count's mansion.

Erica looked up at the full moon. Dylan turned on the radio. George Thorogood and the Destroyers were playing the song 'Bad to The Bone'.

Ralph remarked, "My, this is one bad-ass song."

Erica turned to Dylan and said, "Okay, keep driving straight ahead for a couple of miles and then turn right when you come to the signpost."

Dylan nodded his head in agreement. They then all sat listening to the DJ talking about the storm. He then played a song by Kiss entitled 'Crazy Nights'.

Ralph then spoke in a heightened voice, "Shit, this song is quite fitting. I reckon we are in for a crazy night."

Eddie began to sing along, *"crazy, crazy nights"*.

Erica then turned off the radio and said, "Shit, I ain't that crazy."

All three brothers began to laugh. Dylan then turned right at the signpost. Erica then said, "Okay, follow this road for a mile and then turn left at the old graveyard."

Ralph closed his eyes for a few minutes. A draught of cold air suddenly ran down his spine. He had a bad feeling and then a vision of a creature coming out of the dark shadows and attacking him. Ralph jumped and then opened his eyes. Panic fears fluttered his mind. He then spoke in a heightened voice, "I must admit, I got me a bad feeling about this one. I reckon the strange old guy has got us all spooked."

Once more Erica gazed at the full moon. She then turned to Dylan and said, "Okay, head down that road."

Dylan gazed ahead. His mind whispered 'My, it is a bit remote. All I can see is wind swept trees'. Dylan continued to drive. Erica then said, "Shit, we are here. Turn left." Dylan did as he was instructed. Now in view was an old large mansion. Dylan parked the Cadillac and they all got out.

Ralph looked up at the moon. He then spoke, "Shit, the full moon always makes me mad." Ralph then opened the boot. He reached inside his holdall and then began handing out weapons. He picked up his favourite weapon, his pump action shotgun. Ralph then said, "My ballistic baby, its never let me down, locked and loaded." Ralph then handed Eddie his twelve-gauge shotgun. Ralph then said, "This beauty puts one-inch holes in people; made for door breaching. If the old guy's out we just use this to blow the locks off." Ralph then handed everyone a semi-automatic pistol.

Eddie turned to his brother Ralph and said, "Do we really need this much fire power to put down an old man?"

Ralph replied, "Better to be safe than sorry. Always expect the unexpected." Ralph turned to Dylan and Erica and said, "Remember, aim for the heart if you get a shot at him before me which, may I say, is very unlikely." Ralph closed the boot.

Chapter 26

All four then turned and walked towards the mansion. Suddenly, the front door opened. Erica turned to Dylan and whispered, "My God, this old place is sure spooky."

Ralph continued to walk inside the mansion, as the rest followed with great caution. Inside the mansion it was damp and cold. The only light came from four candles sitting on a table. A draught of cold air suddenly ran down Erica's spine as she inhaled the damp air. Ralph turned to Eddie and said, "Shit, can you smell that? It's the unmistakable stench of death."

Suddenly, the front door slammed shut and then a crack of thunder and lightning echoed all around the mansion. Erica jumped as panic dears fluttered her mind, she reflected a shade of terror.

Dylan turned to Erica and whispered, "Are you okay?"

Erica replied with an expression of pure horror "Shit, this is so unreal." Suddenly, another crack of thunder and lightning. Erica jumped out of her skin once more. Standing on a cold floor she inhaled the unwholesome air. Erica then began to cough. She could hear the howl of the wind as the storm raged fiercely. Dylan put his arm around Erica as anxiety twisted her face. She stood rooted with fear.

Ralph then spoke with a shade of impatience in his voice, "Look, Erica, get a grip of yourself. Remember, we are here for the money."

Erica took a deep breath. She then spoke as the noise of the thunder and lightning pounded in her ears. "Look, ain't any of you big brave men frightened? Cause I certainly am."

Ralph nodded in confirmation. He then spoke in a heightened voice, "I never lapse from my moral code. I show no fear, as fear can get a man killed. I never hesitate, I shoot and then ask questions later, okay? The thunder and lightning can take your mind off the job at hand. Look, the quicker we find the treasure the quicker we can get the fuck out of this hellhole."

Erica nodded her head in agreement. She then said, "Okay, that door leads to the dining area." They then all entered with extreme caution as the light was poor.

Ralph gazed with a shock as the table was set out with four plates. Knives and forks also sat on the table, four candles flickering. The room was cold and draughty. Ralph turned to Erica and then spoke in a heightened voice, "The old guy must have guests. What you reckon?"

Erica shook her head and then replied, "Do the maths; the table is set out for four people- there are four of us."

Ralph laughed then said, "I guess the old guy has already eaten."

Eddie looked to his brother Ralph and said, "Okay, now it looks to me like this old guy is one step ahead of us. He knows we are here, in which case we lose the element of surprise."

Ralph then stood motionless. He had an uneasy feeling but remained calm. He then spoke to Erica in a heightened voice, "So, through that door is the corridor that leads to the treasure?" Erica nodded her head in agreement. Ralph stepped forward and then opened the door. Slowly, he then entered the corridor. The rest then followed.

Erica began to cough. She then said, "My God, I don't remember this place being so rancid and smelly." Ralph agreed that it was rancid and smelly as a draught of cold air ran down his spine. Erica gazed along the corridor. There were no pictures, just a dark, damp corridor complete with mould and cobwebs. Panic fears fluttered her mind. she then whispered, "It's all been changed. These walls were full of pictures of his ancestors. They have all been removed."

A loud laugh began to echo along the corridor, it was the Count. All four stood rooted with fear as the Count began to speak, "Welcome, all, to my mansion of madness. Four flies caught in a web. Erica, my dear, the pictures, as with the treasure are all an illusion; the wine I gave you was drugged. There are no millions, I am quite poor. You have all been deceived. Now you all stand at death's door; hell awaits you all, it is but your time to fall." Suddenly, he stopped talking and became silent.

Ralph suddenly saw red. His anger rose, then he shouted, "God damn you!" He moved forward and began to open fire in the direction of the Count's voice. The crack of his shotgun echoed all around. He continued to move forward, shooting at every shadow.

Eddie then shouted to his brother, "Calm down, you're wasting precious ammo."

Ralph listened to his brother's words. He then turned to speak to Erica. Her heart was pounding, panic fears fluttered her mind, anxiety twisted her face - horror beyond imagination. The noise of the shotgun was pounding in her ears. Ralph began screaming like a madman. His face reddened with rage, he repeated his words again and again. Suddenly Erica could hear what he was saying. She was conscious of his annoyance. She then shouted, "I don't know what the fuck is going on, do you?"

Ralph took a deep breath and then spoke in a heightened voice, "This old bastard has set us up. All of this was a trap. All I want you to do is lead us to the treasure room. If there is no treasure then we are all getting the fuck out of here. Is that understood?"

They all agreed. Dylan's eyes were wild with terror. As they walked along the corridor towards the treasure room, Erica remembered the Count saying he studied the dark arts. Her mind whispered, 'he drugged me. The treasure - is he telling the truth?'

They all soon arrived at a door. Ralph turned to Erica and said, "Is this the door?"

Erica replied, "You heard what that old bastard said. I have no idea. He claimed he drugged me. Must be the door to his library, that's if he has got one."

Ralph tried the handle, it was locked. He then turned to Eddie and said, "Okay, breaching shotgun, lose the lock."

They all stood back as Eddie opened fire. He shot off the lock and the door opened. They all slowly stepped inside the room. Inside the room sat a few candles which gave off little light. Erica felt a sense of compulsion; the room was completely different. She then had a macabre vision as she gazed at the various coffins. Erica stood rooted with fear at the sinister sight.

Ralph took hold of Erica and began to shake her vigorously. He then cried out as panic fears fluttered his mind. "The treasure - that old guy did drug you, there is no treasure." Erica began to weep hysterically.

Eddie, with a cry of wild malice, shouted "You bastard!" He raised his shotgun and began blasting away at the coffins. Splinters of wood flew off in every direction. Ralph pushed Erica to one side, then joined in with his brother, shooting away at the coffins until they both ran out of shells. Ralph then inspected what was left after the onslaught. The coffins had all fallen to the ground, the tables they had sat on were all broken, shot to pieces. All looked at the remains of skeletons shot to pieces.

A blood-curdling scream echoed all around the old grim mansion. Ralph turned to Eddie and then spoke in a heightened voice, "Better load up our shotguns as I reckon we have just pissed off the old guy." They both reloaded their shotguns. Ralph then announced their visit was over. "Let's get the fuck out of here."

There was an unmistakable stench of death and decay as they all left the room. Dylan put his arm around Erica, trying his best to remain calm.

The Count was now livid with wrath; the light in the corridor began to fade rapidly, the far side was now in complete darkness. Suddenly, the Count once more spoke in a loud voice, "From amongst the dark shadows you have desecrated my family's remains. I pity you all, for now I must kill you all in the order I see fit. You will all have to come amongst the dark shadows where I await. There shall be no paradise; hell awaits all four of you. Is there any one of you brave enough to enter the dark shadows? Maybe you, the eldest brother, big bad Ralph. Walk this way if you are not chicken, that is. Are you all ready to die?"

Ralph then replied in an angry heightened voice, "You're an old bastard. I am going to fill you full of lead." Without a thought he moved forward into the shadows. He then opened fire. He adopted a defensive stance as his eyes met with the Count's. The Count began to snarl as Ralph again opened fire, hitting the Count in the chest. Ralph continued to fire; the impact knocked him off his feet. The Count fell to the ground, his motionless body lay still. Ralph took his eyes off the corpse for a brief second and it was gone. Ralph stood rooted with fear, his mind whispered 'no human gets up from that'. Ralph then heard the Count whisper, "I just did. Now it's time to die."

Before Ralph could react, the Count sank his razor-sharp fangs into Ralph's neck. Ralph screamed out in pain. He then dropped his shotgun, blood dripping from the wound. Ralph applied pressure to the wound. He then turned to face the Count and their eyes met. The Count's eyes were wild with terror beyond imagination. Ralph gazed into the Count's bloodshot, livid, burning eyes.

Ralph's eyelids flickered spasmodically. Frowning in confusion, he then mumbled, "You're a real vampire." The Count had heard enough. Ralph's mind was paralysed with fear and then, with superhuman strength, the Count ripped into Ralph's larynx which killed him instantly. He hesitated and then stumbled back onto the cold, damp floor. The Count then lifted Ralph's body up. With hideous strength, he threw the lifeless body along the corridor. His body landed at the feet of his brothers.

All three looked down at Ralph's frightful mutilated body. Eddie's anger suddenly rose; he expressed his annoyance and then shouted "God damn you!" His face reddened with rage.

Dylan's mind whispered, 'Shit, he must be a real vampire'.

Suddenly, the Count began to laugh out loud. He then spoke in a heightened voice, "Dylan the fake vampire; I reckon you never thought you would meet the real deal. All three of you must be expressing such fear as the dark shadows draw ever so nearby. Eddie, have you a wooden stake? Would you not like to avenge your poor departed brother?" Eddie, without warning, raised his shotgun and began firing into the shadows.

Dylan knew he had to somehow escape the mansion of death. He then grabbed hold of Erica's hand and said, "Let's get the fuck out of here."

Erica nodded in confirmation. Panic fears fluttered their minds as they rushed down the corridor of death. The sound of Eddie's shotgun echoed in their ears.

Eddie turned and watched as Dylan and Erica disappeared into the shadows, moving lightning fast. The Count now stood behind Eddie; a draught of cold air suddenly ran down his spine. He felt a breath blowing on the back of his neck. A thought flashed through his brain: stood behind him a mysterious cold-hearted killer with death cold sinister eyes. A voice then whispered, "Are you nervous?" Eddie had a vision of his mutilated brother. His bottom lip began to tremble. He then turned around screaming like a mad man. With wild strength he struggled violently. The Count clawed Eddie's arm and he then lost hold of his shotgun; it then fell to the ground. Eddie then reached for his semi-automatic pistol, gripped by a hot flush panic. The Count then grabbed him by the throat; a wailing, choking scream echoed all around. The Count snarled as he clawed Eddie's face; he pushed Eddie against a wall. His head struck so hard he died instantly, his lifeless body falling to the damp floor.

Erica and Dylan managed to escape the mansion. Both intoxicated with fear they ran towards the Cadillac. Suddenly, the Count appeared before them. Dylan reached for his semi-automatic pistol as did Erica; they both aimed and then opened fire. The Count then simply disappeared. The wind began to howl, their hearts were pounding. Erica turned to Dylan and said, "Shit, where has that old bastard gone?" Her eyes were wild with terror, anxiety twisted her face.

Dylan had a fixed expression of horror. He then replied, "I will stay here in case he returns. You run over and start up the motor and then we will get the fuck out of here."

Erica gazed into his fearful, cold eyes and then nodded in agreement. Her heart was pounding. She ran towards the Cadillac, reaching inside her pocket for the keys. Suddenly, she felt the Count's presence; he appeared and whispered, "Nobody escapes; you must die." Erica turned as the Count grabbed hold of her arm. Erica screamed as she grew more and more hysterical. Erica then reached for the silver cross; she struggled and then pulled it off the chain. She thrust it into the Count's head. He screamed out in pain and then disappeared into the shadows. Erica opened the car door. She then got in and started it up. Erica then hit the gas pedal, driving like a bat out of hell.

Dylan could not believe his eyes; his mind whispered 'judgement'. He then shouted, "You fucking bitch!"

Erica continued to drive away from the scene of carnage. Erica then reached into her pocket and produced a mobile phone. Erica then called the emergency services: a multiple homicide, brothers attacked and killed by a creature. She gave the address and hung up.

Chapter 27

Dylan stood awaiting his death, knowing there was no escape. Suddenly, the Count appeared from the shadows. Dylan pointed his semi-automatic pistol at the Count. The Count moved slowly closer and began to laugh. He then spoke in a heightened voice, "Put it down and expect your fate. You know it has little effect on me as I am a real vampire. You killed a dear friend of mine, poor Henry, now you must decide on your death - quick or slow, I give you the choice."

Dylan stood rooted with fear and lowered his weapon as the Count moved closer and closer. Oh, such dark hypnotising eyes; the Count had powers beyond human comprehension. The Count could read the minds of the fearful; he then spoke, "Yes, Dylan, no costume; face to face with a real vampire. How does it feel? I can hear your heart pounding." Dylan's mind was paralysed by the hideous sight. His heart began to pound faster and faster. the Count then moved at super speed and strength; with razor sharp claws he ripped out Dylan's heart. The Count then held it in his hand and began to laugh. Dylan's lifeless body fell backwards onto the ground.

One hour later a patrol car arrived as the Count faded into the shadows. Erica drove to the Sheriff's department and gave a statement about the brothers all killed by a vampire. The mutilated bodies were all found, but the existence of a vampire was totally unbelievable. Everyone believed Erica was insane and she ended up in a mental ward. Erica was questioned again and again but would not change her story. "It was a real vampire" she explained.

Two detectives gazed at her through a window as she sat on a chair in a locked room. Detective Bishop, a tall well-dressed man with tender looks and gleaming white teeth spoke in a heightened voice to Detective Jones, a solidly built man with a strange looking forehead "Okay, the woman is a complete fruitcake. She claims an old guy killed the three brothers. They went to the mansion to rob him, as they believed he had lots of treasure and was an easy target. She claims there was no treasure, and the old guy was really a vampire. Did you see the pictures of those dead guys?"

Detective Jones replied, "Yeah, they were ripped to pieces. One guy had his heart ripped out of his body; must have been a maniac or a wild animal. She claimed the older brother, Ralph, shot the old guy with a pump action shotgun and he got back up. The locals kept clear of the mansion, claiming it to be haunted by a demon. Can't say I have come across a case like this one, have you?"

Detective Bishop replied, "Shit, all of this is like a Count Dracula horror movie." Detective Jones agreed and they both left the ward.

Erica climbed into bed. She lay motionless; fear had paralysed her mind. Oh, such sinister events that had unfolded before her. Panic fears fluttered her mind as night-time began to call. Erica's eyes were wild with terror as all the lights began to fade. Suddenly, out of the shadows a familiar malignant face of such sinister death and cold eyes; it was the Count. Erica lay gazing at the Count unable to scream or move; her body was completely frozen.

The Count smiled and then said, "Hello my dear Erica, revenge is a dish best served cold. Your friends are all dead; their mutilated bodies will all rot in hell. As for you, I can hear your heart beating, pounding faster and faster. Can you feel the pain?"

Erica, with an expression of horror, placed her hands on her heart. Perspiration was leaking all over her body. She began blinking and frowning, anxiety twisted her face. Suddenly, her heart stopped beating. A cruel smile as the Count faded away.

Author's Note

I have always enjoyed writing and started off with poetry. I became a member of the poetry society I completed over five hundred poems on a variety of subjects. I then became a member of the guild of international songwriters and composers.

I have always been a prolific writer and have a vast collection of poems and short stories. My completed poems have been published in the Standard newspaper for the last twenty years. I often had people contacting me telling me how much they enjoyed my poems. Some of the poems I wrote to my amazement predicted future events. I believe we all have a degree of psychic potential that lies dormant until it is activated.

I have experienced such potential over the past years. I remember having a vision of a helicopter crashing, I then turned on the television to find it breaking news. Another example is when I think of someone I haven't heard of for a long time and then suddenly they contact me. I often listen to music and lots of occasions I have thought of a song I haven't heard in a long time; I would turn on the radio and the song will be playing or about to be played, I remember many years ago riding to work with a friend I had told him I had a vision about being crushed by metal. After work, we were riding home when a heavy goods vehicle loading with metal pulled out in front of us the driver hit his brakes just missing us. My first book "Five Fives Beyond Imagination" came to me in a series of visions unlocking the mysteries that have haunted mankind throughout the centuries. I believe in the power of numerology; numbers compose the very foundation of reality; throughout the centuries people have believed it is possible to predict future events. I have studied numerology for many years, it is based on the belief that numbers are not solid but vibrations and energies that move. Vibrations influence our lives with either the dark shadow side negative experiences, separation or light or light positive experiences connection. Your destiny can be determined using numerology, Philosopher, Pythagoras studied numerology, he believed as I do, numbers are the essence of life.

I was born in October my collective year which shows my qualities are bringing wisdom to the World. My personal year table is the number five which represents communication each number contains emotional, mental physical and spiritual dimensions therefore numerology is such an amazing representation of life. The basis of numerology is that we are influenced by our birth name and our birthdate, the numbers five and eight have influenced me throughout my life. An example of this is in 2014 I had two accidents, I added the date and the month together and came up with the numbers five and eight. I believe when these numbers clash my luck turns bad as together these numbers add up to thirteen. I mentioned earlier about my poems, some of which predicted future events. I remember gazing at the front of a newspaper at the sad face of princess Diana.

I put pen to paper and wrote a poem about the princess in the Summer of nineteen ninety-seven, recalling the end of the poem of which I still have; "Life goes fast when you are harassed, you sealed your fate when you made that date, don't cry Di it was meant to be". Two months later she went on a date with Dodi, and they were harassed by the paparazzi and they both died under tragic circumstances. Another strange thing that happened to me when I was autographed pictures of famous actors in 2003. I got a dozen pictures in my bar room. I placed them on the floor suddenly a large fly appeared on the face of Charles Bronson.

I chased it and then hung up the pictures only for it to return the same picture. I later found out the actor had passed away. In 2003, I sat watching the movie the bodyguard, later about midnight, I picked out a random episode of an eighties show entitled Thriller. The episode I put on was about a killer who would meet women and then drown them in their bathtubs. Later that night I heard the news about Witney Houston who had also died in a bathtub. In the past I have had dreams about older celebrities and the following morning turned on the news to find out they had passed away. I have read, prediction is very difficult especially about the future. I once worked at a large warehouse that employed hundreds, the canteen staff started a weekly raffle each week I would by one strip of five tickets and the draw took place. I won for nine weeks on the run, prizes such as a one-hundred-pound hamper. The bizarre thing was I would write on the back of the copy ticket this is the winner before the draw and that ticket would win the prize. I visited a local social club which was full of people buying raffle tickets. I brought five tickets and then the draw took place I won first prize and then was invited to pick out the next ticket. The bucket was full of tickets the guy mixed them all up several times I then picked out my other ticket. I sat down with my two prizes someone else picked out a ticket and yes, I won again. The last prize was up for grabs another person picked out a ticket and again it was mine I sat on a table with all four prizes I won all four prizes with five tickets impossible people thought. I remember the faces around the club how could someone walked into the club and win all four prizes, people then began to shout "fix" as what I had done was beyond odds. I became so confident believing I just couldn't lose, a friend asked me to go out for a drink and I agreed we visited a pub called the Travellers rest inside the pub they were selling raffle tickets for a cash prize. I informed my friend that I would buy some tickets and return later for the draw, and I would give him half the money. We returned later, I wasn't disappointed I kept my word and gave him half the money.

On another occasion, a friend told me had never won anything in his life we were drinking in the Cheshire Yeoman a man entered the pub selling tickets for a meat hamper. I informed my friend if you were to buy a ticket this minute you will the meat hamper. He agreed and to his total amazement, he won for the first time in his life. I expected to win every time and did, I won again and again even believed I hadn't there was a second prise with my name on it. I had a bizarre winning streak that continued for many years, I then started filling in a pool's coupon. I started off with eight from eleven, the week I change to eight to ten I won. I could believe I accidently put eleven crosses on the winning line that would have won me lots of money.

The company in question sent me a sum in good faith acknowledging my mistake. I remember thinking to myself perhaps I wasn't destined to win such money. My lucky and unlucky numbers have always been five and eight. These numbers have always played a part in my life. I used the same numbers on the EuroMillions the week I changed the numbers they came in I should have won millions. I was missing two numbers five and eight the lucky star numbers I had always used. I remember visiting Morrisons supermarket on several occasions I challenged myself to guess the price without adding the shopping up as I was putting items into the trolley. I remember informing the lady on the till the correct price she replied after scanning then your right "I bet you couldn't do that again". I informed her I already had on several occasions.

In 2003 I was driving towards Ellesmere port town centre I then had a vision of a woman stepping out in front of a car. I returned home and then turned my vision into a short story. More and more visions they just kept coming every day I was writing short stories. I was once in bed having worked a nightshift, I could see characters and a story unfolding I knew if I didn't write the story onto paper, I would not be able to sleep I was writing at a prolific pace and found myself in a trance like state. I wrote nonstop for over an hour and when the story was completed, I looked at the number of pages in amazement.

I had drafted a complete short story entitled Wits about it was a truly amazing horror story. I remember competing in the Great north run I met lots of celebrities including the inspector off the Bill, I had a vision of a young man wanting to compete in the London Marathon, his Father was a Gangster controlling the North of England, he eventually grants his son permission to run the Marathon if he is escorted by a trusted bodyguard. Things go wrong in the South, and then all hell breaks loose between the North and South. This is the best Gangster story ever written, full of twists and gang warfare. As with all the short stories I have written I can picture the characters as though I was watching a movie, the ideas I had for these short stories are all original. I was most prolific in the year 2003 every day I was writing I wrote a story entitles "The Judgement Angels and Demons" and then a science fiction story. I made the mistake of sending some of my short stories to publishers' ideas no one had thought of, and then later similar movies appeared to what I had written. I purchased a DVD entitled "The Knowing"; I watched this movie in disbelief was about a professor played by Nicolas Cage his name was John. In the movie he predicted future events in the story I wrote the main character was in fact professor John and yes it was about future disasters written in 2003, I continued to write more and more stories and only on one occasion have I stopped writing halfway through a story as it was the most frightening story.

I mentioned early on I could see all the characters and the surroundings like I was on a film set, the story was about the supernatural. Imagine being on a film set of the most frightening film ever made. This is the reason I stopped writing and switched to another story. I sent off a thriller to the BBC and various publishers this was a mistake on my behalf, I remember thinking I have over five hundred short stories I just wanted feedback. The BBC board of directors contacted me and said they may use my story in the future and my suggestion has been recorded for the benefit of all BBC senior management and producers. One of the first stories I wrote after the millennium was entitled "Five Fives beyond imagination", I had a vision of David Burns travelling to the fifth dimension to meet Cavoc. Later I decided to write Nostradamus into my story every time I wrote fiction later, I researched and found it to be a fact. For instance, I wrote Nostradamus was in Montpellier on a certain date and John Dee in Paris. On another date to my amazement, fiction turned to fact as they were there on these dates. I finished the story whilst cruising around the Caribbean.

In the same year I also went to Ibiza, the night-time entertainment was poor, my son Bradley asked me to play cards I had not played for a while and soon ran out of games. He then said I will shuffle the pack and you must pick out the ten of diamonds. I have no knowledge of card tricks but picked out the correct card until I picked out all the tens impossible, I thought. My daughter, Shanna had made friends with a group of teenagers who all looked like characters out of the Harry Potter movie. One, informed me that he could do card tricks, I continued picking out all the kings. People began to look in amazement, I soon had an audience. The Harry Potter double examined the deck and then shuffled it several times he then said, "OK pick out the queen of spades". I concentrated on the deck of cards and to everyone's amazement I picked out the correct card. I remember his shocked face and his words "my god how did you do that"? I cannot explain how I picked out all the correct cards, but the word impossible had no meaning to me. I signed the contract to have "Five Fives beyond imagination published" on the 31/10/2014. I have been contacted by various famous authors one sent me a message saying your book is not good it's great. I've just read it hurry up and publish another book and I will buy it. I also had another message from another American author who explained she kept having visions of five fives she then mentioned the fall of 2014 about the time I signed the contract to have my book published.

This was such an enlightening year, 44 days later the 14/12/2014, I lay in bed dreaming about my book, and then I felt a strange presence in the room. I suddenly opened my eyes and sat up, I turned to the right and there stood before me, were two angels I gazed upon them mesmerised by their radiant beauty. I remember their smiling faces such a hypnotising display my eyes suddenly flickered spasmodically and they then faded away. I was so confused as to why they visited me on this date. One month later I uncharacteristically decided to tidy out old letters then found out the answer I was looking for. A letter from a solicitor dating back to the 14/12/2010, this was the date of an accident I had whilst driving towards a roundabout. I stopped to give way to the traffic when a large van crashed into the back on me, the driver was going too fast and never hit his breaks on time. The van pushed me onto the roundabout I managed to steer my car left avoiding other traffic. I suffered whiplash and believed it could have been a lot worse. The angels visited me on the anniversary 4 years to the day. I believe in the impossible and that I was visited by two guardian angels. Ten days later I dreamt of the number 347 repeatedly as if it was some sort of message. I have been predicted future events all my life but was not prepared of what awaited me when I visited Chester to be interviewed by a reporter from the standard newspaper. The date was the 13/05/2015, I parked outside Chester and then walked to the standard office. I met the reported who asked me why I started writing I explained to her in 2003 I was driving along and then had a vision of a young lady stepping out Infront of a car. I informed her after that I wrote a short story about the vision and then kept having more dreams and visions this is how I wrote 500 more remarkable short stories. I finished the interview then visited the blue bell in which was featured in my book the manager gave me a guided tour of the inn this was the oldest inn in Chester. I remember thinking a draft of chilly air ran down my spine this place is spooky. I then walked around Chester handing out leaflets advertising my book for some strange reason people kept asking me the same question repeatedly "why you started writing"? I informed them it was after having a vision of a young lady stepping out Infront of a car. I then noticed the time had flown by; it was time to leave Chester for some reason the subway was closed so I made my way to St Oswald's. The road was terribly busy, I gazed all around and noticed two Asian men walking towards the traffic lights then I noticed a young lady in her twenties she was speed walking with her exceedingly small dog on a lead she was dressed in light pink with green vest and matching shorts. I gazed over at her my mind was saying get across the road as quickly as possible. I noticed a break in the traffic and without hesitation I jogged across the road if I had not, I would have stood next to the young lady waiting for the lights to change. I crossed the road and as I went to walk away, I heard a loud bang, I turned around and gazed in shock and horror as the young lady had been hit by a blue Peugeot 307. This happened at 15:31. I remember the small dog stepping over the body when more and more people arrived and an ambulance service. She was at the lights by herself, my mind whispered you may have prevented her from crossing, or you could have shared her fate. The answer to this question I will never know had the vision in 2003 finally come true? A reporter from the Ellesmere port pioneer who was also doing a story on me, he informed me if I needed anything else he would contact me. 2 weeks later I contacted him and asked him if her required anything else for the story, a brief silence and then he replied in a shocked voice, my that is very spooky he said I have just finished you story and was about to contact you to see if you had a brighter photograph. I then informed him, spooky is something I had always done.

I am friends on Facebook with a lot of award-winning authors one an award-winning Canadian author contacted me with a message you are interested in numerology do you know the Bible code number it took what boffins with the aid of computer to produce the answer which was the number 7. I replied to her that had produced the same conclusion with a pen and a piece of paper after the millennium. I remember it was easter I sat watching three Biblical movies back-to-back. Later, I started to apply deep thought about the movies I had just watched, three words came to me Jesus, cross and Gospel. I then applied numerology, each word when added up came to the same number 74, I then thought of the Bible which was thirty, so I then timed 3×74=222 and then 3×222=666. I then investigated the 74 words spelt out GD, Bible 30 using the 0 it spelt out GOD. I then found out one more word Jewish which was 74, so I timed 4×74 =296 which spelt out BIF, spelt backwards it spelt FIB. I then noticed two words, Baptist and Priest they both came to the number 87 timed by two 2×87=174 again GD. I believe numbers are the key to unlocking the mysteries of the universe. The Bible code number seven is one of the most significant numbers because of its spiritual perfection. Oh, such hidden messages and meanings of codes. Christians believe seven is a Holy number, Genesis says that God rested on the seventh day and that mankind and mankind was created on the sixth. There are seven Continents, seven Oceans, seven Heavens seven colours in the Rainbow, seven worders of the World and seven days in the week and so on. Indeed, number seen is truly extraordinary. It has also been written the number seven is of spiritual enlightenment, inner wisdom pure energy of the mystics. It is related to my star sign, Libra which has been mentioned for its psychic abilities. The award-winning Canadian Author contacted me about the Bible code number seven as I was about to go on Holiday to Majorca. Seven letters I printed off my boarding pass only to find out a was sitting on seat seven. I arrived at my hotel and the room number added up to seven, I often went on Holiday by myself so I could chill in the Sun and write a book. I sat in the Sun a Lady and her Husband asked me if I was an Author, I replied "yes", I informed Her I was writing my second book my first one had been published. She said was a speed reader complete with a high IQ, she then informed me how she would love to read my published book. I lent her a copy to read, she thanked me and began to read, her eyes lit up, wide eyed she read on and suddenly stopped. She was a tall, beautiful Lady, she turned to me with an expression of amazement and said, "How on earth did you think of this"? The Lady was well and truly hooked on the story, she continued reading. I met her later, she kept tight hold of the book as if it was a rare treasure, she then said, "name your price I will pay anything for this book as I want to read it again and again". The Lady then handed me twenty euros one very good sale. The entertainment team then turned up with two big dices and asked me to roll them I was left with the number seven. All through the holiday the number seven kept coming to me in some shape or form. I arrived at the Palma de Mallorca airport it was very large and busy with nearly twenty million passengers using this airport a year. I asked a group of stranger's directions to the checkout which was quite a distance from where I was. I could not believe I later boarded the plane and was sitting next to them, imagine the odds on this happening. I arrive home and later visited a cool trader store I purchased various items and the Lady on the till said that's strange seven pounds seventy-seven pence.

I remember attending a street party me and my son played football with a couple of police constables, they brought raffle tickets and believed the prizes where outstanding. What could I say? I informed them of the will to win and the prizes already had my name written on them. I had done this for many years, I grew with confidence as the draw took place and wasn't disappointed, winning the first and second prizes, the luck of the draw was with me once more. I remember being informed by someone that they never dream, I myself have had lots of dreams the Native American Indians considered dreams as an important source of information about future events, interpreting and understanding is the key to unlock your dreams. There are many levels of existence happening at the same time, it is conceivable that dreams pick up material from other time frames or parallel realities that we are not aware of in our conscious world. My dreams are so vivid, some supernatural, providing information about future events. I have also had out of body dreams witnessing spiritual beings of light and darkness. Imagine flying through the clouds and then looking down on a natural disaster and then later turning on the television and finding out your dream had become reality. Premonitions occur in the land of dreams because of time, it is different in the higher dimensions, the causal mechanism. This tuns action from one place to another, the event witnessed in a dream later it materializes in our domain. Some people adapt a memory, trained to remember and write down the dates of such dreams, examples yes, I have many here are my favourites.

On the 9;3;16, I dreamt I was walking along in a Latin American Country the radiant sun was shining in all its glory. I looked up at tree filled with bananas, I then turned to someone and said the trees are blocking out the sun, and then total darkness. The following day I turned on the television to watch the news, I then found out there had been a Solar Eclipse in the region I had dreamt of. The next dream was so vivid as are all my dreams on the 24;3;16, I dreamt I was in America, riots broke out all over the Country, so I then left on an aeroplane. For some reason I lived in France near the Belgium border, my dwelling was an old farmhouse. I gazed out of the window awaiting a nuclear explosion, the fallout destroyed everything in its path including me. Days later I read about some terrorists that had planned to attack a nuclear plant in the area I had dreamed of. The next dream was on the 9;4;16, I remember two neighbours shooting at each other from their houses and then two Elephants appeared and then two dinosaurs, was a message of mankind's extinction? On the 11;4;16 I lay in bed dreaming of the Grand National, the dream switched to a Baseball team of forty, everyone had to queue up to receive a number and sign their name. I signed and was given the number three, as soon as I signed my name my alarm clock went off. I got out of bed and then went downstairs to the kitchen and opened the cupboard and a loaf of bread fell out onto the worktop, only three pieces of bread fell out of the wrapper. Soon after that I got into my car and turned on the radio the DJ then began to talk about the number three. The horse that won the race had odds on it 33-1. The next dream was on the 12;4;16, I was on a building site high up walking along a scaffolding, I stopped and looked over the edge. I put my hands on the rail, which was not secure, I fell over the edge. The following day I attended a risk assessment course. The course began with a DVD with a man falling off a scaffolding the same as my dream. The next dream was on the 10;6;16, I visited the Whitehouse to meet Donald Trump he revealed to me he was like a coin, he had two sides, one good, one bad. He informed me he was possessed by evil but was still a good mam. Later I remember thinking but Donald Trump is not in the Whitehouse. It was three months later when he was elected President.

The next dream on the 16;6;16, was very vivid and supernatural. Aeroplanes were going missing they simply vanished from the sky, in my dream they were being transported to a mystical dark realm. A demonic monster had amassed a graveyard of aeroplanes. Suddenly a new plane appeared the monster began to rip open the cockpit with huge claws and supernatural strength. I could hear the passenger's screams, the monster then began to feed with every feed became angrier, it then became larger and more insane. The creature then stopped and announced it would travel to the dimension of the humans and feed at will. The monster in my dream could turn on an armour coating that could stop any weapon forged by mankind. The next dream was on the 7;7;16, I dreamt I was walking along the streets of America watching events unfolding, suddenly large black stones hit the ground all around me. I then turned and saw bullets, later I read the story of the Dallas police officers ambushed, twelve shot and five killed. On the 8;9;16, I wrote a poem with the words "imagine as the dark nights draw in and the supernatural events begin".

I went to bed and wasn't disappointed at 05;09, in the morning I felt a strange presence. I couldn't sleep and opened my eyes to see a face looking at me. The face was that of a 18th-century man, the face was in a circle I watched as began to move across the room it then disappeared through the corner of the ceiling. On the 9;9;16, I was visited by Angels in the land of dreams. I then looked at the date of my first visit 14;12;14, if you takeaway 14-9-12-9 and 15-16, you are left with the number nine. On the 19;9;16, I had a nightmare it was so vivid, imagine a very old large mansion with lots of people living in it including a wicked witch. I stood outside in my dream looking at the top window she stood in a boarded -up room. She was dressed in a purple dress and a grey cardigan matching her grey hair. She hates children and was angry and frustrated as she could not find her scarf, she uses to strangle them. The witch would then make it look like an accident. Her face was full of warts, her eyes as dead as the night such a sinister sight. My alarm clock for some reason did not go off at 05;30, instead it went off at 06;00. Autumn is the time for the supernatural, my next dream on 13;10;16 was very enlightening a magical, beautiful dream which I believe was a message from beyond. I was looking through a magical giant book every time I turned a page over, I visited that Country. It was like a out of body experience an atmosphere of bliss and enchantment the book gave such heavenly light. The book revealed information about the different Countries, cultures and population. I got to the last page and suddenly the magical light faded as it then revealed all the Countries weapons of mass destruction. The dream was magical, beyond words I feel lucky to have witnessed such a dream. The message at the end a vision of an arms race and mankind's will to destroy itself with such weapons of mass destruction.

The next dream was on the 16;10;16, I dreamt I was watching the news and its coverage of America and its allies invading North Korea. I watched the sky filled with bombers and then the tanks and infantry. People all around were expressing their horror. The war had just started and then the news reporter mentioned the death toll so far it read sixteen thousand. The dream then switched to a giant Tower block on fire in this Country. I stood outside watching the fire out of control, I remember in the dream a person asked me for help I just stood there watching people burn I replied no, fearful for my own health and safety. Was this a prediction of a future event? The following year the Grenfell fire happened, I dreamt of a Tower burning on the 16;10, the Tower burnt on the 14;6, take away 16 from 14 and 6 from 10, you are left with 24, Grenfell had 24 storeys. The next dream was amazing on the 7;1;17. In the land of dreams I was visited by Angels and then taken to Heaven on a guided tour through the pearly gates oh such majesty and enchantment, an amazing dream. I remember feeling the ultimate bliss as the Angels spoke to me, they explained to me how everything operates in detail. I remember everything was so bright I was shown a queue of people awaiting passage to Heaven. Next a giant set of scales I watched as they judged the next person in the queue. The scales gave off a dazzling light. I was then informed they were the scales of justice, if they turned dark then it was below you go. There was also a place between Heaven and Hell in which you could enhance a second chance. The deeds you declare some of which fair, the Angels will decide upon your final ride. I cannot remember everything that happened in the dream. The following day I wrote a poem about my Heavenly encounter.

The next dream on the 15;3;17, I believe became reality I dreamt the president of Russia met up with the president of Turkey. Later, they visited England and came to my house, they both entered and then sat down taking whilst I made them a cup of tea. Suddenly the dream switched to Turkey, I entered a bar, I noticed a man sitting alone upset drinking vodka. I walked over to the man and asked him if everything was okay, he explained to me back in Russia he had fallen asleep and then a massive fire had broken out. He escaped to Turkey, but his girlfriend was being held captive until his return. I helped him back to Russia and aided him in the rescue of his girlfriend, it was as if I was a secret agent. The man thanked me and then gave me a black bag and told me to give it to President Putin. The dream then faded and then I was in the presence of President Putin, he stood before me and then said, "Hand me the bag", I handed the bag to him, he then emptied the contents onto a table revealing a toy missile, a Star -wars toy and six toy Russian agents. I then handed him a copy of book "Five Fives beyond imagination". As he held it in his hand the cover slowly began to fade. A year later the same month, March dreams are spontaneous psychic events, messages from the subconscious a tantalizing glimpse of the future. I cannot explain why this one dream predicted so many events that have unfolded in March 2018, I read Turkey wants to buy Russian made S-400 Triumf anti-aircraft missiles worth billions. This has created a rift with NATO, the United States has threatened to impose economic sanctions on Turkey in a bid to dissuade Ankara from going ahead with the deal. The missile out classes cruise missiles and Ballistic missiles. I then read about a fire in March 2018 in a Russian shopping centre, the death toll was sixty-four and six bodies were never recovered. We then have in March 2018 Sergei Skripal, an ex-spy sixty-six years of age and daughter aged thirty-three with a Russian-developed Novichok nerve agent. Russian agents came to this Country and carried out this unbelievable crime. I dreamt of the contents of the black bag a missile, Russian agents and a Star-wars toy. The newspapers on the 26;11; 2020 completed my predictions Russia has successfully tested a terrifying new 9,000mph Star-wars missile that can blow up Satellites in space. Imagine the odds on all this occurring from one dream that was so vivid it's as if I lived it.

On the 20;6;17, I lay in bed dreaming of Whales washed up on a beach. I later turned on the television to discover Whales had died due to plastic pollution. On the 26;6;17, I dreamt someone was knocking on my front door. In the dream, I left my bed and answered the front door stood before me was six friends from my past. All six were young once more, one of them then said, I have lost a key have you found it? The key to Eternity. The next dream was on the 28;8;17, a visit to a different dimension. I was on a cruise ship docked in a strange land, my departed Father appeared and informed me he was to be my guide. We visited a land of green, everything was clear in a land of no fear. I gazed at a city of green I took photographs of what I had seen. The climate was hot the sun shone bright, oh such glorious golden rays of light. I walked for many miles; I addressed the many smiles; I saw the faces as if I was there, I spoke to people without a care. This was a truly amazing place, could it have been Heaven. My late Father Leslie Cunliffe, Months before he died, he mentioned his lucky number was eight he died on the 8;12;13. On the 8;9;17, I dreamt I was in the sky looking down at a hurricane in America. Oh, such devastation and then calm, I watched a flock of flamingos being rehomed ahead of the hurricane. The following day I turned on my computer and the first thing I saw was the flock of flamingos that featured in my dream.

The next dream on the 15;10;17, I lay in bed having a dream which kept repeating itself again and again. I could see the letter M and a white car driving, it then lost control it came off the road and then exploded in a field. The following day I turned on my computer to look at news. I noticed the car I dreamt of that had exploded in a field after losing control. The letter M stood for Malta, a journalist by the name of Daphne Caruana Galizia who died from a car bomb just like my dream location Malta. On the 2;11;17, I dreamt of rain and floods around the UK, after the dream we had rain and floods. I sat writing my Author's note on the 1;4;18, I then went to bed and began to dream, I dreamt I was in an old house it was dirty and dark. I lay in bed in the dream, but it was so cold, so I got out of bed and opened a wardrobe and got out some more blankets. I the noticed lots of people in the corner of the room doing the Ouija board, they were getting lots of messages of which I cannot remember. Suddenly a large soldier ant appeared and came towards me from out of the board, I went to kill it and was then informed it couldn't die. The dream then switched to a hotel of sin, it was full of evil spirits. There were lots of strange things happening. I entered a lift to go to my room. I remember I could not get out until I memorised the number 4006. My predictions are numerous dream prophecy, a connection between the subjective mind and the external Universe. I read that some wild-talented individuals can by inward concentration, using the right techniques foresee external events that have not happened yet. The occurrence of prospective dreams cannot be denied. Synchronicity appears to happen at random; to able to precipitate them at will would almost be impossible.

I remember in March 2016 builders arriving at my house to do some work. I woke up with a song playing in my head again and again the song was by Genesis entitles "That's all". The builders arrived with a large radio they turned it on and then the song I was thinking about was playing. Another example on the 29;3;17, I watched "American werewolf in London". The following day, I turned on the radio and the DJ played the theme tune to the movie. I had a vision of an old episode of Supernatural, the one in which Dean said, "I shot the Sheriff, but I didn't kill the Deputy". I had an urge to move a settee and found a DVD disc. I put it into the DVD player and to my amazement the episode I was thinking of came on. Later I sat watching an old DVD, the best of the Bangles, the hit "Walk like an Egyptian" came on. I watched it twice and then wondered why only two people were featured doing the hand movements. One, Princess Diana who died eleven years later and Colonel Gaddafi who died in 2011. My daughter sent me a message as I was listening to the song "American pie". I read it as the song played the day the music died, it read did you know David Bowie has died? I then went out to my car and turned on the radio the news was on and an American said "it was the day the music died". I visited my mother's house; I had a bad feeling something was going to happen to me. I walked into the kitchen and then gazed into the back garden and saw my mother trying to pull out a dead plant. I had a vision of her failing backwards and without thinking, I rushed to help her I then walked into a glass door. Blood poured from a wound, I eventually stopped the flow of blood, I then thought how numerology plays a part in life's events. The date 4;2;17, added together spells BC which is my mother's initials. On its own 4 is D for David, 2 is B for blood and 1 is A for accident and 7 G for garden. Philosopher Pythagoras believe numbers are the essence of life as I do. I have been on cruises all over the World and have had lots of strange things happen to me.

I remember booking a cruise to the Crimea months later Russia invaded Crimea so that was cancelled. This destination was replaced with Romania. The cruise ship docked in the morning; I woke up to explosions I then went on deck. I could see fighter jets and helicopters and at sea a frigate firing at a boat. The captain of the cruise ship then apologised; he went on to say he had no idea it was in fact their national arms day. I got of the ship and walked six miles into town to witness the military bands and their display of weapons. I visited Israel and then Palestine the birthplace of Jesus. I remember buying a gold star of David necklace from a shop in Bethlehem. I remember speaking to the guide with concerns about our safety there was men everywhere armed with Kalashnikov rifles. The birthplace was in fact a cave, I took some amazing photographs and then it was time to go. Crossing the border was an absolute nightmare. I sat at the front of the coach and witnessed a car full of people cross over a white line you weren't supposed to cross. Suddenly Israeli soldiers appeared with lots of weapons shouting at the top of their voices. I remember thinking please don't open fire they did not I then boarded the ship. I put on the necklace, I remember going to sleep and dreaming of the necklace disappearing without trace. I woke up and it was gone, I search the cabin but to no avail.

In October 2016 I made lots of friends on Facebook, one sent me a message about Angel number nine. I was due to fly to Lanzarote, which is nine letters, my seat number was 33c, the c represents the number three again nine. My minibus was number thirty-nine, I arrived late the reception was closed I complained to the manager and was awarded the best room, number 315 yes again adding to nine. I met lots of people someone said it had been raining until I arrived and that I had brought the sun with me. A couple from down South spoke with me, the lady informed me she was a Gypsy, we exchanged stories she listened and then said, "Go to church and pray for answers to find out your true purpose on Earth". I stayed for nine nights the evening I left it poured down with rain, the whole time I was there it was sunny. I arrived at the airport and spoke to a couple of strangers. I later found out I was sitting next to them on the flight home, coincidence I had done this before and believe it to be impossible. I wonder what odds a betting man would have given on this happening again and again.

A famous American contacted me with a message reading you have the gift of prophecy, but you are without Jesus, you are in terrible danger, "you are open to the Jezebel". Another American pointed out to believe is to receive and most awakened do not look beyond the borders of their own equilibrium. On the 9;11;17, I visited a shop and purchased a DVD entitled "Conspiracy" the main actor was Val Kilmer. I remember rushing into Asda with a trolley that had a used coffee cup in it, I picked it up and noticed it had my Christian name on it. I quickly did my shopping and was at the checkout when a Woman in front of me struck up a conversation about Water ship Down, the movie. I mentioned the book and the haunting soundtrack Bright eyes. Later I sat down and watched the movie in disbelief as Val Kilmer visited a Library in search of a book of which he stole and ended up in jail, the book was Water ship Down. Once again, the impossible. In my first book I mentioned the World would end in 2025, which adds up to nine representing the letter I, two add two is the letter D, and five the letter E, which spells out die. My predictions have a habit of becoming reality, so in my next book I decided to extend the date to the 2050, the number two is B, the number 5 in E, add together number 7 which is G, this spells out BEG. I read about a Christian conspiracy theorist who claimed the end of the World would start on the 15th of October and end in 2024.

I dreamt on the 16;10;16, the signs would start on the 16;10;17, I guess I was right. I looked out of my window and witnessed lots of People gazing into the sky, the Sun was bright red. A storm had been blowing, I turned on the Radio and the DJ said, today is so spooky, no birds, darkness like something out of a Stephen King novel. The dream I had about President Putin became reality. I looked at date of the dream the number six, March 2017, one year later in March 2018 President Putin unveiled six new strategic weapons. I read a book on Rasputin and the fact he mentioned before he died that he would be reborn as the leader of Russia. I remember thinking about Rasputin being reborn as President Putin, I then wrote R -reborn, AS- Putin.

In July 2019 me and my daughter entered a Morrisons superstore we split up with our separate trollies and then met up at the till. We both had different items, she went first her bill came to £ 14;57, and then mine £ 14;57, the Lady on the till could not believe it, I kept the receipts as I couldn't either. On the 24;3;19, I purchased a chain in the middle of it an Angel and at the end of it a bell. I hooked it to a post in my back garden, I then dreamt of it being knocked off by a bird of prey. The following day I went into my back garden and found it had been knocked off I then investigated the sky and gazed at a bird of prey hovering above my garden. On the 19;9;20, I placed a story on Facebook about a dream in which an aeroplane crashed, I wrote the clue which kept flashing before me the letter C, seven days later a plane full of cadets crashed in the Eastern City of Chuhuiv. The next dream the number 59 came to me and then two Russian double Agents enter a base, a Russian sergeant claims there is Rat in their base. The Russian sergeant has personal issues with one of the Agents and opens fire on him with a high-powered weapon. The stray bullets hit highly flammable liquids and explode, panic is now on display as emery forces take advantage and invade the camp, I then dreamt of the battle between them. Could this have been a vision of the Russian invasion of the Ukraine and were does the number 59 come into play. I was intrigued so I went the internet and found out Ukraine forces pushed back Russian invading forces in several areas in 59 minutes. I had another book published towards the end of 2019 and then on the 13th of November 2019 the ultimate nightmare of which I posted on Facebook on the 15th of November 2019. A very strange and vivid dream, I believed it would come true and informed family and friends, but no one believed it possible. I cannot remember how it started but the rest I can, I visited the Cinema with a beautiful Lady to watch a movie. The both of us separated I then found myself in a laboratory I saw what I believed to be dead people who had died from a virus. I watched as they began to move, I then ran out of the place only to meet up with the Lady. We walked for a while until we arrived at a Church there was hundreds of people burning their dead wearing masks. We moved quickly from the darkness to a zone of light only to witness ruined temples and pictures of fallen Angels I remember thinking some of the building looked oriental. We continued to walk until we arrived at a building filled with people dressed in clothes from the fifties and sixties. We sat down as a giant jukebox played music from that era, I believe the message was that people from this era would be mostly affected by the Corona virus. I informed people the virus would spread across the World and be here in the UK, no one believed it possible, but I have witnessed the impossible. The world found out about the virus on the 31st of December forty-seven days after my dream. The word Corona six letters apply numerology sixty-six, add six and you are left with the number of the beast 666. I mentioned the date of the dream the 13th and we have the 31st one and three, these numbers mean something to me the answers are in my first book Five fives beyond imagination. The book was published in 2014, the story was about a shape shifting creature from a different dimension by the name of Cavoc, each letter represented the end of days the first letter China the third virus. I believe the virus was manufactured as a bioweapon and the timing of the release onto the World was carefully planned for maximum effect. I read Chinese scientists discussed weaponizing Coronavirus in 2015, a Genetic bioweapon I believed it was released onto the World to cripple the World's economies. I wrote in my book Five fives beyond imagination China would be the first choice on ending the World, since then they have become so aggressive creating an arms race and constantly polluted our planet Earth.

I remember many years ago sitting chatting about China with Kevin an intellectual friend, I read in February 2019 China's aging population is a threat to its future we both believed China would do something to relieve it of this burden population control virus killing off the weak and old. In March 2021, I dreamt of scientists in a lab seeking a vaccination for the corona virus, I then kept getting the number two flashing before me in the dream. The dream then switched to a warship happily sailing on a calm sea it felt so relaxing and then suddenly it is hit by missile after missile I could see lots of explosions until it sunk. We had an incident with a British warship in June 2021, HMS Defender- a type 45 destroyer- was involved in a confrontation with the Russian military while sailing near the Crimean Peninsula. The ship was shot at, and Putin said even if Russia had sunk the UK warship, it would not have caused World War three. I believe this dream will become reality in the distant future and a lone warship sailing on calm waters will be sunk without mercy. Will 2025 be the year China has an amphibious fleet large enough to invade Taiwan. The next dream was more of a nightmare, I was driving a car as the dead began to rise from their graves, I was being chased by ghosts I then speeded up and escaped them. The dream then switched I was driving through a town all the bars and stores were boarded up. An economic collapse I witnessed poverty there a saw outdoor traders trying to make a living, I then saw someone selling goods I had not seen for many years. I still have hundreds of short stories of which I am expanding, anyone of these original stories could be major box office hits. This book "Death Date Heartless Fate", I remember being in a room in Bulgaria as I wrote about the Counts vengeance, it all went dark and then the crack of thunder and lightning of which I had never seen or heard of it was so loud. The Weather had changed flash floods, more thunder the room was shaking and then darkness, I remember thinking "my this sure is spooky". Most Authors hear their characters speak and reported visual or other sensory experiences of their character's when they were writing. A fifth of Author's had the sense that their characters was occupying the same physical space. In "Death Date Heartless Fate," I could see all the characters as if I was on the set of a movie, I believe this to be so amazing. The story has a message "what goes around comes around", I enjoyed the comedy, fear and the mystery and sincerely hope the readers also enjoy this book.

To Julie,

Many thanks.

David Cunliffe.

"LIMITED EDITION."